MAMIE BRANDON

MAMIE BRANDON

JACK SHERIDAN

CUTTING EDGE

ISBN-13: 978-1-957868-89-9

Published by
Cutting Edge Books
PO Box 8212
Calabasas, CA 91372
www.cuttingedgebooks.com

CHAPTER ONE

THE heat was almost unbearable. The flat, with its lunch-room and its highway, seemed crushed beneath the weight of some great, sprawling body, from which all stir of life had fled save for a tiny, feeble pulsing, as if there were a remnant of nerve still functioning within its core.

Mamie took the old rag from its nail by the refrigerator and held it under the tap, kneading it slowly to get it good and wet. When it was heavy, soggy, she listlessly began to scrub the counter top again. She leaned forward ponderously, rubbing the surface with short, circular movements, then paused momentarily about half-way down the stretch and examined her hands. They were getting red again! she thought bitterly; all red and dish-panny! She sighed with discontent.

Outside in the baking flat nothing stirred. Now and then a car would come down grade, bursting forth from the pines, and come racing past the lunch-room and round the curve behind the stone bluff to the west. Or a truck and trailer would come thundering down grade and past.

Mamie knew most of the drivers on the route. Sometimes as they went lumbering past, they would cut loose with a single, sharp blast on their horns. And other times, mostly at nights, they'd stop, have a cup of coffee or two, maybe even a sandwich or a bowl of chili. They'd drop a nickel in the juke box and sit around for a little while, just batting the breeze, snatching a few minutes' break on the run. But to-day the summer's heat was too much; there was no stirring outside. The highway lay baked, supine, silent, exhausted.

Mamie got to the end of the counter. She lumped the rag in a sodden pile and doubled back, lining each little cluster of catsup and mustard bottles in place. Finally she stood again at the far end, and sighed heavily. Automatically she rubbed her sweaty palms flat against the soiled uniform, damp against her flanks. She picked up the dirty rag and, half-turning, tossed it to the nail.

Mamie's gaze remained upon it for a moment. Then she shrugged. She moved dully around the end of the counter to where the mirror was. It was just a fragment of looking-glass tacked in the centre of the door upon which the word "Toilet" had once been hastily daubed as if in after-thought. Mamie stared at her reflection objectively. Not too bad a puss, she comforted herself, not too bad. Her twenty-eight years were only shadowed yet. She ran the flat of her hand under her chin, where the little roll of fat kept threatening to show. She grunted. She leaned closer, staring intently into her eyes. They were on the greenish side. She frowned. Green eyes and brown hair—what a lousy combination!

She moved back now, smoothing the smudgy dress into place. She let her gaze go sliding down the length of her figure. If it was bust, she grimaced, she had plenty of that! Two big, well-formed breasts crammed into the hot, holding mould of the tight bodice. She reached up and cupped them in her palms for a moment, hefting their weight. There was a trace of satisfaction in her eyes. Her hands travelled down over her waist, her gaze following tardily. She was big all over, no getting away from that: big swelling hips, big rounded, fleshy thighs. She was a big, sturdy girl—she remembered somebody saying something like that once, somewhere along the way. Well, she had enough to get by with; that was for sure! Guys went for dames with plenty of meat on them, meat in the right places, that is. A fat, foraging drop of perspiration edged in cautious spurts across her chest and slid into the deep cleft between her breasts. With a grimace Mamie ran her finger down the crack. She wiped her hands on her thighs, trying to smooth out the wrinkles as best she could.

The model A pick-up kidded to a stop. Mamie watched him as he jumped down as he came towards the lunchroom. He was tall, lean, blonde. He wore a pair of tight-fitting blue jeans and a T-shirt, soiled around the neckline. Cautiously, with a little quickening inside her, she watched him come. A vagrant thought crossed her mind. As long as she had known Frank Parks, he had always worn the same things. Just them jeans and that thin cotton shirt!

He stepped inside, pausing to let the door bang hard against his heels. He always did that. He came across the floor, came round the end of the counter.

"Hiya, Mamie!"

His arms slid round her middle and he pulled her to him roughly in a quick, possessive motion. She could feel the blood in her break loose and come charging upwards. There was a sharp, almost painful pounding in the back of her head, like birds' wings beating. He pulled her hard against him until she could feel his chest muscles cording against her, cutting sharp against her breasts. His lips covered hers and he pressed his body tight, his hip bones sharp, insistent on her thighs. Her hands hung limply at her sides as the first wave of him engulfed her. Then she stiffened. Her fingers curled and rolled up into little, knotted balls. Suddenly she put her fists against him and pushed violently with all the force she could muster. She broke free and stepped back, sideways, so that the edge of the counter came jutting between them, blocking.

"You stop it!" she whispered hoarsely. "Stop it, stop it!"

Frank stood solid, smiling lazily. He stood where he was, watching those breasts rise and fall with her pressured breathing.

"Why stop, Mamie? You like it!"

"You shut up! I don't know what right you got come busting in here like that!" The color rode high in her flushed face. "A

3

body'd think I was cheap! I got some pride left!" Mamie flung her words wildly.

Frank slid himself on one of the stools along the counter. He put his bare, browned arms out on the surface before him. Mamie glanced down and caught the glint of the fine blonde hairs on the backs of his hands. She tore her gaze away with force.

"Sure thing, Mamie. You got lotsa pride." He spoke very softly. He took a toothpick from the little glass bowl on the counter and slid it far back to one side in his mouth. He let his eyes drift down from her flaming face, on down to the low-cut V of her dress, over the swell of her hips to the fullness of her thighs. He grinned. "You got lots of something else, too, baby! You ain't going to waste it … "

There was a tentative question in the way he said that. Mamie set her jaw hard. He better get one thing straight; she wasn't no whore, no easy pick-up! She was Mamie Thomas and she did have plenty of pride left, no matter what he was thinking! She wasn't going sneaking off behind no shed, no, sir, not even with him, Frank Parks! Not even if he was built like a brick-john! She tried to keep her eyes off those blonde hairs that glinted on his arms.

"What're you gonna have, Frank?"

He watched her narrowly. She sure was a hard cookie to figure out, this Mamie! She wanted it! He could see it plain, could feel it in her kisses, could tell, that's all! He could swear she was hot for him! He ran his tongue along dry lips.

"What you got racked up against me, baby? What's so hard to take?" He paused. "You and me been friends now for a long time. Ain't no reason why we can't be … Look, you afraid maybe I ain't able to deliver or something? Only one way to find out, kid, you gotta take a chance!"

Mamie swallowed. She had to say something.

"It ain't just you, Frank." She fought desperately to think out the right words to say, so he would understand it wasn't personal. "It ain't just you. It's just … when I let myself go whole-hog … "

she faltered "…it's gotta be with a ring, with everything that goes along with it, see?" She wet her lips gingerly and brought her eyes down to him again. He wasn't smiling any more; he was watching her. Her words gained strength and momentum. "You got the right idea, Frank. I ain't got nothing against a good roll in the hay… only, it's gotta be with the right guy, see? You missed out on one thing. I got a helluva big price-tag on me, see? You can see the price easy; a ring, a place of my own, and that old 'Mrs.' tacked on my handle. I know what it's worth, see? I got it all figured out. I been doping it out for a long time. I know what the score is, this going on and on, never having nothing you can call your own! I got a bellyful of living like that! And it ain't for me no more, see? With me things is gonna be different. I been keeping my eyes open. There's guys around with the things I want. The way I see it, I got something they'd kinda like to have, too. Like you want it, Frank, only I ain't just gonna give it for the asking no more. The guy that gets what I got… he's gonna pay my price, see?"

She stopped talking. She looked down into his eyes, watching her. Frank took the toothpick from his mouth and flicked it over the counter.

"Sure thing," he said quietly. "Sure, I guess I see what you mean."

He got up and crossed over to the juke box. He studied the titles for a moment, punched one of the buttons and inserted his coin. She stared at the muscles in his back, at their ripple when he used his fingers. The music started and he came back and slid himself on the stool before her. His eyes were intent on her face as he spoke.

"So you got it all figured out nice and pat, ain't you? Well maybe it ain't up to me to tell you, kid, but from where I'm sitting, I got a feeling you been forgetting a couple of items. Seems to me you been forgetting you're a dame, first. Just plain dame. I don't know, maybe you're a horse-trader, too, but mostly you're a dame. All that stuff you got stacked up inside you, in here…"

he tapped his broad chest "…you ain't reckoning what's going on inside there much. You figure you can turn the juice on and off whenever you want to, but it don't work out like that, baby." He leaned forward a little. "Maybe you don't remember me, kid. Take a good gander. It's me, your boy friend, Frankie Parks, the guy you was kissing a little while back, remember?" A wry grin twisted his face. "I ain't saying you ain't gonna get what you want, one of these days. I ain't saying you will, and I ain't saying you won't. Only you better start doping out what you're gonna do about that other business, too. 'Cause what you're packing around ain't the kind of stuff you can forget easy-like. That stuff don't pack up no good on no shelf, remember that!"

He scratched his chin idly. His voice was low and steady.

"It's like this, between me and you, baby. There's been things getting ready inside us for a long time now. Sooner or later it's gotta be you and me together, no matter what else you got doped out. And when the pot gets ready to boil over, it's me that's gonna be hanging around. Me, Frankie Parks." He ran his tongue along inside his lower teeth. "I'm gonna be around…because I ain't about to give up, see? Me and you's got some mighty unfinished business together, baby!"

Mamie flushed.

"Go on, gimme a cup of coffee, Mamie." He brought the whole thing to a finish abruptly.

Mamie filled a cup and brought it over to him. She shook slightly and some slopped over on the counter. She got the rag from its nail, and leaned over, dabbing at the mess, and he found himself looking into the cleft at the top of her dress. She tossed the rag back on the nail, came round the counter, opened the door with the piece of glass tacked on it, and disappeared, closing the door firmly as she went. Frank listened to the juke box absently.

The screen door banged shut with a staccato crack. The older man crossed the floor and sat down at the far end of the counter.

He took the soiled menu in his thick fingers, he glanced at the listings casually, then he shoved it back behind the catsup bottle. He shot a brief look down to where Frank sat, caught the young man's nod and returned it with one as slight. He made no attempt to speak.

Frank eyed him with open curiosity. Brandon must be around fifty now, he figured. Karl Brandon was one of the local ranchers. He had a pretty fair-sized place up in the pines. He worked as a ditch-tender for the power people, too. He was an old-timer, been around these parts for years. Not many people seemed to know Brandon very well; he kept by himself, most of the time, never talked to anybody unless he had to. Most people figured Brandon was surly; some of them even said he was mean and cruel. Well, that business a few years back was enough to make anybody curl up inside! He did have a kind of sullen look about him. His eyes were dark, sunken deep in his head, and his hair, under the inevitable black hat, was what people in these parts called "iron-grey." His lips were thin, tight, devoid of color.

Mamie came out of the toilet and sauntered by. Frank lifted his eyes.

"Why, Mr. Brandon!" She was purring, as smooth as you please, swinging along with that funny, exciting walk of hers. "You been quite a stranger! I ain't seen you around for more than a week now!"

She sounded faked, eager, forced. Suddenly Frank, listening, got the idea, smash, right between the eyes. Mamie was leaning over the counter now, her two hands flat on the surface, her whole body tilted, aimed down at Brandon. He might be an old bastard, Frank thought savagely, but he sure wasn't too old! He was helping himself to a good look-see right now! And she was letting him get a good healthy one, too! Frank got to his feet suddenly and hurled a nickel across the counter. Mamie glanced in his direction briefly, her surprise shadowed in her eyes.

"Thanks for the tip!" Frank said too loudly. He strode to the door and kicked it open. Mamie's eyes followed him to the model A, saw him slide his body under the wheel.

"I never liked that young punk!" Brandon muttered.

Frank could see inside the lunch-room. He could see the old guy reach up and make a pass at Mamie, still leaning at him that way! Frank started the engine with a grinding roar; he kicked the gears into reverse, swung round and pressed the light truck out to the highway. He knew what he ought to do, all right! He ought to clear the hell out of this damned country! He ought to go back down to the valley, to Colfax even, anywhere away from Mamie! She and her goddam bargain basement ideas! Well, to hell with her! "I got some pride left," she had said! What a crust! Then she went out hooking for some broken-down old bastard like Brandon! He couldn't shake that picture of Brandon reaching out for her like that! And her, just standing there knowing damn well what he was after, letting him, too! Why, the old man was so hot in his pants he couldn't even sit still! Damn her! Damn her straight to hell!

Inside the lunch-room she let Karl Brandon reach up with his big hand and touch her there. She figured he could get some pretty good ideas, maybe. She watched his thick hand with its coarse black hairs, its stubby fingers with uneven nails, as it came up from the counter. She watched it with a kind of detachment, as it reached over and took hold of her. And, then, when she had let him, he became bolder, cupping her breast in his palm. Now she felt his fingers creeping down inside, rough upon her flesh.

She reached up with one casual hand and took the fingers away.

"Now, Mr. Brandon, you mustn't do that! After all, it ain't like I was a common chippy! I got some pride!"

She smiled at him slowly, taking the sting from her words. She straightened and patted her hair into place. The motion pulled her breasts high, a challenge directly in front of his eyes, as she had known it would. He wet his lips.

"Mamie," he said thickly, "there's something I gotta say. I been gonna say it for a long time now, only I ain't known how. Mamie, I gotta have you! I gotta have you! I need you lots!"

Mamie stopped patting her hair. The job was done! All these months of letting him look, letting him cop a feel now and then, getting him all steamed-up like he was now, all the days spent getting him ready so it would pay-off like this...and, now, here it was! He was asking her! Popping the question in the middle of this screened-in hot house! Everything she had wanted for so long, everything she had worked for, everything she had set her heart on, everything was in the bag! The house of her own, the ring, the whole shooting works!

"I got me a real nice place, Mamie. You'll live good. I got nice new furniture; everything I got is brand-new, almost." He went on and on in a dull kind of monotone. "You ain't gonna have to want nothing up there, Mamie. I been waiting for somebody like you. I been waiting a long time for you. I want you damn bad. Ever since I first seen you, Mamie, I been wanting you like that. I want you to marry me, Mamie. I want you to come home with me, to be my wife."

There it was; Bingo! This was it! This was the step that took her over the line! She could see herself so clearly now. She was a woman with a position. She turned her face away from his eyes for a moment and gazed around the room. Her eyes fell on the dirty rag hanging from its nail. That was the past. She shifted her eyes to the refrigerator, white, cool, clean. That was the future. He wanted her. Like Frank Parks, like all the others, he wanted her. Only he was ready, able, willing to give in return. She brought her eyes back to Karl Brandon, waiting for her word. She saw him quite clearly, just as he was, an old man, practically old, with big, thick hands and great, heavy wrists, the coarse black hairs furred like cuffs on them. She had a fleeting memory of other hands, other wrists, with blondeness on them. Almost hastily she said yes, she would marry him, very quietly, very firmly.

Brandon was all for a quick marriage. There was no use waiting now, since everything was agreed between them. They would drive over the summit and get it done in Reno this Saturday night! It only took a few hours to make Reno; you didn't have to wait there, as you did in California. That way, by going off on Saturday evening, by getting back on Sunday to the place, he would lose no time in his chores. She figured she would have to work through Saturday. That would give Bill Randall a chance to find somebody else. Bill Randall had been real nice to her all these months. She had to do that for him. Yes, if Brandon wanted it this way, they could get married on Saturday. He got up, fumbled across the counter and took hold of her face, drawing it up to his. His kiss was rough; she was surprised how little response there was in her. She tried to look as she figured he expected her to look. He released her, turned and went out briskly. The screen door slammed behind him.

Mamie stood behind the counter in the lunch-room and watched him go. While she was standing there, savouring her triumph, Bill Randall came in through the back door. Since he owned the joint, he figured he ought to drop in now and then. Though, he silently admitted to himself, since Mamie had been working there, his calls were nothing more than routine. They were simply check-ups—to see what she needed, to look over the supplies, stuff like that.

"Hi! What's new and startling!"

"Oh ... Bill! You scared me!" Mamie spun round, her eyes wide. "I'm sure glad you come around to-day. I got some news for you, Bill. I'm gonna quit—Saturday."

"But ... why? What's the trouble! Something wrong?"

He was completely befogged. She had been working here almost six months now. They had been pretty good friends all the way ... or so he thought. There had been no funny stuff, just plain friendship. So far as he had known, everything was shipshape. Having her here holding down the joint had given him lots of time to work the place in the pines with Ruth. He was used to letting the joint go perking along with her, used to leaving the works in her hands. He was fond of her, damn fond of her, come to think of it!

"There ain't nothing wrong, Bill. Honest. Only, you see, I'm gonna get married."

"Going to get married!" Bill echoed after a moment. His wits began to stir, to work again. He grinned cunningly. "It's Frank Parks, I bet!" he crowed.

She looked at him almost coldly. "No, it ain't Frank Parks! I'm getting married to Karl Brandon Saturday night." She ran her fingertips nervously along the counter edge, waiting for the shot to strike.

It had been a bull's-eye. Bill stood rooted, his eyes stretched wide. Finally he came around to seat himself on one of the stools.

"So ... it's gonna be Brandon, huh?" His voice was steady, almost flat. "How come it's Brandon, Mamie?"

" 'Cause he's asked me!"

"I'm sorry. I had no right to ask that."

She felt all confused. "That's okay. I'm sorry I barked at you. I guess I'm all hot and tired."

Bill was thoughtful. "Brandon isn't what I'd call the romantic type," he remarked casually. He was feeling his way with extreme caution. "He's certainly not young, not like someone else I know who seems to be carrying the torch around here recently."

"Being young and full of piss and vinegar ain't everything!" Mamie exploded hotly. "There's a helluva lot of other things that count." Her tone veered and became almost plaintive. "After all, Bill, I got my future to think about!"

The room was very hot, very still. "You know, Mamie, it's lousy, living without loving," Bill remarked. "You know you don't love Brandon, Mamie."

She watched a car speeding east along the silver-coated road before she permitted herself the answer.

"No … " she admitted. "You're right. I don't love him. I don't think I could love him, ever!" She paused; her tone became hard, even. "But he's got things I been wanting. He's got things that matter to me, the only things!"

"What about Frank?" He put the question softly, with an edge of whetted steel to cut through her defences. "He's in love with you. You know that."

She wheeled on him instantly, pinning him down with blazing eyes. "He's hot to sleep with me, if that's what you mean by 'love'! Love!" She threw back her head and laughed brassily. "There's a word that sure gets a helluva kicking around!"

"I do think Frank is in love with you, Mamie. I think he really loves you, down underneath." Bill Randall tried to recapture her eyes. "I'll admit the kid's easy, maybe. Could be he's been on the wrong track with you. But, Mamie, don't you see? The kid just doesn't give a hoot right now, not about anything. It's only because he's all screwed up inside; he can't figure out what's what. I don't know why; maybe he's been on the bum too long. Maybe he's been too long by himself, on his own. A man gets that way, Mamie, all twisted up like that, if he hasn't anything of his own to work for, to really live for. He needs settling down. The way I see it, you could do that for him." He pushed forward and went on doggedly. "That's what you could do, Mamie. You're the only one who could, the way I see it. You could get him to settle down, get him started in the right direction. With someone like you, he'd wake up and get next to himself."

Mamie blocked him with an outburst.

"Stop it, Bill! For God's sake, stop it! I ain't interested, that's all; I just ain't interested!" She clamped her mouth shut until the anger subsided. When she spoke again her voice was quiet and there was a kind of tremble, at first. "I ain't saying you're wrong about Frank; I ain't saying you're right, neither. The only thing

I know is, that with me and Frank it ain't no dice, Bill. It just ain't gonna be him, Bill, that's all. I ain't getting no younger. I'm pretty damn near thirty now; there's times I feel more like forty. I'm getting awful tired living like this, Bill, counting out days with nothing but a half-assed wish to go on." She shook her head slowly. "Uh-uh, Bill. I guess I just run out. I ain't got no more time left. I can't afford to sit on my behind waiting for anybody to wake up no more."

Bill raised himself wearily from the stool. He walked over to the music box and bending forward he scanned the title list carefully. Finally he turned and glanced back at her, standing exactly where he had left her. She looked all caved-in, he thought with sudden compassion, she looked tired, worn-out completely.

"Well…" he said with a tired smile. "I sure wish you all the luck in the world, Mamie." She managed to return the smile. "You've had a pretty rocky day, Mamie," he offered. "Why not knock off for a while? Take a break. I'll be around here. I'd better get used to this place again."

She nodded with a grateful smile. "I think I'll take a walk," she said. "I'll go down there, where the pines are. It'll be cool there, and maybe I'll get some thinking worked out."

The next morning he came by early, gloomily prophesying that he would never be able to find anyone who could begin to take her place. "What I'll probably get in here is some curvy babe whose big ambition is to be the pin-up queen of the Trucking Association! The toast of the truck and trailer crowd! Miss Fast Freight."

Mamie struck an exaggerated pose. "Well…" she smirked. "I ain't done too bad! Just the other day Charley Washburn was asking me for a picture for his cab this winter. Said looking at me would help keep him warm over the summit! 'Course, I wasn't sure exactly what he was getting at, making a crack like that."

"Did you take him up on it?"

"Who … me? Not much! Last time he was here he said he had one of Betty Grable. I guess she'll do the trick. I ain't exactly what you'd call the Grable type!"

"Maybe you're just self-conscious about things," Bill grinned.

"Yeah … maybe that's it." The smile seemed to die a little on her face. "Yeah … maybe you got something there. Maybe I am."

Bill stared at her. She was a queer one! He had a hunch he knew what she was thinking.

"Well, take it easy, kid. I'll try and be back in a couple of hours or so."

A big diesel truck came rumbling down out of the pines as he spoke. He watched it swing off the asphalt and come rolling to a stand-still. A large barrel-chested man in a leather jacket and a pair of dirty khaki trousers jumped out. Bill shoved open the screen and thrust out his hand with a ready grin.

The driver pumped the hand lustily. "Long time no see, Randall! Hiya doing?"

"When did you get back on the truck?"

"Oh, 'bout six weeks now."

"I'd been wondering what became of you. Sure good to see you again."

"Well, I been out of the army some time now. Didn't do nothing at first. Me and the old lady, we kinda took ourselves a good long vacation at first. You know what I mean … " he smirked and nudged Bill in mock confidence. "Before I came back from the other side I wrote her and I says, 'Take a good look at the floor now, baby, 'cause when papa gets back you're gonna be looking at the ceiling for a long time!' He threw back his head and roared with laughter. "Well, now it's back to the grind. I got me another mouth to feed! Jees, it's sure good to be on the road again!"

Bill kept shaking the fellow's hand. "Well, I'm sure glad you're back on the job safe and sound, fellow." He let go of the hand and turned, leaning in the doorway. "Hey, Mamie! Here's Mac back!

Take good care of him." He clapped Mac on the shoulder. "I gotta go, boy. Sorry I can't stick around."

Mac watched Randall strike out across the gravel and then came on into the lunch-room.

"What's it gonna be?" Mamie put on her best customer smile.

"Coffee and a couple of sinkers, I guess." Mac said, his eyes traveling over her with experienced skill. "How long you been around, kid? Don't remember you." His tone was easy, familiar.

She set the plate and cup in front of him. "Oh, I don't know. 'Bout six months or so."

"Bill Randall's a good joe, ain't he?"

"Yeah, he sure is an all-right guy. This ain't been such a bad place to work in."

He caught the dismissal in her tone. "You leaving here?"

"Tomorrow. I'm gonna get married."

"Well, well, well! Getting yourself hitched up, eh?" He looked at her closely for a minute. "It's all right, kiddo, this here marriage stuff. Ain't nothing like it." He was very serious. "I got me the damnedest, sweetest little old woman out, believe you me! And the prettiest damned kid in all California! That's no bull I'm slinging you, neither!"

She smiled faintly. "You was saying to Bill you was in the war. Army or navy?"

"Me? I was army. Army Air Corps. Drove a truck. Same goddam thing I done in civilian life! Ain't that a laugh?"

"I guess you seen a lot of things, interesting things, huh?"

"Sure. I been around plenty. I was on the other side of the pond for a couple of years. England, 'bout a hunnerd miles up from London."

The screen door whined softly as he was talking. The woman hesitated for a moment on the outside and then entered. Mamie hadn't heard a car. She looked out past the stranger and saw why immediately. The girl had come up on horseback.

Mac was well under way now. "…and them flying bombs, they was the damndest things, kiddo, something terrific!" He was holding up one hand, to show her how they operated. "They come along just like this…buzz-buzz-buzz…Then the motor cuts off…you don't hear a damn thing…longest goddam minute in the world…" He twisted his hand, banking it, running it sharply towards the floor. "Down she comes, boom!…and you've had it!"

"Had what?" Mamie stared at him.

Mac looked at her blankly. "Had what? Just…you've had it!" He shrugged helplessly. "Kinda like you'd say 'That's that!' or 'period!' Like the Frenchies say, 'Feenee!' See? It's all over! Done! You've had it!"

Mamie nodded. "I get it, I think." She shot a quick glance over at the woman. She could see she was listening to them, only she was pretending she was looking at the title cards on the juke box. She was small, well-moulded; she carried herself very well. She was a kind of blonde, Mamie figured, a sort of a…what do they call it?…ash-blonde. Her riding costume was simple, a man's big plaid shirt with a pair of man's jeans. She was a lady; you could see that. Mamie figured she must be around twenty-five more or less. Definitely, very definitely, a lady.

"Well, honey chile, guess that's about it for this time." Mac got up and fished in his pocket for a coin. He tossed it across the counter. She caught it, rang up the sale and flipped him the nickel change.

"In other words," she grinned, "you've had it!"

"What?" Mac threw back his head and his laugh was a throaty roar. "That's the ticket, kiddo! Right on the ball!" He leaned over, "You know, you ain't too bad on the eyes, kiddo. Now, if I wasn't a respectable married character…I could be making a pass about now! Ain't it hell?"

"You tramps is all alike!" Mamie cried in mock indignation. He backed towards the screen door.

"Well, be good, kiddo! Don't do nothing I wouldn't do!" He sobered, remembering. "Oh, about that getting married business. I hope you and the guy gets along swell, see? There ain't nothing like it—you believe me!"

He was standing with his hand on the screen door hook. Now he shifted his eyes and let them run up and down the back of the other woman. His glance swung over and connected with Mamie's eyes. He clicked his tongue and whistled, low and full of meaning. He was grinning as he went out.

The young woman half-turned at the sound of the whistle. "Are they all like that?" she murmured.

"You mustn't mind them." Mamie grinned. "Them truck drivers are all a little screwy, I guess. They don't mean nothing by it. Kinda helps pass the time mostly, I guess."

"Oh, I don't mind being whistled at—don't get me wrong!" The woman smiled. "To be frank, it's when they don't whistle that I'll start worrying!" The young woman came over and held out her hand. "I'm Ruth Randall," she said quickly.

Mamie's eyes widened. So, this was Bill's wife! "I'm Mamie…Mamie Thomas." She wiped her fingers on her hips before taking the extended hand. " 'Course, it's really May, but I don't remember nobody ever calling me that. It's been Mamie ever since I was a kid."

"I figured you'd be Mamie," Ruth said. "You see, Bill's talked about you so much." She seated herself on a stool and began to toy with the little glass bowlful of toothpicks in front of her. "I'm really very sorry I've let all this time go by without ever coming around to get acquainted," Ruth went on. "I should have made friends with you a long time ago. I guess some of my good manners got left behind in Auburn when I came out in the hills. You'll just have to forgive me."

Mamie was trying to figure out the angle. What had brought Ruth Randall round at this stage of the game?

"I hope we'll be friends, you and I, good friends," Ruth said simply. She patted the stool at her side. "Come round and sit here." Mamie took her place at Ruth's side.

"You know, Bill thinks you're pretty wonderful, Mamie. He says there's only one person like you in a carload." Ruth made her compliment easily, candidly. Mamie shot a quick, veiled, measuring glance at Ruth's face. Ruth was apparently quite sincere. Mamie went relaxed.

"Bill's a good egg. I liked him a lot. I mean, I like him," she amended hastily. "I like him a lot. Still, I suppose he's told you all my secrets. Bill, I mean."

Ruth shot her a narrow glance. Then she reached out impulsively and covered the other woman's hands, idly clasped in her lap.

"Not all your secrets, Mamie. But he did tell me about you getting married to-morrow night, to Karl Brandon."

Mamie met her cool eyes levelly.

"Yeah." Her tone was even. "I'm gonna get married. Tomorrow night in Reno, to Karl Brandon, like you said."

Ruth got to her feet. Now was the time for talking.

"I suppose I've really no business to butt in where I'm not concerned, Mamie, but I'm going to say what I came to say. I don't know this Karl Brandon at all. I've no idea what he's like, except from the things Bill has told me, from what I've heard. But I have known Frank Parks a long time. It's because of him, because I do know him that I wanted to tell you a couple of things myself."

"It won't be no use." Mamie's voice cut in, sharp, warning.

"Please ... Please, let me say what I have to say. It won't take long. It might mean something to you; it might not. But I've got to say it."

Mamie shrugged. There was a dead silence. Ruth took silence for assent.

"Bill thinks Frank Parks is in love with you, Mamie." Ruth gripped Mamie's shoulder. "Is he, Mamie? Tell me. Is Frank in love with you, as Bill says?"

Mamie made no reply.

"There are some things I'd like to tell you, if you'll let me. Maybe they're not important; maybe they are. I know they seemed important to me." Ruth hesitated, but Mamie betrayed no feeling whatsoever. "When we first moved up on our place, Frank Parks came to work along with Bill and me. He wasn't much more than just a kid then. I became very fond of him right off, right from the start. I felt towards him like a sister, if you know what I mean. After a while, the three of us being together all the time, Bill and I thought we knew him pretty well.

"Frank was born up here, you know, up in the hills. His mother and father took him down to the valley when he was quite small. After they had been there a dozen years or so, the parents were both killed in some train accident. Frank was about thirteen when this happened. After that, he was completely alone. He ditched school and started to ramble on his own. You know the kind of a life that must have been. He's always been physically older than his age, too. He had his first woman when he was only fourteen; he told me that himself. He knocked around the valley for several years, working in the fields, in the canneries, riding the rods and all the rest of it. Finally, he got tired and, I suppose, a little curious, and came back up here. There were jobs to do on the railroad down in Colfax and sometimes he worked on the places around here. This took a couple of years or so. At length, Bill got acquainted with him down in Baxter one day. He was in between jobs then; Bill needed another hand to help us clear off the place. And that's how Frank came to work for us. That was almost four years ago. He was around twenty-two or so.

"He stayed around for quite a while. He seemed to like us. Bill's only a couple of years older than Frank; they had a lot in common. Being round Bill seemed to steady Frank a lot. He talked a bit, after he got to know us, but his talk was always about things he had seen or done, never about what he wanted from the future. It was almost as if he were afraid to look forward; as if he were taking refuge in the past. I remember one night he went into town. He got good and drunk that night. It was the first, the only time I had ever seen him really drunk. It frightened me at first, and then I felt terribly sorry for him: he was so much like a little lost boy...

Frank was propped in the doorway, the weight of his body full against the frame. Something made Ruth glance up from the table where she was reading in the light from the little oil lamp.

"Why, Frank!" A wave of snagging fear ran through her. He was tight, awfully tight, she realized instantly. Bill was down at the barn, too, out of earshot. But Frank just stood there, slumped against the door-jamb. His breath was a series of long, heavy gasps.

"I'm sorry, Ruth," he managed thickly. "So sorry, Ruthie." He grinned foolishly. "I'm pretty damn potted!"

He lurched forward with that. She sprang to her feet and ran to his side. She eased him down into the chair. He pitched forward heavily, over his bare arms outstretched on the table-top. Then, after a moment, he pulled himself erect with an effort; he looked down at her, crouched at his side.

"Hiya, Ruthie!" His head wobbled. "Sure am plastered; I'm pickled; but good, baby!"

Instinctively she reached out and stroked his blonde hair. "Sure, Frank." His head had dropped forward again. Suddenly she could see the muscles in his back working convulsively; it came to her with a shock that he was crying. She put her arm around his waist.

"Oh, Frank boy, what is it? What's the matter?"

He couldn't say anything for a while. He just sat there, crying. He stopped finally, he raised his head abruptly and looked down at her.

"I guess I'm a goddam fool!"

"What's the matter, Frank?" She faltered a little. "What is it that's going on inside you?"

He stared over her head. "I don't know." He was empty of all feeling now. "It's something I don't know. It's like I can't find something I lost." His gaze came back to her. "What have I lost, Ruth?" He reached over suddenly and seized her arms, pinning them at her sides, his voice scaling the incline of despair.

She turned her face from his desperate look.

"I haven't got it, Frank," she confessed sadly. "I can't give you the answer. It's something you've got to find out for yourself. You will find it some day. If you're big enough to know it when it comes, to meet it and take it, you'll find the thing you want."

He got to his feet unsteadily. "I'm awful sorry, Ruth," he said simply and turned and left the room.

Ruth looked at Mamie. "He went away that night and never came back to the place again." She paused for a long moment. "I've seen him now and then. I've seen him down in town, and once in a while when I'm out riding I've run across him on the river path. But it's nothing more than a case of hello and goodbye, that's all. It's as if he pulled himself back into a kind of shell that night so far as we are concerned. I never mentioned that night to Bill. Somehow, I felt it was something between Frank and me. Somehow I felt, too, that you ought to know, especially after what Bill told me last night."

Mamie swallowed. "And ... ?"

"From what Bill tells me, I think maybe Frank's in love with you, Mamie. I think maybe he's on the way to finding out some of the answers, at last." She took Mamie's hands in hers. "Don't you see, Mamie?" she cried, "he's all mixed-up—lost. Somebody's got to back him up, to give him assurance, confidence in himself. If it is you he loves, then it's only you who can bring him peace and happiness. With you he can be somebody, do things, stop all this terrible waste! Oh, I'm so very sure of it!"

She fell into an abrupt silence. Mamie slowly pulled her hands free.

"I'm sorry," she said coldly. "I ain't in the rescue business. You see, I got my questions, too, and I got my answers. I dug them up all by myself, a long time ago. Karl Brandon's the answer to my questions." She hesitated. "I been kinda sorry for Frank Parks, sure I been sorry for me, too, for a long time. Only, you see, I ain't sorry for me no more. I been working hard to get what I wanted all this time ... " her voice slanted fiercely, " ... and it's gonna take a damn sight more than a guy like Frank Parks to change anything now!"

"I'm sorry you feel that way." Ruth walked to the screen door, paused, then turned and held out her hand. "I'm not sorry I came, though," she said truthfully. "After Bill told me what you said yesterday, I felt you ought to know everything there was to know about Frank before it was too late." She kept her eyes on Mamie's face. "You see, I have such a lot of faith in Frank. He's a nice good kid down underneath, when you break down that front. I guess it's just that I'm on his side, that's all."

Mamie came slowly across the lunch-room and the two women stood close to each other at the door. "You're a kind person," Mamie said suddenly. "I think, maybe, you know what's what."

Ruth colored. "I know I've had an awful nerve butting in."

"Somehow, it ain't quite like butting in." Mamie put out her hand and touched Ruth. "You been telling me all this stuff about Frank Parks. I can see why you done it. You been hoping I'd change my mind, maybe, about to-morrow. But it ain't gonna be changed. I been a long time figuring out all the angles on this getting married business. You see, this ain't no first time with me."

Ruth glanced at her with a tiny flicker of surprise. Bill hadn't said anything about that.

"I was married once before," Mamie said. "He was a kid; we wasn't neither of us more than kids. He was a good-looking guy, like Frank, and I guess I went for him plenty, looking back now. He didn't have a bean. All he had was them good looks. That was enough for me… in them days. Well, to make it short, it lasted about a year. All the time we was married I worked, slinging hash, just like I been doing here. That's about all I ever been able to do. I ain't had no schooling like you." She stumbled and picked herself up instantly. "I made enough dough. There wasn't much, but it was enough for a cheap room, some food, and a bed. But I always had one big break; I could climb in with Joe." She shot a sharp glance at Ruth. "I ain't holding nothing back. I like men; I like men lots. I figured just sleeping with Joe was plenty. Just to be with him, to have his arms hugging me tight all night, that was all I wanted. I didn't mind working my head off all day, just so's there'd be the nights with him. Well, one day I found out I wasn't the only one climbing in with Joe. So I beat it. I ain't much on this sharing business, see?" She took a sharp, barbed breath. "We busted up. I got me a job in a joint down near Las Vegas and I got me a divorce. Somebody was telling me later on he got kinda bottle-happy. They was right. I seen him just one since then: in North Sacramento once. I was working in a gin-mill when he comes in with some whore. I seen she was keeping him, like I did. I felt kinda better after I caught that set-up. I even kinda got over missing him at night!"

There was nothing Ruth could say. This was out of her ken.

"So that's it, honey. I figure I been through the mill and I ain't looking to shack up with no drifters. It ain't nice what happens to drifters, or to their women, neither. The way I got it doped out, somebody's gotta change sooner or later in a set-up like that. You and Bill got the right slant there. Only the way I seen it, it's the goddam women who do the switcheroo, see? It's them that gives in, if they stick!"

"I'm so sorry..." Ruth's hand touched her lightly.

Mamie's voice became tense. "You don't have to. I ain't looking for sympathy. It's just I figured you asked for it; now you got it. You see this Parks from your side of the fence; you got him just waiting for somebody to come along and give him a big boost. Well, it don't make no sense to me that way. I can't help seeing him like that Joe was, a good-looking, simple bastard who ain't got nothing but his looks. I ain't anxious to hook up with no more Joes, never." She looked at Ruth steadily. "All I want is for everybody to mind their own damn business. Let me mind mine. I'm gonna do what I'm gonna do, no matter what, see?"

Ruth's eyes softened. "I think maybe I understand, Mamie...a little, anyway."

Mamie felt better now; all harshness faded from her eyes. "We're gonna be neighbors pretty soon," she offered, building a careful bridge across the gap.

"Yes. And friends."

"Friends...from to-day."

Ruth reached out and squeezed Mamie's arm briefly. Then she went out to where the horse was tethered. She swung herself up on his back. "So long, Mamie!" she called, as she prodded the animal out to the highway.

CHAPTER TWO

THE sun was just edging down behind the big stone pile to the west when Brandon came back to the lunch-room on Saturday. Mamie was the first to recognize the truck as it came rumbling down round the curve. She and Bill had been standing side by side, saying nothing, simply waiting for him. Brandon turned in off the highway and came up close to the building. He shut off the engine and just sat, making no move to climb down from the cab. Mamie stooped and picked up the little striped suitcase.

"Well, Bill, I guess this is it!"

She put out her hand and Bill nodded as he took it. He pressed it with unaccustomed tenderness and cleared his throat noisily.

"Best of everything, Mamie. I mean that."

He opened the screen door and she went on out. He watched her thoughtfully as she crossed the gravel strand to where Brandon still sat in his truck. Even now he made no move to get down, to help her. He simply leaned over and thrust open the heavy door. Mamie grunted a little, lifting the suitcase high, and shoved it on the floor, hard against the seat. Then she reached down and took hold of her tight skirt. Hoisting it high above the rolls of her stockings, she clambered up to her place beside him. For her wedding trip Mamie was decked out in her best. She wore a cheap, dark suit, which had already started to wrinkle, and a white blouse all frilly down the front. Pinned firmly on her dark hair was a tiny black patch of a hat with a wispy veil that came almost to her shoulders. Bill Randall's bouquet of baby roses, the one he had brought her from town the night before, rode high on her shoulder.

Bill waited until the big truck began to move out to the highway. He saw her turn once and wave. He returned it slowly, letting his hand fall to his side limply. The truck wheels lumbered on to the asphalt and then began their rhythmic singing east. The machine crossed the flat and disappeared into the pines that furred the beginning of the long grade up to the summit.

Bill Randall sighed, suddenly decided to close the joint up to-night, even if it were a Saturday night. He felt a sudden, quickening desire to be in the house in the woods with Ruth, a crying need to have her arms around him tight, holding him firm and secure.

It was almost nine o'clock and very nearly dark when Brandon finally shut off the engine and pushed open the door on his side of the cab. The flickering neon sign above them splashed a dull, quivering reddish glow over everything. Mamie peered out into the vermilion night. The chill off the mountains came pouring over her through the opened door. Brandon stood down on the ground, right below her, waiting. She shoved open her door and swung her feet to the running-board. She shivered in spite of herself.

"I figure we better get a place to stay, before anything else," Brandon commented. "Saturday nights it gets pretty crowded round here."

She nodded, and picked up the suitcase. He went on before her, heading up the walk towards the first cottage. Brandon rang the bell. She paused just behind him and set the suitcase down on the edge of the porch. She glanced round. The auto court was a squared U. There were a couple of rows of one-room huts, with a space between each for an automobile. A man finally answered the summons of the bell. He was a very thin, needle-like man, partially bald, with spectacles shoved high on his forehead.

"Yes ... what is it?"

"We want a place for the night ... me and my wife, that is." Brandon tripped over the unfamiliar latter.

"You and your wife, you say." He leaned forward to check them shrewdly. "Sure you're married?"

Mamie felt herself flush as anger dashed over her. The dumb fool! He didn't think she'd be here if they weren't?

"This here is a respectable place, this is. No funny business allowed here, even if it is Reno."

Brandon's thin lips compressed. "Look, mister. The lady and me is getting married in a few minutes. We're trying to get us a place before it's too late, see!"

The man studied them. "No," he decided finally. "I can't afford to take no chances. People all the time come around, and just because this here's Reno they think everywhere's a good-time place." He found himself looking at Mamie, standing quietly in the background. "Look ... I'll tell you. You folks leave a dollar deposit and I'll hold a place for, say, an hour. When you get married and all"—he stole a sly glance at Brandon—"you bring back the licence and you get the place. Okay?"

Brandon took out his purse and handed over the dollar without further comment.

The man smiled benignly.

"You can leave your bag here, if you want."

"We'll take it with us!" Brandon turned his back on him and stalked past Mamie down off the porch. The man raised his eyebrows slightly, dropping the glasses into place again; he shrugged. Mamie reached down and picked up the bag and followed Brandon down the walk to the truck.

At nine-thirty, or pretty close to it, on a Saturday night in Reno, they were married by a wayside justice of the peace. The wedding took place in a small frame house on the eastern outskirts of town. It was a yellow house, on whose exterior signs had been plastered to proclaim the justice's willingness and ability to undertake the task of union any time by day or night. Witnesses and ring supplied for a modest fee.

They were joined in the living-room, quickly and with dispatch. There were four people and the justice in the room at the time. The judge wore rimless glasses that caught and held the reflection of the room lights in such a way that, standing where she did, Mamie never once saw his eyes. She could remember that a long time afterwards. She stood before him in her rumpled suit with the white blouse all frilly down the front and Bill's bouquet beginning to wilt and hang. Brandon stood at her side in an ill-fitting brown best suit, and now and then, while the judge mumbled through the required words, she studied Brandon. His hair was combed nice, she thought. In the bright light of the room it looked almost blonde instead of iron-grey. She ran her eyes along his shoulders. They were big, hard beams of strength. A tiny rocket of excitement came soaring within her. She tried to concentrate on the words as they rippled out with practised ease over the lips of the man who read before them. She wondered vaguely if there would be something about "all my worldly goods" as there was sometimes. She tried to remember if they had been in it the other time. But it was too long ago. Brandon nodded once and she heard his voice, as if it were miles away, almost the voice of a stranger, saying, "I do."

There was little to the cabin actually. There was a toilet and just one room with a big, double bed. Brandon had gone into the toilet and left the door slightly ajar. Mamie stood in the centre of the room and listened to the sounds of him in there. She had a slight twinge of annoyance, but she was not embarrassed. She crossed to the dresser and carefully took off her hat with its veil. Brandon came out of the toilet and moved round to the other side of the bed. He stripped off his coat and hung it carefully over the back of the only chair.

"Well," he remarked, as he started to undo the buttons on his shirt, "here we are, Mamie, just me and you."

Mamie stood and watched him with a kind of detached fascination as he undressed. They were man and wife. She glanced down at the ring once, as if she wished to confirm this; then she looked back at her husband. He had removed his shirt and was laying it carefully over the coat. He straightened, naked to the waist. He was massive, big-boned, well-built, with heavy, knotted muscles, and hairy. Her breath clotted suddenly; she felt the tug of her rising desire. She had never seen a man with so much hair on his body. It came spiralling out of the gouge of his navel in a thick, bushy path and went spreading out over his lower ribs. It widened, matting over his chest, so thick she could hardly see the small discs of his nipples. He slid off his boots, his trousers and his shorts; he stood for a moment naked, except for his socks, scratching the hairy bowl of his belly. His legs were muscled and big, smoky with the shadow of the hair on them. Mamie watched as he sat on the bed, his back to her, slipping off his socks. Then he swung around and, raising the covers, slid down in the trough of the bed. Mamie remained, riveted in the centre of the floor. She became conscious of his eyes on her, and she smiled slowly, gingerly wetting her lips. Her eyes were hazy, narrowed, like cats' eyes, pinpointed with the quickening hunger in her. She had almost forgotten; it was like the first time with a man, alone, just the two of you.

"You don't mind ... " Her words flipped lightly. " ... I'd kinda like to turn the light off ... "

Brandon grunted. Mamie knew suddenly he very much minded. He had pushed the covers back so that they lay low across the puffed rise of his belly. He watched her intently. She forgot about the lights; she disrobed with unaccustomed haste, feverishly, almost clumsily. After a short time she switched off the light and slid down cautiously beside him, her hip grazing his as she took her place.

That slight touch of their bodies was as if she had inadvertently pressed some hidden spring; his great arms closed upon her like the jaws of a steel trap. He seized her with a strength, with a terrible intensity, that shattered her own mounting desire, plunged her into open panic. She fought him savagely for a few moments, struggling to assert the advantage as she had always done before. But she had misjudged him. He won in a sudden, smashing triumph. Her resistance broke and crumbled. She yielded, spent, and he took possession of her in his own furious way. He had stripped her of every defence, scattered her every emotion in those fierce, recurrent, maddening waves of hunger.

Brandon's love was a new kind of love to her, a terrible, urgent, dominant, undeniable thing. It was as if he had raped her, she realized with a stab of surprise. Yet she had come to him, had wanted him, her own desire high and ready. But it had been he who had taken her after his own fashion, harshly, completely, impersonally. It was as if a tremendous hunger had been dammed within him for a timeless age without release, without gratification. His love was cruel, brutal, ravishing. For the first time in her life, Mamie had been possessed. She lay exhausted and tearless, drained and a wife.

Brandon wanted to get out of Reno before the heat came pressing down from the mountains. So they rose early the next morning and had their wedding breakfast in the café alongside the Motel. It would be a long drive back over the summit. Brandon figured to make it back to the flat by noon-time. They climbed up into the truck and Mamie slid over to sit close at his side. He pushed her away with a rough, off-hand move. "Gotta keep my arms free," he said gruffly. "Damn hard truck to handle on the curves."

When they hit the grade on the other side of the lake, the truck slowed down, reluctant to take on the increased load. Brandon shoved the gears into low and they crawled along noisily, slowly mounting the incline towards the rocky crest. As they neared the top Brandon pulled over on the shoulder of the road; they sat listening to an angry bubbling down inside the hood. Brandon got out and cautiously took off the radiator cap. The steam, released, came shooting like a geyser. Mamie opened her door and climbed down and walked across the black roadway. She stood on the soft, sluffy dirt shoulder, looking down. Donner Lake was a flat, blue plate, rimmed with green, at her feet. After a few moments she felt him coming up behind her; they stood together, gazing down over the lake, over the trees, over towards the rim of snow-capped mountains, towards the patch of forest where Tahoe lay.

"Gees, it's sure beautiful, ain't it, Mr. Brandon?"

He stared at her blankly. Then he glanced back out over the spread of the country.

"Yeah, I guess it is, like you say," he conceded. "Only, all I know for sure is I'd like to get my hands on some of that there timber. That stuff sure ain't doing nobody no good like it is!"

Mamie found herself conscious of each individual tree in the endlessness before her. She saw with her husband's sight and each tree had the initials K. B. cut deep in its trunk. She drew a slow, full breath.

"No..." she said quietly. "I guess it don't do nobody no good." She swung away from his side abruptly.

He followed her back to the truck, climbed up into the cab, and started the engine. They moved forward and went over the top. They coasted down the long grade, past the rocks, tunneling finally through the thick, wooded belt near the flat.

"Want to stop and get some coffee?" Brandon turned slightly.

"That would be nice." She was pleased and brightened in her corner. The truck came roaring through the pines and suddenly they came charging out into the brilliant sunshine of the open meadow. Over to the left she could see the lunch-room, white and squat. Brandon drove the truck close to the building, and they ground to a whirring stop.

Mamie jumped to the ground, ran to the screen door and pulled it open wide. Brandon walked slowly round the machine, peering closely at the tires.

Bill Randall was leaning over the counter. He glanced up as she burst into the room. A broad grin went sweeping across his face.

"Well … welcome home!"

Mamie ran over to the end of the counter, as if she were going round behind it. Suddenly she caught herself, grinned, and dropped to a stool.

"We're gonna have some coffee, me and Mr. Brandon," she announced. Brandon had entered and now stood quietly behind her. Bill thrust out his hand.

"Congratulations, Brandon!"

"Thanks." Brandon accepted the hand and even managed a faint, inconclusive friendliness. Bill glanced down at Mamie sitting in her open pride.

"Sure glad to see you get back safe and sound."

"It's sure good to be back, too." Mamie confessed. Brandon had seated himself at her side. They waited, saying nothing, while Bill fussed with the coffee urn and finally came slowly towards them, balancing the two brimming cups. He set them down with tense care and then stood back, surveying them with frank curiosity.

"So now you're Mr. and Mrs.!"

Mamie flushed a little. "Yeah, that's it! We even got us a piece of paper to prove it!" The way she put it, it meant nothing. She managed to scrape up a tight little smile to cover her words. Randall would know what she meant. She turned slightly, almost defiantly, and shoved her hand with marked possessiveness between Brandon's arm and his body, her fingers locking round his hard biceps. She nodded with a quick little jerk of her head, as if she wished to underscore her words, to impress them on his mind.

Outside on the gravel there was the sound of a car coming up; then silence spilled in again. Bill watched Frank Parks with narrowing eyes as he came striding across to the screen door. Bill's brow furrowed. Frank came on in, pulling the screen door wide, stepping inside letting the door hit hard against his heels, as he always did. Mamie heard the identifying slam. She glanced up from her coffee and caught the tight look on Bill's face. The color went draining from her cheeks; her eyes widened. Brandon went on sipping his coffee at her side, unconscious of the tension around him.

"Well, well … so it's the newly-weds!" Frank's voice was steady and humorless. "Congratulations, Brandon!"

Brandon twisted his head slightly and brought his cool gaze to Frank's face. He nodded once, curtly, and went back to his coffee.

Mamie forced her eyes up the length of Frank's body, towering over her. Her eyes moved slowly, up past the big silver buckle on his belt, past the smooth oval of his stomach, past the hard chest under the snug shirt, to his neck, and, finally, to his face, his eyes. He was looking down at her with a taut, unfamiliar expression. It was a curious mixture of jaunty cockiness, tempered with hurt, tinted with cruelty. A confusion came piling within her. There was a thick vein in the dead centre of his forehead; she had never noticed it before. Now it stood out dark against the tanned smoothness, rigid and corded, each pulsing beat measured in its throbbing.

"Thanks, Frank." Her words were almost inaudible.

He swallowed hard and set his jaw. "Thanks for what?" he snorted. "It's what you're supposed to say, ain't it? Congratulations to folks that get married!" His voice soared, became almost shrill. "You know something?" He leaned slightly forward, his eyes cold and piercing. "You can go plumb to hell, for all I care, Mamie … you, Mamie Brandon!"

Mamie stiffened. There was a sharp crash as she raked her cup from the counter. Brandon was up and round her, in front of Frank Parks in an instant.

"Maybe you better be getting the hell out of here!" Brandon snarled. "Maybe you better be making tracks, mister!"

Mamie sat in a stupor, unseeing, her eyes on the shattered bits of the cup at Frank's feet. Randall had moved down to the far end of the counter, watching, prepared. Frank stood his ground arrogantly, his legs braced apart firmly, looking down at her, ignoring the inflamed face of her husband. Finally, he shifted his gaze slowly and looked at Brandon; there was a glint of contempt in his eyes. He spun on his heel and walked easily to the screen door.

"You remember ... I'm gonna be around," he promised very softly.

Mamie sat rock-like. Frank pushed on out, letting the screen door slap shut with a crack behind him. He stalked to the pick-up and clambered up on the seat. Brandon had followed him to the door and stood in its frame. Frank started the engine on the model A and leaned out over the side. "Remember ... I'm gonna be around."

Brandon kicked the door open angrily. He came carefully, on light cat feet, to the side of the small truck. Bill stepped through the screen door, never taking his eyes from the scene before him.

"You come nosing round my wife," he heard Brandon say, "and you're a dead duck! Remember that!"

Brandon brushed Bill to one side and re-entered the lunch-room. Bill stood quietly while Frank threw the gears into reverse, his rear wheels chewing two deep gashes in the gravel. He swung the model A round, shot out to the highway and disappeared behind the stone bluff. Bill thoughtfully smoothed the gravel back into place with his toe then wandered back to the lunch-room.

Mamie sat stunned when Brandon and Frank went storming out. She glanced down at the broken pieces of cup, and from somewhere far off she dimly heard Frank's voice coming to her with a promise: "I'm gonna be around," he was saying. They had gone away now; she tried to hear what they were saying. But her mind refused to help, refused to sort out words from sounds. After a moment or two she stirred slowly. She moved down round the end of the counter, to the refrigerator, and took down the dirty rag. She came back out front and, stooping down, she began to gather the scattered bits of china. Almost mechanically, she dabbed at the coffee puddle on the floor. At that moment Brandon returned.

"Get the hell off the floor!" he commanded. "You ain't no goddam waitress no more! You're my wife!" Mamie flushed painfully. She heard the screen door again and saw Bill Randall's legs come next to those of her husband.

"Never mind the cup, Mamie," Lill spoke quickly. "I'll get that stuff later."

Brandon glared. "I'll pay for the cup," he said sharply. "My wife's kinda upset to-day!" He drew the purse from his pocket and, forcing it open with fingers that trembled, he dug down into it. He fished out a quarter and held it out towards Bill.

"A cup isn't that important to me, Brandon," Bill refused curtly.

Time hung suspended for a tiny second. Then Brandon stepped forward and flung the coin to the counter. He reached down and gripped Mamie tightly by the fleshy part of her arm and dragged her sharply to a standing position.

"We're heading for home you and me!" Letting go of her, he turned and stamped out of the lunch-room, slamming the door violently in his wake.

The room was very still. Mamie managed a thin, uneasy smile.

"It's a helluva mess, ain't it?" she observed heavily. "I guess you and Ruth'll have plenty to talk about now."

Bill flushed. "He's just a little hot right now," he offered limply. "I wouldn't worry too much. After all, it was that damned hot-head Frank Parks' fault..."

Mamie looked at him thoughtfully. She laid the dirty rag on the counter.

"Who knows?" she said flatly. "Maybe it wasn't all his fault..." She sighed. "I'm real sorry this had to happen here, in your joint, Bill. But it did, and if it hadn't happened here, I guess it would have somewhere else."

She crossed to the screen door, stood looking out through the mesh at her husband, perched impatiently behind the steering wheel.

"Damn dirty bastard!" She spat the words through her teeth; then turned and glanced at Bill and softened instantly. "Thanks, Bill, for everything." She tossed him a semblance of a smile. "Well... happy days!" She flipped it wearily.

Mamie marched out into the blanketing heat of the midday sun, and climbed up on the leather seat beside her husband.

Karl and Mamie Brandon rode down the highway away from the lunch-room in a thick, coagulated silence. The stone bluff moved closer, closer until at last it towered over them, sharp and top-heavy. The truck sped through its shadow and went rumbling out into the sunlight, up the slight grade into the dusk of pines.

Mamie was waiting for Brandon to say something. She waited alertly for him to start raking up the scene, fresh and bleeding behind them. But he said nothing. After a little while they came to a reddish, dusty road leading to the woods. They swung into the rutted trail. When they had gone about a half mile into the woods, the truck poked its snout out into the open space before the house.

Brandon had planned his house well. It stood solid on the crest of the rise in the centre of a large clearing. The pines and scrub oak ranged themselves along the edges of the clearing, a dense, protecting wall of green, some fifty yards from the house itself. The clearing was well-tended and clean. To the left of the house, over by the far rim of the space, there was a large wooden barn, and off behind was a large, cultivated plot, with vegetables interspersed with a few emaciated fruit-trees. Three cows stood in the corral near the barn.

The house itself was redwood. It was low and flat, with a porch, three steps off the ground level, running the width of the building. Mamie could see what was apparently a back porch jutting from the rear, with a kind of pathway leading to a small shed-like building and an outhouse.

Brandon edged the truck up close to the front path any raced the engine noisily before he cut it off. The stillness of the place came rushing in on them. It was very hot.

Brandon slid his body round so that his feet were only metal running-board. He sat there for a moment, running his practised eye critically over the place. Then he eased himself to the ground. He walked round to the front of the truck and stood, legs apart, surveying the house, the barn, everything in general. He apparently found all in order, precisely as he had left it the day before. Mamie sat high above him in the muggy cab, sat very quietly. He came round to her side of the truck and pulled open the door.

"Well … this is it! You're home."

Mamie Brandon swung her legs out over the step and jumped down beside him. She looked curiously at the house, baking in the dry, oppressive heat. Brandon brushed past her, going to the truck, and pulled down the suitcase. He set it on the ground at her feet and turned and went up the path alone, up the few steps to the porch. Mamie stood alone, a little unsure. She reached down and picked up the bag. After a moment of indecision she followed him. By the time she had reached the porch he had already unlocked the door and gone inside. She noticed he had left the door slightly ajar. Mamie paused at the top of the steps and tried to slow her breathing. She shifted her weight and set the suitcase on the porch floor. She could feel a thin trickle of sweat trailing aimlessly down the inaccessible middle of her back.

She crossed the porch and rested her hands, palms flat, on the rough-hewn railing. "You're home!" Her mind went back to retrieve his words. The incident at the lunch-room had been a sharp, ugly thing; the sting of Frank Parks was still in her, smarting. What the hell right had he to say anything! Brandon had not mentioned the affair. For that she was dimly grateful. She did not feel in the mood for a row. Her resentment towards Frank faded. She gave a tiny snort; all that storming and furore kicked up by a look, by a couple of words from a man who was nothing, nothing at all to her!

Mamie stood now, her feet planted firmly on the porch of this house, her house. This belonged to her, to Mamie Brandon. These were the things she herself had made real, had held out for, had won for herself by herself. She had bought them in her way; she had paid for them. She held the receipt, signed by the county clerk's hand. No Frank Parks, no Bills, no Ruths, no Joes from the past could touch her now. She was safe and secure, now and for ever.

Mamie Brandon bent over and took a firm grip on her suitcase handle. She crossed the porch, stepped over the threshold of her house, and as she entered, she stuck out her foot and kicked the door shut behind her.

CHAPTER THREE

THE entire face of the gravel apron was criss-crossed with tire marks and skid scars. Bill started to work at the corner nearest the building and raked steadily, erasing the souvenirs of the day's traffic. He worked silently, thinking over the events behind him, impersonally, judiciously. By the time he had reached the shoulder of the road, the long shadow cast by the stone bluff had crept stealthily eastward across the flat and lay parallel, waiting for him. Bill paused, leaning on the rake handle. Then suddenly, without quite realizing why, he leaped hastily, throwing his body prone on the grassy strip beside the parking.

The battered, hybrid roadster with no fenders came careening off the highway, skinning past him as he dived. Bill scrambled to his feet, fighting to press his temper down. He came stalking to where the tow-headed kid and the girl sat.

"I guess you'll be surprised to find out I just finished raking this all down!" he barked angrily.

They both gazed at him serenely. "It looks awfully nice, too, Mr. Randall," the girl conceded. "You see, I came. My brother Arthur, here, brought me out from Dutch Flat."

Bill looked at her, at the brown, wavy hair that framed her sun-tanned face. He glanced past her, at Arthur. Arthur was a wiry kid, with a straw-colored thatch of unruly hair and a face of the same pattern as hers. Only, where her face was smooth, tanned, and clear, his was splotched with a handful of freckles.

"You might move this crate!" Bill's ire still simmered. "And then you might grab on to this rake. Cover up those marks!"

The kid pulled the car up with a quick, frantic spurt, then swung an abnormally long pair of legs over the side of the car and dropped to the ground. He came over and took the rake. The girl swung her legs over the stripped side of the machine and Bill's eyes caught a wayward glimpse of bare, browned thigh. She came over to him shaking her long hair back on her shoulders.

"I came, just like you wanted," she repeated.

"That's good." He ran his eyes over her sharply. She was a helluva good-looking kid. Almost too good-looking for a job in a joint. Still, with Mamie gone he needed someone, anyone. He headed for the lunch-room. "If you'll come on in, I'll try and give you the general idea."

The kid was earnestly raking the gravel. "You stick around, Arthur," she commanded. "I don't think he'll want me to stay around to-night."

"Okay, sis."

She followed Bill into the building and gazed critically around. Bill watched her curiously.

"Like it?" he ventured drily.

"Yes. It's nice. Looks just like a lunch-room," she replied a little acidly.

Bill winced. He moved past her, to where the clean uniform was hanging.

"I'd like you to wear this when you're on the job."

She took the dress and held it up to her shoulders. "It's kind of on the ample side, isn't it?" she remarked with a frown. "Certainly not what you'd call form-fitting!"

He could remember Mamie in it. It sure had been then!

"Maybe you could take it in or something," he offered lamely.

"Take it in?" She sounded dubious. "Yeah...maybe."

Bill skirted further discussion about the uniform. He went on, pointing out the cash register, the coffee urn, where the cups and plates were stacked. "The sink's behind here, behind the partition." He disappeared behind it and talked from there.

"I'd like the things washed up as soon as the customers finish. Understand?"

"Sure."

Bill glanced round. "There's a small room off the back door where you can stay, if you ever want to. The other gal used to stay out here all night now and then."

She glanced towards the back portion of the small place. "Oh ... I don't think I'd want to do that." She hesitated. "No ... you see, Arthur's going to bring me out and come for me at night. Thanks, anyway."

Bill scurried on. "Keep the bottles lined up on the counter. Keep toothpicks in the bowls. Keep the counter clean—all the time. Lights off when you don't need them. Board up the screens at night before you lock up." He spilled out the instructions. "One more thing—the juke box." He pointed to the corner.

"Got anything good on it?" she asked.

"What?"

She was over at the juke now, stooped forward, reading the titles. She shook her head slowly, in a regretful sort of way.

"That Lombardo stuff! It really ought to be chucked out, Mr. Randall! It's so icky, so old!"

Bill said nothing.

"What were you going to say about the juke box?" she prompted.

"It goes on the blink now and then," he said jerkily. "When it does, there's an 'out of order' sign."

She smiled. "Don't worry! Arthur can fix it."

"Arthur who?"

"Why, Mr. Randall! Arthur's my brother—he's right outside there!" She nodded in that direction. The tall kid was coming towards the building with the rake in hand. "Arthur's awfully clever. I think he's kind of cute, don't you?"

Bill started slightly. The kid was indecently tall, Bill thought, tall and rangy, like Frank Parks. In fact, come to think of it, he reminded Bill of Frank Parks a lot. Only, where Frank was older, solid, developed, the kid was still forming, still mostly all legs.

"He's very … cute!" Bill said flatly.

"Yes, he is." She smiled. "You won't want me to stay around to-night, will you? You see, Arthur and I always have a date in town every Sunday night … down at Baxter, at the dance."

" … with your brother?"

"Oh yes. I always go with Arthur."

"You have no boy friend, then?" Bill was curious.

She regarded him with cool, grey eyes. "When I find a fellow like Arthur," she said, "I'll have a boy friend. Okay about to-night?"

Bill felt a sudden confidence in her, in the way she put things together. Everything was going to be okay.

"Sure … sure, kid. Go on along. You be here bright and early to-morrow, though!" He glanced round the room and then back at her. "That's about everything, I guess."

She reached out as if she were going to hand the uniform to him. He pointed to the nail. "It goes there!"

"Okay!"

She tossed it easily, unerringly to the mark. She crossed to the screen door. Arthur ranged just outside, resting his chin on the end of the rake handle. She took the rake, setting it just inside, against the wall. She smiled at Bill and then let the door slam shut.

"Arthur, wasn't it just too sweet of Mr. Randall to let me off on my very first night?" They moved across the parking to the car. "I think he's an old dear!"

Bill heard that very clearly. The engine coughed and came up racing and spitting, drowning out their further talk. Bill bolted across the floor and flung open the screen.

"Hey! Wait!" The engine died down. "What's your name?"

She yelled back to him. "It's Binnie!"

"What? Minnie?"

"Binnie. Binnie. B-i-n-n-i-e! Like the movie star!"

"Oh. Binnie! Okay!" Binnie … like the movie star! He might have known it would be Binnie or Bette or something like that— something like a movie star! It was a wonder Arthur was Arthur, he thought bitterly. It's a wonder he wasn't a Gary or a Guy or a Gregory—something like a movie star, too!

Bill Randall let the screen door slam loudly. He stood looking at the white uniform and wished devoutly, fiercely, that Mamie were back. Mamie had never made him feel old! Mamie had a way of eliminating time from the day's routine. This Binnie, now, she was different. She and her Arthur! He didn't feel old, not exactly; that wasn't it. He felt exhausted, beat-up, worn-out!

He snapped the lock on the door and put up the boarding round the screens. He paused in the frame of the back door and surveyed the place. It did look just like a lunch-room, as she had said! He grunted. He switched off the lights and went out, pulling the back door shut. He came round the building and started walking out across the parking to the road. His flashlight hung from his belt and the stock kept whacking against his groin with every step. But he walked on, letting it bang away, only vaguely conscious of its annoyance. His mind was busy with other things. Just beyond the stone bluff, he turned off the highway and cut up the path in the shrouding darkness, the beaded cone of his light darting from pine to pine preceding him. Finally he came to the fence round the place. He vaulted it easily and went across the clearing, up to the house. There was a light in the window.

Bill drew a deep, relaxing breath. It was always good to get home. He gazed round the open section with satisfaction. Everything in good order. Suddenly Keno barked once sharply, and came racing round the edge of the house, leaping and dancing with welcome. Bill stooped and rubbed the little dog gently behind the ears. The door above them opened; Ruth came out on the porch. He could see the silvered line of the long zipper down the front of her housecoat gleaming in the reflected light from the hallway.

"Hello, darling!" she said. "I'd begun to wonder where you were, I thought maybe you'd been kidnapped by some wild woman!"

He straightened, climbed the steps and swept her into his arms. She was so cool, so complete, so wonderful! He kissed her long and hard. "Oh ... sir!" She pulled away and caught her breath. "You'd better be careful! My old husband is liable to come home any time!"

"Slut!" He hugged her tight and kissed her under the ear.

She was mock serious. "You know, Bill, I've got the makings of a bad woman in me. What's more ... I think I like it!" They laughed and Ruth broke away. She went on ahead, back into the house. Bill glanced down at Keno.

"Keep your eyes peeled, chum. I got a feeling we're going to be busy inside!"

Ruth pulled her legs up under her in the big, chintz-covered chair and lit a cigarette. Bill came into the room a moment later, crossed over and plucked the cigarette from her lips.

"Bill, you've got an awful nerve!"

"Always the ever-lovin' thoughtful little woman!" Bill dropped into the cushioned cup of the chesterfield and settled back, puffing clouds of smoke. "There's times when I just don't know what I'd do without you, wench!"

Ruth got another cigarette and lit it. "You'll pardon my saying so, but you look positively beat-up to-night, Mr. Randall!" she observed.

"You can say that again, baby! I am. This lunch-room business is too much for an old man, I guess."

"Yeah. Practically decrepit, you are!" she snorted. "What about the new girl ... what's her name?"

"It's Binnie, darling—just like the movie star!"

"What about the girl?"

"She's going to be all right. She's a darn nice kid. She'll be all right. She's no Mamie, though!" He drew heavily on his cigarette and expelled the smoke from his nostrils. "We had a prize mess down there to-day, kiddo."

"Mess? What kind of a mess?"

"A rip-snorter! Our Mamie came back from Reno with her brand-new husband this morning. Freshly wed!"

"And…?"

"Well… they came in and got some coffee. Everything was peaches and cream. That is, it was until your old boy friend Frankie Parks blew in!"

Ruth gripped the arms of her chair. "Oh, Bill!"

"Yeah, that's how it was! In comes young Frank, hotter than a firecracker. He says 'Congratulations!' only the way he says it you could scrape ice from it. Brandon's just as cool, casual. Finally Frank goes off the deep end. He tells Mamie, for no reason at all, that as far as he's concerned she can go to hell. Well, naturally, that brought the old man to his feet. He jumps the kid and tells him to beat it—but fast! Frankie begins to get on to himself about then. Only not before he gets in a parting shot. He tells the two of them he's not through. He's going to be around, he says. That Brandon was crazy mad. He chased Frank outside and told him if he pulls any funny business in the future he's as good as a dead duck. That's the way he put it—a dead duck."

"How stupid of Frank!" Ruth burst out. "How stupid and thoughtless! How terribly cruel!" She reviewed the scene in her mind and frowned "Bill. What kind of a man is Brandon? What's the real story behind him?"

Bill gazed at her thoughtfully. "Brandon?" He hesitated. "Well, it's a long story." He paused again, to try and arrange his thoughts. "He's got a damned nice place, I know that. At least, that's what everybody says. I've never been on the property." Bill grinned sheepishly. "He's been around these parts for years.

Brandon was little more than a kid when he and his father settled in the hills. They worked up at the old saw-mill on the river. After the mill folded up and the old man died, Brandon junior found himself with a goodly chunk of dough in his jeans. He bought that section of his long before many people lived round here. I guess he picked it up for a song in those days. He put up a little shack and that's where he lived. The house came later after he had met the woman."

Ruth's brows shot up. "A woman?"

"Yes, there was a woman. Mamie isn't the love of his life by any means. It was about ten years ago, if I remember right. She was a school-teacher, of all things, from Sacramento mento. Brandon and she met somehow, and before long had fallen for him. I guess he fell for her, too."

A look of disbelief had spread over Ruth's face of smiled thinly.

"That's the way it was," he said.

"Well, it is a little hard to believe." She looked at him hastily. "From what you've already told me about him, I mean."

"I know. But they say she was very pretty, and, remember Brandon was younger then. Too, he was pretty inexperienced; that's important. At any rate, he met her and before the summer had run out, he had asked her to marry him and she had said yes. There was only one hitch. She had one more year to teach, according to the contract of her job. So they had to wait until she was finished."

"What on earth do you suppose a woman like that saw in Brandon?" Ruth was wondering.

"Just one of those things, I guess." Bill cleared his throat noisily. "Well, once she had said yes, Brandon really went to town. His property sits on a hill, as you know, and he picked out the highest part of the ground and cleared it all off. He worked like a beaver, all by himself, cutting away the undergrowth, hacking away the timber, until he had the whole top of the knoll just as he wanted it. On the very top of the rise he laid the foundation for this house of theirs. She took to coming up from the valley every Saturday, staying through Sunday—all discreet and above board: she stayed down at O'Malley's in Colfax—and they spent all their time up on the place. The house began to shape up, and by the time the first snows came that winter, the house itself was just about done. They had worked like oxen, the two of them, all winter, all spring, furnishing the place. She had a lot of definite ideas, they say, and Brandon must have been daffy with love. All she had to do was want something, apparently, and he would get it. She worked out what she wanted for each room and he bought it. There were crates of stuff all over the platform down in Colfax that spring. By the time summer came the house was done, all ready to move into."

Ruth was listening, absorbed. He paused for a long time and then picked up the thread again.

"She sure must have had a way about her, that woman. She wanted a bang-up wedding with all the trimmings. Finally she sold him on the idea of getting it done down in Colfax—in a church. She was going to wind up her job on a Thursday, I think it was, and she would drive up from the valley on Saturday. The wedding was set for that Sunday afternoon."

Bill lit another cigarette. He expelled the smoke with force.

"It never came off. Oh, she finished her job all right and started out from Sacramento just as she had planned, all by herself. Only she left a day earlier, see? On Friday instead of Saturday. I guess she figured she'd surprise him or something. Well, that Friday night she piled into her car and started on her way. It was dark when she started and raining to beat hell. A couple of miles this side of Colfax she came barrelling round that big curve down there and ploughed into the rear of one of those big gas trucks. It blew sky high and her car, drenched with gas, flip-flopped a couple of times and the whole works burned to a crisp. There wasn't enough left of her to bury!"

Ruth's hand was over her mouth, her eyes dark with horror. Bill went over to the fireplace and bent down, stirring the logs. He came back to the chesterfield and dropped down.

"That's all I know about Karl Brandon," he said briefly. "He's barricaded himself away from people ever since the accident. That's been over ten years now. He's been a hermit."

"Living in the house they planned together," Ruth added wistfully.

Bill shook his head.

"No, he's never lived in the place itself, not in that house. After the accident he built himself a room in the rear of his barn. He boarded up the house. As far as I know, the house is just the same as it was the day of the accident. All the things she put into it are still there, new; they've never been used."

Bill leaned over and unlaced his shoes. He kicked them off on the rug. Ruth raised her gaze slowly and met his eyes.

"What about Mamie, Bill? Does she know all this?"

"I don't think she knows any of it. I had it on the tip of my tongue to tell her the other day. But she got to talking and I could see it wouldn't be any use. Maybe she's better off, in a way, not to know. She'll find out in her own way, in her own time. And that'll be soon enough, God knows!"

"You don't think he loves Mamie."

"Do you ... after what I've told you?"

She shook her head. The room was silent. Bill got up and walked over to the big window. He stood there, staring out into the night.

"But then ... " he reasoned cautiously, "Mamie doesn't love him, either. That's one reason you couldn't talk to her the other day; she's set her course knowing that from the start. Nobody could tell her anything. She thinks she's got everything she wanted; she wouldn't listen to anything that might threaten to change anything. No, she's going to have to find out for herself. I like Mamie; I'd hate like hell to see her get hurt." He turned and looked down at Ruth, his eyes troubled. "There's nothing we can do but just sit here and watch it come. And it will come. Because, just as sure as God made little green apples, there's nothing but grief in that place on the hill."

Ruth was small, almost child-like in the depths of the big chair. "You know, Bill…" she worked her thought slowly. "I've been wondering, ever since I talked with Mamie. I wonder if we really know what kind of a person Mamie really is." She raised her eyes. He had swung round and was gazing down into her upturned face. But there was no surprise in his eyes. She saw quite suddenly that he had been wondering the very same thing.

CHAPTER FOUR

RANDON was standing in the centre of the room, waiting quietly. He was smiling quite broadly.

"Well, this is it! You're home, Mamie!" he repeated. He came forward and, taking the suitcase from her hand, set it down. He straightened and put his vise-like arms about her middle and drew her close. His lips found hers; she closed her eyes. In spite of the power and the urgency of his embrace there was no upsurge of feeling. Finally he broke away and gazed at her. He had noticed nothing of this passiveness.

"Come on!" He brushed past her and started across the room. "Maybe you'd like to see the place, huh?"

Mamie let her gaze wander about the room. Two large, roomy chairs, covered with a gay chintz, were set at angles to the open hearth. At the side of the chair to the left, the one nearest the double windows, there was a paper and magazine rack, with a few newspapers stuffed down into it, along with a couple of magazines. That must be his chair, she thought; the other one would be hers. The hardwood floor was highly, almost unbelievably polished in the spaces between the throw rugs; a bookcase to her right was partially filled with books which looked pretty old. There was a long, low table on her left; its surface was mirror-like, free of objects save for an old copy of a newspaper. She opened the paper casually; the headlines seemed strange. Her eye fell on the date line. It was almost ten years old! No wonder the news sounded funny!

"Ain't you coming?"

She had forgotten him in her absorbed perusal of the room. She hurried to his side with an apologetic smile. He turned and preceded her down a small corridor.

"This here's the bedroom." He stepped aside to let her pass.

She entered, her eyes wide. She thought she'd never seen anything so beautiful, so gorgeous! It was a large, airy room with big windows; there was a new-looking bed, a double bed with a nice bedspread. She could see it was a good one! A walnut dressing table, topped by a huge circular mirror, was set up to the wall on the other side of the bed. She uttered a shrill cry of delight. She pressed round to the dresser, pulled open one of the top drawers. Inside there was a complete set of combs, brushes, all the usual paraphernalia. She picked up the largest comb. It was made out of ivory, with a heavy silver backing. The initials E. B. were cut deep in the metal. E. B.—this stuff must have belonged to his mother, she thought suddenly.

His eyes found her with the comb in her hand. He flushed a little, coughed slightly.

"Come on!" he urged, almost brusquely.

She laid the comb gently on the sleek dresser-top and followed him into the hall. He pushed open the door opposite, the first on the left. "Bathroom," he labelled simply. There was a big tub, and an incomplete attachment for a shower. The washbowl was glistening white. She flashed a quick glance around.

"Ain't no toilet." He intercepted her question. "Couldn't get hold of one. Have to use the place outside." He moved down the hallway. "Here's a kinda bedroom, too."

She leaned through the doorway. There was a small couch in the room, a chest of drawers, and a couple of faded prints tacked on the wall. That was all. She suddenly got the idea that this might have been planned for a nursery, a kid's room. She joined him at the end of the hall. He pushed open the last door and she brushed past him into the kitchen.

It was a huge kitchen, large, well-ordered. Up against the wall on her left there was a giant wood-burning stove; beyond it, a large tiled sink with two taps and an auxiliary hand pump. All along the walls, around the room, there were built-in cabinets and shelves, piled with canned foods and cartons. Against the wall on her right, a big, noisy refrigerator reminded her instantly of the one in the lunch-room. Only this one looked newer. Everything looked so new, she thought. Or, what was more to the point, it all looked as if it had never been used.

He led her through a barren room that jutted out like a growth on the back of the house. This would be the washroom; there was a small washing machine, one of the tray types, set up on one of two stone tubs. He opened the screen door.

"I guess you know what that there is." He made a gesture towards the lean frame of an outhouse.

She did. She made a grimace to herself and tried not to think of the coming winter months. He struck out towards a little square shack. He bent down and fitted a key into the lock. The door swung open with a protesting whine.

The shed housed a collection of everything under the sun. There was a work bench and a mess of odds-and-ends of tools hung in rows above it. There were crates and boxes, old hunks of iron parts for cars, and machinery, piled all over the place. A big barrel overflowed with old clothing and rags. Tools, wires, ropes hung from nails and hooks along the walls. Her wandering eye hesitated on a large, double-barrelled shotgun, wrapped in sackcloth. There were no windows and the air in the room smelled musty.

"I keep lots of junk in here," Brandon explained needlessly. "Most of it's just ranch stuff."

She swept the contents of the room with a disdainful look.

"You ain't seen the barn yet."

He started across the clearing. She came up behind him, a little sluggishly. She was getting tired. This had been a long, hard day. Yet, there was a spurring, vicarious thrill in all this, seeing the place for the first time.

"Got vegetables out there." He flung his arm in the direction of the uneven rows off towards the trees on their right. "Spinach, carrots, beets, stuff like that. Them fruit trees, they bear pretty good." He had dropped back and was matching his steps with hers. "You can?" he asked.

"Can what?"

"You can ... put up stuff?"

She shook her head slowly. "No, I don't know how. There's lots of things I gotta learn, I guess."

He stopped by the hewn-timber rails of the corral. The three cows stood close to each other, and surveyed her with cold uninterest.

"I suppose I gotta be learning to milk them cows, too," she ventured.

He turned and glanced at her. "I take care of outside work," he informed her briefly and definitely. "You got your hands full just taking care of the house."

That took care of that! Mamie felt vastly relieved. But she wanted him to know she was ready to do her part.

"Have you ... have we got chickens?"

"Yeah, a few. They're over there, behind the barn."

"Maybe I could take care of them, couldn't I?"

"If that's what you want," was all he said.

He pulled open the door to the barn. It was a nice barn, she guessed. Not too large, but nice. She moved across the floor, heading for a little door under the overhanging loft. She went through into the tiny room. There was a small oil-stove, a basin and pitcher beside a low, single couch. A pantry's opened door revealed a supply of foodstuffs.

"I didn't know you had a hired hand?"

"I don't. I been living out here myself," he said simply.

She looked at him with open surprise. Why on earth had he been bunking up out here when he had that swell house to live in? This Brandon was sure a queer duck! They went out into the blistering heat. He led her round to the other side of the building and showed her the small flock of chickens whose guardian she had become, by request. Well, there weren't many of them, thank God! But there were enough.

A path took off from the edge of the chicken yard and trailed down to the trees, dipping out of sight behind the green wall.

"What's that?"

"Goes down to the old river-bed."

"River-bed?"

"It ain't really a river. Nothing but a dried-up crick most of the time."

Suddenly she remembered Ruth's words. "I see Frank now and then along the river trail..."

Their first week passed. And the second became the third, which in turn was the fourth. There was an ease in the rapid adjustment to their living together. It was entirely Brandon's show. It was Brandon who set the pattern and Mamie who accepted it without hint or question. As he told her that first day, he worked the farm. He took care of the stock, the vegetable garden; he handled the hundred odd things about the place.

Twice a week, as regular as clockwork, on Tuesday and Friday nights, he went off after dinner on his patrolling inspection of the ditch line. He had been assigned a section of the great wooden trough that brought the waters down from the mountains to the powerhouse near town. This section was his responsibility; he was paid to maintain that section, to guard it against leakage or damage. It was a job that paid well and kept him out most of the night.

At first she missed him acutely these nights. The bed seemed hollow, empty, cold with his absence. But as the weeks stretched out, she found she kind of welcomed the break, was grateful for the chance to be alone with herself in the house.

During the day, while he was outside around the place working and during the nights when he was away, all those moments when she was alone, she devoted herself to the house. The house became mistress to her, admired always, cared for with increasing appetite and satisfaction. She would move through its rooms, caressing them with glittering eyes. She would sit alone in the bedroom studying each little detail, as if she were trying to memorize each little item. The things she adored ranged themselves before her eyes: the drawn curtains with their tie-back ribbons, the dressing-table, the heavy silver-handled articles with the curious initials E. B. She kept the house immaculate, doing her chores with hands and fingers that made each duty a service. There was no tell-tale track of dust permitted anywhere. There were no wrinkles permitted on the covers of the beds. The dressing-table was polished, free from any touch of living.

He paid scant attention to the house. That was, as he had said, her look-out. What she did within the house was her business. He asked nothing more than to have his meals and the comforts he demanded. As far as the house was concerned, he stayed clear. Except for one incident. It occurred quite by accident one evening as they sat before the fire.

He had his eyes closed, head tilted back on the chair top. She was relaxed, thumbing through one of the magazines from the rack. The fire crackled and spat. A tiny ember shot out and skidded across the shining floor. She sprang hastily to her feet, dropping the magazine to the floor. Quickly she brushed the glowing spark back under the grate.

Brandon opened his eyes, roused by the commotion, and watched her.

"What'd you do with the little brass dog that was there on the mantel?"

She turned, one hand on the edge of the mantelpiece, and looked down on him, surprised at his tone. He was angry, she realized. She tried to collect her jumbled thoughts, to remember.

"I … I put it over there … on the table."

"Why?"

"I don't know. I … just thought it would look better there."

He said nothing for the moment; then he pulled himself out of the low chair and crossed the room to the table. He picked up the brass figure, came back and, reaching directly in front of her, placed the dog in its original position.

"I don't want nothing ever changed around here, understand?" His words were careful, each underlined separately.

"But … why?" she stammered.

"It don't make no difference why. I don't want nothing changed, ever. I don't want no changes, see? I want it like it is. Don't ever change nothing."

He offered her no explanation. When she went to bed later on, he was already asleep, his great, hairy back set against her. He made no effort to speak to her the next morning.

She got used to these recurrent silences of his gradually. She came too, to accept the well-defined, unalterable precision by which he lived and had his being. There was no deviation from plan for any reason whatever. Monday, he worked around the place; Tuesday, he worked around the place most of the day and that night he went off to inspect the ditch line; Wednesday, he slept late, worked around the place until noon and after that went down to Baxter for a short time; Thursday, he disappeared into the woods and was gone all day sawing and chopping; Friday, it was the place again and the ditch patrol that night; and on Saturday, around noontime, he climbed up in the truck and went down to Colfax, further away, to get what provisions they would need for the coming week. Sunday, he worked the place, the same as any other day.

She made no attempts to accompany him on the trips to town. It was a short trip to Baxter on Wednesday and there was nothing there anyway—a gas station, a general store, and a few odds and ends. Saturdays he made the longer jaunt to Colfax. Once or twice she had had a slight urge to go along those first weeks, but for some reason she had let it pass. He had never asked her to go along and she let it stay that way. She was content. The novelty of complete seclusion had not yet worn away.

CHAPTER FIVE

I<small>T WAS</small> the last Saturday in August. The heat had reached a peak. Bill Randall came slowly along the side of the highway from the stone bluff, squinting in the glare, peering over towards the white box-like structure that was his place. He recognized Frank Parks' model A parked out front. With a slight frown he quickened his pace to the screen door.

Frank was sitting on a stool inside talking to Binnie. Bill put his hand on the big shoulder.

"Hello, Frankie boy! What's up?"

Frank seized Bill's proffered hand. "Hiya, bud! Nothing's exciting! Just been batting the breeze with the gal friend here. Say, Bill, you done all right!"

Bill glanced at Binnie. She looked so radiant, so cool in that spotless uniform. She had taken it in; now it fitted like the paper on the wall! The kid had a nice wall to fit, too!

"You haven't been letting this character fill you full of bull, Binnie? He's an artist at it."

"Don't worry, Bill; I know it when I hear it!" She laughed and went behind the partition, leaving them alone.

Bill sat down at Frank's side. "What have you been doing, Frank? I haven't seen you around for a couple of months almost."

Frank eyed him warmly. "Been doing some railroad work again—down in the yards at Colfax. Just finished up, as a matter of fact."

"Yeah?" There was a brief silence. "New what?"

"Don't know exactly; ain't made up my mind yet."

Bill probed cautiously. "We can always use a good hand up on the place for a while, Frank."

Frank smiled. "No, thanks, Bill. Tell you the truth, I been kinda thinking about going down to the valley for a spell. Kinda curious. Must be about time for the crops."

"Yeah ... guess it is."

"How's Ruth?"

"Good. She's fine."

"That's swell." Frank paused. "Seen Mamie around?"

"Not since you have. You still thinking about her, Frank?"

"No ... not exactly. I just been wondering if she. got everything she was wanting?"

Bill stood up. The conversation made him uncomfortable. "I guess so," he said.

"I guess you're right."

Frank took three toothpicks from the bowl. He broke them into little segments and began to piece out a vague design.

Binnie came out from behind the thin wall. "Everything's been awfully quiet, Bill."

"I shouldn't be surprised. It's too damned hot!"

Binnie chuckled. She glanced down at the man in front of her. "Really, you are a nuisance! All you can do is make a mess." She leaned over and picked up the bits of toothpick. "You're worse than a baby, honestly!"

He grinned at her. She cupped her palm over the bits of wood and went to the ash-can to drop them in. Then she came back, glanced at Frank's face and colored briefly. Bill watched the interplay. Good God! he thought, I hope he isn't going on the make for her; why, she's nothing more than a kid!

Binnie crossed over to the juke box, put a coin in the plunger. She glanced at Bill and smiled.

"I've got a big surprise for you. I finally enticed the guy to change a couple of the records. You listen. Now this one's really something!"

She shoved the plunger, and after a moment or so the music came rolling softly into the room. The three of them listened absently. It was a good piece! Bill had to concede. Funny how right she was, even about a damn-fool record like this! He gazed at her with a surge of fondness. Instinctively he glanced at Frank. But Frank was looking out beyond her, beyond the room towards the highway. The piece drifted to an end.

"How's Art, the boy wonder?" Bill asked.

"He's off in the mountains, cutting timber. He'll be back to-morrow."

"In time for the usual Sunday-night spree?"

"That's right, sir!" she giggled.

"Still no other guy around?"

"Good gosh, Bill! I told you once, until I meet that right guy … Arthur's good enough for me."

"What kind of a guy is this 'right guy' going to be?" Frank asked.

She hesitated, confused. "I … I'm not sure," she said slowly. "But I'll know him when he comes along."

Frank gazed at her for some minutes. She was looking at Frank. They were both very serious. Frank shifted his gaze to Bill.

"You was saying you could use somebody up on the place for a while. Offer still go?"

Bill nodded.

"You got yourself a boy!" Frank got to his feet. "I'll be seeing you later on, Bill. Sometime this afternoon. Okay?"

"Okay, Frank, sure."

He went past them out into the sunlight. He walked round the model A and climbed in. The light car rolled slowly down the highway.

"You know, Bill, I think he's a very nice … guy," Binnie said evenly.

"He's a great guy, Binnie."

"Arthur's nuts about Frank, you know."

"I didn't even know they knew each other."

"Oh yes." She laughed faintly. "Arthur worked with Frank on some logging deal up in the hills. From that time on all he's been talking about is what Frank Parks says, what Frank Parks does, what Frank Parks thinks. He dogs Frank's footsteps whenever Frank's around. Yes, I like Frank, He's been awfully nice to Arthur. You know what I mean, Bill. An older fellow like Frank must get awfully fed-up having a kid like Arthur tagging around all the time!" She paused. "But if he does, he never shows it. You know, in a way, when you see them together, they're an awful lot like brothers. Don't you even think they look a little like each other?"

Bill nodded. He glanced out to the road. Ruth was coming along the shoulder of the highway, jogging along on the old horse.

"Here comes the wife," he remarked, brightening.

They watched Ruth swing down off the horse. She left him at the grassy strip. She pulled open the door and thumped inside.

"Hail! Well, Billy me lad, I'm back, snooping around again!" She pushed herself on tiptoe and kissed her husband lightly below the ear. She smiled at Binnie. "You're Binnie. I've heard all about you, my dear. You see, my husband happens to be an incorrigible gossip. Though, I will admit, I do encourage him now and then."

"I'm awfully glad to know you, Mrs. Randall."

Ruth let go her hand and stepped back, smiling. "You are lovely! You're quite the loveliest thing I've seen in years! You make me feel all old and dowdy."

Binnie flushed. "You're very kind, Mrs. Randall."

"Please, dear. Don't call me Mrs. Randall. Makes me feel as if I were Bill's mother ... instead of his wife!" She pressed Binnie's arm gently. "It's Ruth ... Ruth ... "

Bill cleared his throat. "Ruth, I've got something to tell you, honey. It's about Frank Parks."

A tiny catch took hold of her heart. "What is it, Bill?"

He smiled at her apprehension. "It's nothing bad," he reassured her gently. "In fact, it's good. He's coming up to the place again, to work for us. For a while at any rate."

"Oh, Bill, that's wonderful!" She looked at Binnie. "Do you know Frank Parks?"

"Yeah, she knows him," Bill said.

Ruth glanced at him curiously. She glanced back at Binnie. She is lovely, absolutely lovely, she thought.

"When's he coming?"

"Be up later to-day," he said.

"Then I've got to be on my way. That room in the barn will have to be cleaned up."

Bill gazed at her. Ruth was terrific! She always seemed to know what to do, even before it needed doing. A wave of tenderness for her swept over him. He stepped forward and reached.

She sidestepped his arms. "Oh no, you don't," she laughed; "I've got work to do." She grinned back at Binnie. "You'd better watch out for this character!" She levelled an accusing finger at her husband. "He's a terrible wolf, believe me!"

They watched her as she scrambled up on Joe's big back. She waved once in their direction and kicked the old horse into an unwilling gallop.

"She's awfully cute," Binnie said. "How long have you been married, Bill?"

" 'Bout five years."

"Is she from around here?"

He shook his head. "No; she's from Auburn. I met her at a dance down there one night. It happened just like that. I met her; I had a dance or two with her and bang! It was all over—I was hooked!"

There was a moment of silence.

"That's the way I'd like it to be with me, when it happens," Binnie said at last.

"How's that?"

"Quick ... and afterwards nice and perfect. Like it is with you and Ruth. I'd like to get married, to settle down, to live like you and Ruth."

He frowned slightly, wondering if Frank Parks were the one to give that kind of life to anyone.

The noise from the outside shook him loose from the thought. It was the old man—Brandon! The big truck was edging down off the asphalt, scrunching on to the gravel strand. Brandon brought the truck close to the building and shut off the clanking engine. He climbed down stiffly from the seat and came to the door.

"Morning, Randall."

Bill nodded. "Good morning, Brandon."

Brandon sat down and scarcely glanced at Binnie. "Cup of coffee and a couple of doughnuts." After a moment he turned and looked at Bill. "You make much out of this dump?"

"I make enough."

Brandon shot him a sharp look. "Nice weather we're having."

"Yeah. Awful hot to-day, though."

Bill fought to keep the astonished crease from between his eyes. The man was being damn near friendly! Thank God Frank had pulled out when he did!

Binnie put the coffee and doughnuts in front of Brandon. He got out his purse and handed her a coin. She turned, rang it up, and gave him his change. Bill cleared his throat.

"How's ... Mrs. Brandon?"

"She's all right." Brandon stopped his munching. He glanced over at Bill. "She sticks pretty close to the place. She don't care much about going out no more."

He shut up tight after that. He finally finished and got to his feet. He looked at Bill for a moment; the old hint of surliness had returned. He nodded curtly and went out to his truck.

"That's a strange sort of man, isn't he?" Binnie commented. "He married the other woman, didn't he? The one who was here before me."

"Yes. That's right. He married Mamie."

"What kind of a woman is she, Bill, this Mamie Brandon?"

He returned her gaze evenly. "I really don't know," he confessed. "I used to think I knew her very well... but now I really don't know."

They were sitting at dinner that night when Mamie asked him about the trip into town.

"Was it nice down in town?"

"It was all right."

"Did you see anybody?"

He stared at her with mounting annoyance. He hated interruptions when he was eating.

"No," he said coldly, "I didn't see no one."

She tried once again.

"I don't see how you could go all the way to town and not see nobody!"

He set his lips grimly. "I said I didn't see nobody." It was final and complete.

Suddenly she made up her mind. She rose and stood by the table, looking down on him.

"I want to go to town with you next week."

He glanced up at her. "We'll see... when the time comes."

"But I want to know now!" Her tone was petulant.

He flared dangerously. "I said we'll see when the time comes. That's all there is to it!"

"But I don't see why I can't know now."

"What's been getting into you lately?"

She held her stand for a moment; then it broke. "Oh, I don't know. I just feel kinda restless, somehow. I kinda want to see some people."

His eyes narrowed. "You want to see people, huh? What people?"

She brought her eyes back to him, bewildered, missing the point. She hadn't meant anybody in particular. "What people?" she echoed. "Why, nobody exactly. Just ... people."

He was gazing at her shrewdly. "We'll see ... when the time comes." The discussion was closed. He went back to his food.

"It's awfully good to see you again, Frank."

He took Ruth's hand. "It's sure good to see you."

Bill was pleased and satisfied. Just like old times, he thought, he and Ruth and Frank all working together. Ruth's eye transmitted a message. Bill took the hint.

"I'm going on down to the barn," he announced. "You stay here, Frank, and visit with Ruth for a while. There's not much we can do to-day, anyway."

He walked away and Frank followed Ruth's lead round to the back of the house.

She sat down on the bench in the sun. She slid over to make room for him. "Sit down, Frank. Let's talk."

"I'll park here on the ground, where I can see you better." He dropped to the earth and drew his legs up close to his chest.

There was a moment's silence. Neither knew quite how to begin.

"I hear you've been down in Colfax, working in the yards again."

"Yeah. It ain't a bad deal; I wouldn't want it permanent, though."

"You're still pretty much the wanderer, aren't you, Frank?"

He glanced up at her soberly. "I guess that's about it." "There's one thing, though. I been kinda figuring I'd sort of like to think about maybe getting married one of these days." He stumbled, confused. "Just thinking about it, understand."

Her face lit up. "Is there anybody yet?"

"No. Nobody yet." He grinned. "You could say I'm in the market, that's all."

She closed her eyes for a moment. She had to say this next thing, but she wasn't sure she knew quite how to say it.

"You don't have to answer this, Frank, not if you'd rather not. But what about Mamie? How do you feel about Mamie now?"

"That's all over."

"Are you sure?"

"Sure. Sure thing. I'm sure."

She said nothing. Suddenly his eyes came to her face and they were dark and wild.

"Sure? I ain't sure! I ain't sure about nothing no more! How do I feel about Mamie? I can't forget her, that's how I feel about Mamie Brandon! I got her down inside me all the time! I got her in me, Ruth! All I do is go around all the time thinking about her, about the way she was, wanting her like that! God knows I been trying to get rid of her! Only I can't, Ruth, I can't!"

There was desperation in his voice. He lurched forward, put his folded arms on his knees and buried his face against them. She looked at him, her heart sick with helplessness.

"It was different with her, with Mamie. For months I kept chasing after her. Sure, all I wanted to do was lay her! I figured she knew the score from away back the first time I seen her. I got next to her now and then and the way she acted I figured that's what she wanted, too. Only she always stopped me; she wouldn't let me get close enough. The more she wouldn't, the more I just had to have her, Ruth. It got like wanting dope or something like that. I was going crazy, just wanting her. It wasn't like when I wanted a woman any other time. When a guy gets like that, it comes sudden. You know what it is right off. It's kind of a good feeling in a way, like wanting something to eat or drink. When it's like that, it's easy. You go out and get a woman, get it out of your system. That's that. Only with her it was different, somehow. With her it was more than just wanting her, simple like that. It wasn't like between a guy and a dame. With her something came right out and grabbed hold of you. It scared you, Ruth; it wasn't right! You got a feeling that when you was wanting her, that maybe it was her instead that was wanting you, that she was wanting it more than you was! I used to wonder, God, where would it end, a thing like that, if you ever got started—with her wanting like that?" His intensity broke; he raised his head and looked at Ruth soberly. "Oh, she never said nothing like that! She never said yes or even maybe. All she kept saying all the time was no. She kept harping on that other stuff, the kind of life she's got with Brandon. It wasn't what she said that scared me, it was that other thing, that funny feeling!" He was silent for a moment and then wet his lips before going on. "I'm scared of her, Ruth! Even with her being married and all, I'm still scared of her. I'm scared one day it's gonna happen just like I know it's been gonna happen ever since we laid eyes on each other the first time! It's gonna happen, Ruth, and I'm scared of her!"

Ruth put out her hand to stop him. But he plunged ahead.

"I knowed from the start she was bad for me, Ruth. There's something that's no good for me in her. I ain't no kid, Ruth; I've had women, lots of women. Pretty damn near all of them were the kind most folks call bad women. There was something that was good in all of them somewheres. But there ain't nothing that's good for me in Mamie Brandon, nothing!"

Ruth was staring down in horror. She gripped him by the arm.

"Frank, stop! You can't believe what you've been saying. She's not the kind of woman you think. She's just not that kind of woman at all." He looked up at her and then away as she went on breathlessly.

"Those are terrible things, Frank. There were reasons why she dared not let herself love you. She wanted you, yes, but clean and honest and right. She wanted you, but she forced herself to go the other way. It was the fighting within her that you felt so strong. Why, Frank, you've never even given her a fair chance. You've never tried to see her side of it for a single moment."

He kept avoiding her eyes. Her voice steadied.

"I think she's made a bad mistake, Frank. There'll come a time when she'll see just how bad a mistake it is. But it's too late to change things now. When it comes, Mamie'll have her problem to fight alone. Nobody can help her. And you mustn't ever, ever interfere. You mustn't frighten her nor confuse her, Frank—not ever!"

He got to his feet and brushed the clinging, soft dirt from his jeans.

"I hope you're right, Ruth," he said slowly. "For Mamie's sake, for my sake I sure as hell hope you're right. Only I don't think so. I'll just go on, hoping I can keep away from her, hoping I can keep as far away from her as I can get!"

Ruth misinterpreted his words and smiled her indulgent encouragement. She got to her feet and they walked slowly around the house to the front yard. He took her hands in his, pressed them firmly, and then released them.

"I'll go down and see if I can give Bill a hand with anything," he said.

CHAPTER SIX

O NE night a few weeks later, the three of them sat lazing in front of the fire. Quite suddenly Ruth made up her mind.

"Bill, I think I'll go over and see Mamie to-morrow."

He glanced at her curiously. "Might not be a bad idea, at that," he said. Bill had not told her, or Frank, about Brandon's visit to the lunch-room.

"She might like a little company," Ruth continued. "It's been almost five months now, hasn't it?"

Bill turned his eyes to Frank. He was staring into the fire with a detached, remote look. Either he had not heard what they said or he was paying little attention. Frank had apparently put all that other business out of his mind in these last months, Bill thought. That was good; over and done with, as it should be.

The next morning Ruth fitted the bridle over Joe's head and swung herself up on his broad back. She spurred the old horse down the path leading into the woods behind the barn. Finally she reached the bottom of the incline and started along the level path. This was the river trail, as everybody in the hills called it. It started from the Randall place and led down the slope away from their clearing, through the trees, along the creek bed for several miles. It curved in a gradual horse-shoe arc, crossing under the concrete highway bridge, cutting back parallel on the Brandon side of the road. At the other end it would rise slowly and scale the side of the hill that marked the beginning of the Brandon property. Somewhere, about midway on that rise, the path would fork. One branch dipped down to the creek once again; the other led up and emerged from the trees in front of the Brandon house.

Ruth always enjoyed the river trail. She sat back now, listening to the melody of the hills, glancing up at the spanning arc of the highway bridge as she passed beneath it. A few miles beyond, when she had almost reached the beginning of the climb to the fork, her eyes picked out the figure of someone sprawled out on the top of one of the big rocks directly in front of her. It was Mamie Brandon!

Mamie gave the appearance of being asleep. But she heard the approaching sounds. She sat upright and recognized Ruth. She scrambled to her feet.

"Ruth Randall!" she cried out with pleasure as the other woman came within hearing distance. "Gee whiz, it's good to see you!"

Ruth pulled Joe to a halt, slid off, and came to the base of the rock.

"I hardly expected to find you here, like this, the outdoor type!" she laughed. "How are you doing, Mamie?"

Mamie prepared to descend from her perch. Ruth stopped her.

"You stay right where you are," she called. "I'll come up there." She skirted the rock, vaulted up to the face of the stone. She gazed about her. The path started up into the trees just a little further on. Ruth realized the fork she had been heading for was up on the hill. The ranch was up there, behind the screening trees.

"Say, this is all right!" She made herself comfortable, then fished two cigarettes from her shirt pocket. "Have a smoke?"

Mamie took one and they lit up.

"Well, Mamie, what have you been doing with yourself? I haven't seen you down in town or anything."

Mamie ran her nail along a thin fissure in the stone. "Nothing. I ain't been doing nothing. I got the house to take care of; that and the goddam chickens!"

"Chickens?"

"Yeah, chickens. I been taking care of them. Oh, it was all my own damn fault. I figured it would be a snap. After all, chickens…they ain't so big. So I said I'd take care of them…and that's what I been doing ever since."

Ruth had been watching Mamie with shrewd, observing eyes. Mamie looked really very well, Ruth thought. The old, wild, furtive restlessness seemed gone.

"How do you like your place?"

Mamie's face was illumined with genuine feeling. "Oh, gee! It's swell, Ruth! Honest it is! You ever seen it?"

Ruth shook her head. "No."

"Then I want you to be sure and see it before you go." Mamie fell silent for a moment. "I ain't never had no chance to show off before." She glanced at Ruth soberly. "Mr. Brandon, he kinda likes to stick alone, I guess."

Ruth caught the loneliness in Mamie's voice. Mamie fixed her eyes on Ruth.

"How's Bill?"

"Okay. He's busy to-day cutting down the woods!"

"That ain't no easy job cutting down trees. Not by yourself."

A second trickled by. "He's not doing it by himself. Frank's with him."

Mamie said nothing for a moment. "Oh," she finally commented. "How is he?"

"Fine."

"That's good." Mamie dismissed Frank lamely. "How's things down at the lunch-room?"

"Getting along okay, I guess."

"What's the new kid like, the one who took my job?"

"Very nice. She's very pretty. Her name's Binnie."

Mamie let her gaze drift around the trees. Ruth turned her head slightly, studying Mamie's profile.

"How's…Mr. Brandon?" she asked quietly.

"He's all right."

Ruth sat up suddenly with a little laugh. "Good heavens, all we've been doing is ask each other how this one is or that one." She covered Mamie's hand with hers. "And how are you, Mamie, that's what I really want to know?"

Mamie pulled her hand free gently and climbed to her feet. "Me? I'm just swell," she clipped. "Let's go! I want you to see the house!"

The three of them started up the trail—Mamie in the lead, then Ruth, pulling Joe. They came to the fork in the trail. Mamie held the lead, puffing heavily as she plodded up the hill. On the crest. She stopped, breathing heavily, and wiped her glistening face with the back of her hand. She turned and watched as Ruth and Joe came over the rim of the hill. They had come out right behind the barn, in front of the chicken pen.

"Well, I see your chickens!" Ruth laughed.

"Yeah. Ain't they the dirtiest, nastiest things? What you don't have to go through to get a lousy egg!"

Mamie started out once more. They headed across the open, towards the house set on the crest of the rise.

"Oh, Mamie! I like that!" Ruth exclaimed with unconcealed delight. "I just love the way it sits up there on the very top like that!"

Mamie flushed with pleasure. "Me too!" she said proudly.

The two women started along the path. Ruth glanced around the clearing; she sought out the vegetable patch, to where the fruit-trees poked up. She caught sight of Brandon, working over there. She could just make out the upper portion of his body. The day was very hot. He had stripped down to the waist and Ruth could see the heavy contours of his enormous physique, even at this distance.

"Why, he's tremendous!" The words escaped her.

Mamie turned in surprise; she followed Ruth's gaze to the patch. "Yeah," she conceded. "For an old man, he's sure built!"

They moved on up the path. Mamie led the way round the house, down along the side to the front. Ruth tied Joe to the porch railing and then followed Mamie up the front steps. A tour of the house followed.

"Let's have some coffee!" Mamie suggested when they were in the kitchen.

She went over to the stove and busied herself. Ruth sat down. In a short while the warm, homey smell of coffee rose in the room. Mamie carried cups and coffee pot over and poured. Ruth kept her eyes on her, saying nothing.

"Kinda different from the coffee urn down at the place!" Mamie ventured.

Ruth smiled. "Quite a lot different."

Mamie sat down and glanced over the rim of her cup. "It's nice, ain't it?"

Ruth nodded quickly. "It's more than that, Mamie," she said. "It's like heaven!"

"Yeah." Mamie repeated the phrase. "It's like heaven!"

Ruth studied the woman across the table as she sipped her coffee. "You aren't ... sorry about anything, are you, Mamie?"

"Sorry?" Mamie met her gaze coolly, levelly. "Sorry about what?"

"What I mean is, you're satisfied with everything?"

Mamie pursed her lips, mulling the question. "Yeah, I guess so. I'm satisfied." She stared into her cup. "It's only ... I get kinda lonesome sometimes. That's the only thing."

Ruth glanced out of the big window towards the vegetable patch. He was still out in the broiling sun, uncovered, half-naked. Mamie caught the line of her vision and they watched him together.

"He don't talk much, that one," Mamie remarked slowly. "There's days when he don't say nothing at all. It wouldn't be so bad if there was a few other people around now and then. People like you, that I could sort of talk to." She faltered. "But … you know how he is. He don't want people to come around. Sometimes I get a hunch he keeps people away deliberate."

"You ought to come over and see us!" Ruth said impulsively.

The same tardy thought rose in both their minds at once.

"I ain't so sure … " Mamie said vaguely.

Ruth did not force her invitation. Frank Parks and how he felt came jogging into her memory. How terribly wrong he had been about Mamie! She turned and glanced out of the window. Brandon was coming towards the house. He had slipped on his shirt and was buttoning it slowly as he came.

Brandon came in the back door and stamped several times on the floor of the washroom to remove the dust from his shoes. "Hey, Mamie!" he called. She made no attempt to answer. He came into the kitchen and stopped short at the sight of the stranger.

"I got company," Mamie announced, coloring.

"Um … " He nodded slightly at Ruth.

"Oh … 'scuse me! This here's Ruth Randall, Mr. Brandon." Mamie completed her formal introduction in lopsided confusion.

"How do you do, Mr. Brandon?" Ruth inclined her head.

He simply nodded and turned to his wife. "I gotta go down to Baxter."

"But this is Sunday!" she protested. "There won't be no place open to-day."

"The place I'm going to'll be open," he snapped. He glanced at Ruth. "I got trouble with my apple-trees."

She nodded. "I know. We've had trouble too."

"Yeah?" He turned to Mamie. "I'm going."

He nodded to Ruth abruptly and went out. They sat still, listening to the sounds of his starting the engine out front. The truck moved away and the racket faded into silence.

"He really don't mean nothing, being short like that," Mamie said. "Have some more coffee!"

"No, thanks, Mamie. I've got to be on my way. Really, I must!"

"Oh, stay!" There was a sudden plunging plea in Mamie's voice.

"I'd love to, Mamie, honestly. But I can't. I've got to get lunch ready for those working men of mine. I'll be losing my job if I don't!" She rose to her feet. "I do wish you'd come over and see us sometime, Mamie," Ruth urged; fully realizing the potential danger but suddenly not caring. "You come over soon, Mamie. And, maybe, I'll be seeing you down in town one of these days." She hesitated. "You know … you really ought to get out more."

"Yeah … maybe I ought."

When lunch was ready to put on the table, Ruth went out to the porch and took down the iron bar that rested on the crossbeam. She beat violently on the triangle. The clattering din went spinning, ricocheting across the clearing, and presently the two men came marching up the rise towards the house, where she waited for them on the porch. She smiled at them affectionately and went on ahead to put the food on the table.

After they had washed up they took their places. She passed the plates and they helped themselves greedily.

"Well, how was the trip over to the Brandons?" Bill asked.

She sat back and watched them. "All right," she said.

"How's Mamie."

"All right."

He glanced up sharply. "What went wrong?"

"Wrong? Why, nothing went wrong. Why?"

"You keep on saying 'all right, all right.'"

"Well, darling, as far as I could see, everything was all right!"

"Sounds funny, the way you say it."

"I can't help how it sounds, lovey; it's true."

Frank had said nothing. He ate silently, devoting his attention to his plate exclusively. Bill glanced at him briefly and then back at her.

"I finally met Brandon," she said.

"Oh?"

"He is a little difficult, isn't he?"

"Why? What did he say?"

"He didn't say anything. He did mention he was having trouble with the apple-trees."

"I guess everybody has bugs this year. Damned nuisance!"

She fell silent once more. After a moment she looked at Bill. "I asked Mamie to come over and see us sometime."

He shifted his glance to Frank. But Frank kept his eyes on his plate.

"Sure," Bill agreed vacantly. "She must get kinda lonely over there all by herself. I don't imagine Brandon has changed his ways much."

"They never have any company. I was the first."

Bill's sympathy stifled his misgivings. "Sure. It'll be good to see her again."

Frank continued his meal, made no comment.

"She asked about you ... both," Ruth offered.

Neither of them answered her. They finished the meal and pushed back their chairs, stretching out to relax. They lit their cigarettes and the three of them smoked in contemplation. It was Frank who finally broke the silence.

"By the way, I'm going down to town to-night," he remarked casually. I'm going down to the dance."

The dance hall was not imposing. Some unknown promoter with an eye to the wants and desire of the younger crowd had tossed together a simple frame building at a vantage-point along the highway a short distance out of town. He put down a fairly smooth floor, erected a sort of stage at one end, and let it go at that. The band was on a par with the hall. It was a five-piece job that some college kids from down in the valley had organized. Their music was brassy and shrill, but their beat was steady; and their intent was good. The dancers from Baxter and You Bet and all the other little places tucked into the hills showed up with gusto each Sunday night without fail. To them, for a little while once a week, it was as if a thousand strings played softly in the night and each couple danced alone across the waxen floor of heaven.

Frank shoved the model A up into a vacant space and went up to the ticket window.

"Hi, Frankie!" the guy inside greeted. "Back again for a little more of the same?"

"Yeah. It's been a long time!"

"That's what the girl said to the sailor, bud!"

Frank grinned and took his ticket over to the door. There were a lot of couples here already; a solid mass was moving around the floor in steady tempo to the music. Frank peered curiously around. There were a lot of stags propped against the wall, and some of them greeted him with a sign or a nod. Frank moved over and leaned against the plank wall himself, watching the dancers wheel by.

"Hi, Frank, what's doin'?"

He glanced at the short man. "Hiya, Corky!"

"Lots here to-night." Corky indicated the mob on the floor.

"Yeah. You can say that again!" Frank kept his eyes on the crowd, as if he were searching for some particular person.

"What you been doing?"

"Nothing much. Been working with the Randalls."

Corky nodded. There was a hung silence.

"Say, Frank. Could you use a snort, huh?"

Frank brightened. "You got a bottle?"

"Corky patted his hip pocket. "We better get outside."

Corky led the way out to the screening shadows of the trees. He pulled the bottle out, uncapped it, and handed it to Frank.

Frank tilted the bottle, gulping with big swallows. He brought the bottle down, wheezing violently. "Jesus Christ!" he exclaimed. "That stuff's terrific! What the hell'd you do—make it yourself?"

"You're pretty damned particular, getting something for nothing!" Corky laughed. He took a generous swig himself. He coughed. "Boy ... that's something!"

Frank's eyes were on the door to the hall. A couple climbed the stairs and disappeared inside.

"You see Art around to-night?" Frank asked.

Corky shook his head. He held the bottle out towards Frank.

"I don't want no more just now," Frank grinned. "I gotta find that kid. Be seeing you around, Corky! Thanks for the drink."

The place seemed more crowded then before. It was stuffy hot, too. Frank could feel the sweat oozing out all over him. He wondered if it were the heat or the whisky. He had a hunch it was the latter stuff.

"Gonna dance with me, Frankie?" The girl murmured in his ear as some man led her out towards the floor.

"Later, kid." He flashed a ready smile. He watched them move out and blend into the pack. He gazed around the room slowly. No soap! Art and Binnie had not showed up, not yet. He went on waiting. The girl who had asked him to dance with her moved past, signalling him violently from the floor over her partner's shoulder. He pretended he did not see her. He waited. Suddenly he straightened and grinned.

Art and Binnie had entered the building and they headed right for the floor. Frank followed them with eyes now bright and alive. That Binnie, she sure was a honey! Frank stared out across the floor. Art and Binnie had been swallowed up almost instantly. He decided to wait until the break came. But before the music had come to a pause, Art came threading his way off the floor. He was alone.

"Hi, Frank!" He reached out and clapped him on the shoulder. They were almost of a size. Frank felt as if he were looking in some sort of a mirror.

"Hiya, kid!"

Art flushed with pleasure. "Sure good to see you!" he said.

"When'd you get back?"

"This morning."

"How'd the job go?"

"Same old stuff." Art's eyes were blue, too, like his.

"You all done up there?"

"Yeah. For a couple of days or so, anyhow. They said they'd call if they wanted me."

Frank's eyes were on the dancers. The music came to an end and there was a slight pause. Then the band picked up and things went on as before. Art was still talking.

"Hey, Frank, when're you and me going down to the valley and have us a high old time, huh!"

They had made one of those trips together once, and a high old time it had been, too! Frank could still remember that one. He'd had a head for a week after. There'd been a helluva lot of liquor and a hunk of women on the side, too!

"You and me'll get together one of these days. We'll pitch a lulu, kid!"

Art grinned. Frank kept watching the dancers closely.

"What'd you do with your sister?"

"Some clunk she knows from Dutch Flat cut in on us. He's always cutting in!" Art grinned. "The poor dope kinda goes for her in a big way!"

"Where is she!"

"Out there on the floor somewhere." Art peered at Frank curiously. "Don't start worrying. She won't go outside with him. She won't go outside with nobody but me."

"She's got the right slant there," Frank commented grimly.

The couple came into sight, moving slowly with the revolving mass on the floor. Frank watched them approach. She was keeping away from the big guy, keeping a good space between their bodies. The guy wasn't much of a dancer, Frank judged.

She wasn't having a very good time, he could see that. He tapped Art's shoulder.

"I'm gonna bust up that little deal right now," he announced.

Art's eyes followed Frank as he went out to the edge of the floor and waited. Frank let them come right up to him before he stepped out. He moved up behind the big fellow and laid his hand on his shoulder.

"Sorry, bud," Frank said quietly.

The fellow stood helplessly as Frank scooped her in his arms. As they started to dance, the guy moved off the floor and took his place against the wall, his face dark and pouty. Art grinned as Frank and his sister swayed with the music. That Frank did everything good, he thought; he danced like a pro. Binnie was a lot happier now, he could see that. That Frank was sure smooth!

Frank said nothing to her at first. He pulled her close to him, so that they would share the common rhythm of the number. She made no effort to pull away. He relaxed and let the drive of the tempo carry them around the slow circle. After a few moments he pulled away slightly and looked down into her face.

"Hiya doing, beautiful?" he said softly.

She smiled a little smile. "Hello."

They danced silently for a while. He glanced down at her again.

"Anybody ever tell you you're a damn good dancer?"

"Lots, she admitted.

A faint shadow crossed his face. "Lots," she had said. Well, he guessed there had been lots! Why not? She was all right!

"I didn't believe all of them," she added after a moment.

"I think you're a swell dancer," he phrased himself carefully.

"I believe you, Frank," she said slowly.

The music came to a crashing finish. He took her by the arm and propelled her across the floor to where Art was leaning against the wall. "Well, if it ain't Kelly and Hayworth!" he said with a laugh.

"Ape!" Binnie chuckled.

"How's about us going outside and getting some air!" Frank suggested.

They stood off to one side near the trees. "What became of Romeo?" Art asked his sister.

"Frank put the skids under him. I guess he got sore and went home!"

All three laughed indulgently. A girl came out and ran across the clearing. She disappeared into the shadows of the trees. Frank whistled, low and full of meaning.

"Not bad, not bad!" he remarked with approval.

Art laughed. "What d'ya suppose she's going off into the woods for?"

Binnie blushed. "I've got a hunch this is where I go and powder my nose!" She gave a tiny, self-conscious giggle. They watched her in silence until she had disappeared inside.

"Gees, I think she's swell!" Frank breathed.

Art glanced at him with a trace of surprise. "You bet she is!" he agreed. "She's the best!"

It was funny how they could talk so easily, so freely about everything but her. They had hashed over women and the times they had had with them, talked it all out bluntly and openly. Frank had never attempted to pull his punches. Art was no kid, not that way. He'd had a few times on his own! Only now there was no way of saying what they were feeling. Their thoughts were on Binnie, but there was something that restricted the words they might have said.

Between them Art and Frank kept her dancing all the remainder of the evening. Corky came sidling up alongside Frank later on, offering the remainder of the stuff in the bottle. Frank, watching the other two, had almost curtly refused.

"No, thanks; I don't want no more." He had walked away, then, out across the floor and had taken her away from her brother.

"Well, I'll be a no-good sonofabitch!" Corky had exploded, and tilting the bottle, he had drained it right out in front of everybody in the place.

CHAPTER SEVEN

ON WEDNESDAY Brandon went to town, according to schedule. Mamie had let him go these past weeks without raking up the old request to accompany him. But on the following Friday, during dinner, she suddenly brought up the subject again.

"I want to go with you to-morrow," she said flatly.

"All right," he said abruptly, almost stunning her with her own surprise.

The next morning she awakened with a tingle of anticipation. She rose hurriedly, straightened the house, and gave him his breakfast. After he had gone to turn the stock out, she went into the bedroom and got out her thin wedding suit and blouse. She took a long tub-bath, and for the first time in a long time she applied her make-up carefully and deliberately. She dressed with extreme care. She got out the shiny, patent-leather purse and the little patch of a hat with the veil and put them ready on the dresser top. Well, she was all set!

She went into the breakfast nook in the kitchen and sat down at the window to wait for him to return to the house. When he finally did come, he gave her a long, penetrating look.

"You got yourself all dressed up!" It amounted to an accusation.

She glanced down at herself. "I ain't got nothing else."

"Well, I ain't gonna dress up, not just to go down to that stinking town." He went stomping off through the house. In a moment she could hear the sounds of him in the bathroom. At least, she thought irritably, he's washing!

He took his own good time getting ready. Finally he came to the door and looked at her.

"Well, ain't you coming?" he asked gruffly. "You gonna sit there and moon all day?"

They went out to the truck. Brandon went first and by the time she had reached the truck he was already behind the wheel. She took her place at his side, sliding back on the cold leather seat. She held the veiled hat and the purse in her lap and remembered to take a good grip on the frame of the window. They bounced and lurched out along the uneven ruts of the road, whipping up a thick curtain of swirling dust. He swung west on the asphalt and she relaxed her grip and settled back. They dropped down through Baxter and on past the road that turned off to Dutch Flat. Finally they pulled over the top of the rise and rolled swiftly down into Colfax.

He drove along the row of small buildings fronting the railroad tracks and pulled up in front of the movie house. She sat there reading the placard. To-night only, Lauren Bacall in something or other. She wondered who Lauren Bacall was, anyhow. Maybe, she'd have time to go and find out. He had climbed down and slammed his door. The metallic crash roused her sharply. She stirred, shoved open her door, and got down. Brandon had gone on up the sidewalk, and she caught a fleeting glimpse of him just as he disaappeared into the general store. She marched up the sidewalk in the blazing sun to the store.

Brandon was leaning over the counter. A young man with pale, watery eyes came across the floor to her.

"Yes, ma'am?" His eyes ran up and down her body.

"Nothing, thanks. I'm with him, with my husband," She nodded at the back before her.

The clerk moved away quickly. The older man, on the other side of the counter, the one waiting on Brandon, now glanced at her. He too did some running of the eye, she noticed.

"I didn't know you was married, Brandon?"

"Yeah; this here's my wife." Brandon did not turn.

"Howdy!" she nodded; her smile was eager.

"Howdy, Mrs. Brandon." The old man helped himself to another quick, curious look which she tried to ignore. Then he went back to Brandon and the order.

Mamie moved around the store slowly. She studied the shelves and tried to think of something extra special she might get for herself, alone. She wanted a kind of souvenir. It had been such a long time! She looked carefully, but there was nothing she really wanted. She picked up a couple of movie magazines from the rack. Here was something she could look at in the evenings. She walked over to the counter and laid a few coins in front of the kid. He rang up the sale and handed her the change. He had cold, wettish hands, she noticed with a sharp feeling of repugnance.

She shoved the magazines under her arm and retreated to the back of the store, to wait for Brandon to finish. She opened the flap of the big purse and fished out a cigarette. She stuck it in her mouth and bent over, scratching the match on the upraised sole of her shoe. The old man behind the counter heard the rasp.

"Please, Mrs. Brandon! We don't 'low no smoking in the store, ma'am." He was cold and unfriendly about it. "Fire, you know."

She felt like a stupid fool, standing there with the unlighted cigarette dangling from the corner of her mouth. She blew out the match and walked across the floor as casually as she could and went outside. Standing in the shade of the extended roof, she scratched another match and lit the cigarette.

Brandon came out of the store eventually. He seemed a little surprised to find her there, still waiting for him.

"All through with the buying?"

"Yeah. Where to now?"

"I gotta go up the street," he said. The way he said it, she got the hint. He was going up the street ... alone!

She shrugged her shoulders imperceptibly. "What you got to do don't make no difference to me," she said independently.

He let the remark pass. "Why don't you go to the pitcher show?"

She brightened with the suggestion. "That would be kinda nice!" then she shook her head. "Naw. It's too damned hot!"

They stood like two strangers in the middle of the sidewalk, uncertain, each waiting for something to occur that might offer escape from the other.

"Why, it's Mamie Brandon! Of all people!"

She wheeled, startled. Ruth Randall, her arms full of packages, stood right behind them. She glanced at Brandon. "You remember Ruth ... Mrs. Randall?"

He nodded. "I gotta go up the street," he said bluntly, seizing the chance at hand. He walked away.

Mamie turned to Ruth. "He's got errands to do."

Ruth detected a feeling of awkwardness. "I'm sorry if I busted up something."

"You didn't. Truth is, we was both trying to figure out some way to get rid of each other. I'm sure glad you came along like you did!"

A curious look swept across Ruth's face. Her eyes went past Mamie to the figure of Brandon, now far up the street. Suddenly she became conscious of the heat burning down on them.

"Good heavens, let's get out of this sun," Ruth laughed. They moved down the sidewalk. "Let's dump this stuff in the car." Ruth crossed to the curb, to the side of the model A pick-up.

"Why, that's Frank's car!" Mamie exclaimed.

Ruth glanced at her. "Yes, that's right. It's Frank's car."

Mamie stood still. Ruth placed her bundles in the back of the truck. "Well, what shall we do now?"

"I been thinking about going to the show."

Ruth shook her head. "Oh no, you don't want to do that. It's too hot to sit all afternoon. Let's go have a beer some place and just talk for a while. All right?"

"Suits me," Mamie agreed.

The two women walked down the sidewalk until they came to a bar. The words "Charlie's Place" were tattooed in gold lettering across the windows. The interior looked nice and cool. They went inside. It was a cheap, ordinary-looking place. There were a few round, pill-box stools on upraised chromium legs set along the bar. Behind the counter a full-length mirror seemed to double the size of the place. They hesitated a moment and then Mamie led the way over to the stools. The bartender came forward.

"Ladies, what's it gonna be?"

"We want a couple of beers, Charlie." Mamie slid herself on a stool with a grunt.

The bartender turned and got a couple of glasses down from the glittering array lined before the mirror. He grinned at Mamie's reflection in the glass.

"Me—I ain't Charlie, lady," he confided. "Me, I'm Pete."

"Hi, Pete. Where's Charlie to-day. Goofing off?"

He drew two brimming glassfuls of beer and shoved them across the counter. Mamie laid a dollar bill in front of her. He rang up the sale and, turning back, laid a little pile of change before her. He leaned over in a confidential way and grinned.

"Tell you something. There ain't no Charlie at all!"

"Ain't no Charlie!" Mamie simulated grave shock. She glanced at Ruth. "You heard that? There ain't no Charlie at all!"

Pete became even more confidential. "That's strictly between you girls and me, remember!" He nodded. "There never was no Charlie, never!"

"Never?" Mamie asked incredulously.

He shook his head. "Never."

Mamie looked at Ruth. Ruth was struggling to keep her amusement under control. But Mamie betrayed nothing whatsoever. She was dead-pan clean through.

"How come?" She gave her head a half-jerk towards the big front windows. "How come they say 'Charlie's Place' if there ain't never been no Charlie?"

Pete shot a quick, nervous glance around the empty bar and then looked at her soberly. "It was the goddam sign-painter that done it," he confessed heavily.

"Sign-painter?"

"Yeah. Him. He wanted some publicity for herself, that's what."

"Publicity?"

"Yeah. His name was Charlie, see? So he puts his own name up there 'stead of mine!"

Silence greeted his admission. Mamie bent a little closer.

"There's a way you could change it, if you want to."

"What!" Pete howled indignantly. "Change the name of this classy joint after all these years?"

"Naw." Mamie paused. "Change your own name, sucker! Make it Charlie!"

He stepped back. Mamie picked up her glass and drained it. She shoved it towards him with an indicating nod. She reached over and pushed Ruth's glass alongside the first empty.

"Come on, brother, refill!"

He took the two glasses and filled them deftly to the brim.

"This here one's on me!" he said. "I always appreciate a lady who can go along with a gag!"

Some man had come in, parked himself at the far end of the bar near the door, and was watching them with detached interest. Pete went down to serve him.

"I wish I could do that!" Ruth said with a slight edge of envy.

"Do what?"

"What you just did. Kid with them like that. I can never keep it up. I never know what to say!"

Mamie began to toy with the glass in her hand. "You get so's you can do it easy," she said. "I guess bartending's a lot like slinging hash. There's always a lot of jabbering that don't mean nothing, really." She was silent a moment. "It's been a helluva long time since I done any of it, though! I'm a little rusty," she said.

Ruth removed her hat and laid it on the counter. "This is the first time I've ever seen you in town, Mamie," she said, principally to get the conversation under way.

"That's easy. It's the first time I been in town. Since I got married, that is."

"Really?"

There was a pause.

"How's everything with you folks?" Mamie asked.

"Just fine."

The silence drifted over them once more. Mamie kept rolling her glass.

"I kind of hoped you'd come over and see us," Ruth said slowly.

Mamie cleared her throat. "I didn't get round to it," she lied.

The fingers of Ruth's mind groped out for a topic.

"Did you ever do any canning, Mamie?" she asked.

Mamie accepted the lead gratefully. "I been trying to learn how to put up vegetables for the winter. But I ain't been doing so good!"

"You've got some fruit on your place, haven't you?"

"Yeah, there's a little. Not too much. There's some cots and apples."

"You ought to can that stuff, Mamie. I've got all the recipes on how you do it. It's not too hard, really."

Mamie felt her interest quicken. "I'd sorta like to try the fruit. It'd be kinda fun seeing if I could do it."

"Hello…"

His voice shoved in between them. Ruth swung round on her stool and looked up into his face. Mamie kept her eyes rigidly ahead, at the reflected image of him in the bar mirror. Finally, because she knew she must, she swung round slowly and looked into his face.

"Hello, Frank," she said evenly.

He looked down at her. Ruth watched her breath snagging a little.

"How you been doing, Mamie?"

"All right. Okay."

"Swell."

He moved round and climbed up on the next stool. Pete came up.

"Well, by God, if it ain't Frank Parks! Where you been keeping yourself lately? What'll you have?"

"Howdy, Pete. We'll have a beer, I guess." He glanced at the nearly empty glasses in front of the women. "Set 'em up all around." The bartender nodded and filled the glasses. "How about having one yourself, Pete?"

"It's a little on the early side for a Saturday." Pete grinned. He leaned forward in a gossipy, curious way. "They been telling me you been dating a pretty slick little chick from the Flat these days. Folks been seeing you around at the dances."

Frank colored slightly. "That so?"

"That's what they been saying."

"Then I guess they must be right," Frank said. Pete dropped the subject. He mumbled something about having to look after a customer and went scurrying down to where the lone man sat.

Finally Ruth ventured to speak. "You all through with whatever you had to do, Frank?"

"Yeah. I'm ready to pull out any time you are."

Ruth glanced at Mamie, toying with her beer glass. "Frank drove me to town to-day," she explained pointlessly. "Bill's painting the kitchen up home. Or, at any rate, he's been trying to."

Frank smiled. He glanced sideways at Mamie and there was no feeling at all. He felt completely at ease, sitting here at Mamie's side. All the old fear of her seemed to have gone away. He was free!

"How's everything been going, Mamie?" he asked gently, fed with the impersonal curiosity of old acquaintance.

She shifted on her stool so that she could take a careful, steady look at him. "You asked me that once before," she reminded him lightly. "Everything's just fine with me, Frank."

"That's swell. I'm real glad, Mamie."

"You been having lots of fun, Frank?"

"Fun?" he echoed. For a moment he wasn't quite sure what she meant. Then he realized she had meant nothing. "Oh, sure. Sure thing," he finished weakly.

"Frank's been working like the very devil!" Ruth said.

"Oh, yeah? What doing?"

"Ruth's making it sound like too much. I just been helping Bill that's all." Frank felt a need for explanation. "We been clearing off the place for Bill's addition. He's figuring on putting some more to the barn."

Mamie glanced at Ruth. "Things must be damned prosperous on the Randall place," she remarked.

"Things have been prosperous down at the lunch-room, you mean!" Ruth giggled. "It makes it nice having that place, too. You see, we lose all our money on the ranch and make it back on the hamburgers and coffee!"

"Maybe we ought to get us a lunch-room," Mamie suggested lightly.

"You don't need one," Frank said. "You ain't planning no additions to the barn."

"We ain't planning no additions, period!"

Ruth reached into her dwindling bag of tricks and shoved another lead towards them.

"Frank, they're having the same trouble with the apple-trees as we are. Some kind of bug getting into them."

Frank sat examining the backs of his large hands. Mamie looked down at them, along the bare arms with the fine hairs curling on them. She snatched her eyes away. Frank was going on about the trees.

"There's some kind of stuff on the market now, some black, sticky stuff. You spray them with it. It's supposed to kill them off as quick as a flash." He glanced past Mamie to Ruth. "We ought to get some. They've got it at Harbin's."

Ruth nodded. "Let's go get some now."

Frank looked at her glass. "Go for another beer first?"

She shook her head. Mamie picked up her glass and drained it.

"How's about you?"

"No. None for me, thanks."

The three of them moved towards the door. Pete made a gesture with his hand. "Come back again—soon." His eyes were on Mamie as he spoke.

"Be seeing you around, hot shot!"

She winked at Pete and followed Ruth out into the sunshine. Frank followed them out, pulling his hat forward to shield his eyes from the glare. The heat seemed worse than it had been before.

"Well, now what?" he asked.

"I thought we were going to Harbin's." Ruth reminded. She linked her arm through Mamie's and they started up the sidewalk. Frank walked at Ruth's right, next to the curb.

It happened without warning of any kind. Karl Brandon pushed through the door of the post office and stepped out on the sidewalk directly in front of them. He came to a dead halt in the glare and faced them. His face had gone dark, the eyes two sunken pools of lashing fury. Mamie froze instantly, stunned with shock, pulling Ruth to a halt. Frank had taken several paces beyond them before he realized what was taking place. He stopped, simply stood there staring at Brandon, his mind slowly beginning to grasp the situation.

With a dangerous, fluid movement Brandon crossed the sidewalk and pushed his body directly across the path of the taller man. Frank went rigid. Mamie almost ran to Brandon's side. With a furious burst of strength she grabbed at his arm and spun him away from in front of Frank so that he was facing her instead.

"Don't you dare!" she spat. "Don't you dare say nothing!"

Brandon stared at his wife coldly, impersonally. He held himself firm for a moment, then wheeled, breaking her grasp easily, faced Frank Parks again.

"I told you once to keep away from my wife. I meant goddam far away from her!"

Frank's face was a hard, expressionless mask. Ruth felt a little clutch of dread seize her heart. "A dead duck!—the phrase came spinning out of the past to her. Her eyes were on that vein in the centre of Frank's forehead, fluttering, pulsing. Hardly conscious of her action, she ran forward suddenly, her body glancing against Mamie, shoving her out of the way. She grabbed at Brandon's arm.

"Mr. Brandon! You've got everything all wrong!" she cried with terrible urgency. "It isn't what you're thinking at all!"

He glanced at her, startled, surprised. She took a single retreating step.

"If you're smart, like I give you credit for, Mrs. Randall, you'll be keeping your nose out of things that ain't your business, see? If you don't, you might be getting hurt one of these days!"

She crept backwards, horror in her eyes. She knew what he meant behind those cruel, ominous words. Frank reached out sharply. For a split second Mamie was afraid he was going to strike Brandon. Then Frank's arm, arrested in mid-air, and fell back to his side. Brandon pulled his stare from Ruth and brought it back again to the furious face above him.

"I told you once. Parks! I'm telling you again—and I'm telling you for the last time! You keep away from Mamie, see? Keep away from her … or you're gonna be damn sorry!"

Ruth felt terribly sick at her stomach. Frank caught a glimpse of her pale, stricken face and moved quickly. He pushed Brandon aside roughly and crossed to her. His arms went around her and he half-dragged her into the shade of the building.

"I want to go home, please, Frank," she whispered. "Please, take me home!"

Frank held her tight and glared at Brandon.

"You simple bastard! You poor, simple bastard!"

Brandon, stung, took a quick step forward.

Mamie hurled her entire weight at him.

"Don't do it, Mr. Brandon! Don't! It won't do no good!" A supernormal strength came up within her; she gripped him by the arms with iron-band fingers. "Don't do it!" she kept crying. "Don't! It won't do no good!"

His eyes widened with surprise, at her overpowering strength, at the hysterical fury behind her attack. She held him fast, unable to move from the centre of the walk.

Frank led Ruth away down the pavement to the model A. Mamie still gripped Brandon by the arms. Finally she forced her fingers to let him go. Brandon remained solid in his place. His strength had deserted him now. Finally he moved, taking slow, almost cautious steps. He was exhausted. He felt as if he would never make it back to the truck.

Frank guided the pick-up close to the house and cut the engine. He and Ruth sat quietly for a few moments, collecting their wits.

"That was pretty nasty," Ruth commented finally. "Frank, promise me you'll keep away from that man! Please, Frank! Keep away from him!"

"For his sake … or mine?" he asked with a touch of bitterness.

She thought she knew what he meant. "For both your sakes."

"That makes the second time," Frank observed after a brief pause. "The first time I guess it was my fault. Well, the second round goes to him. Looks like maybe we got one up on each other!"

It was the unspoken threat of the third, the unknown, that frightened her. "Let it go at that, Frank!"

He looked at her thoughtfully, but he made no further comment. They got out of the pick-up and carried the bundles round to the back of the house. Bill was perched high on a ladder in the centre of the kitchen, slapping paint across the ceiling. He grinned down at them as they entered. Ruth smiled thinly at him. Something's gone wrong, he realized, something's gone wrong—that's for sure!

"Well, what's happened?" he asked simply.

Frank glanced up at him soberly. "You'll have to come down from there. I ain't gonna tell you in here."

Bill laid the brush on top of the ladder and climbed down. Frank turned and went out of the back door. Bill followed. Ruth stood at the big window in the living-room, watching them as they went down the path to the barn together. Frank pushed open the door to the barn and they went inside. He sat down on a bale of hay. Bill moved past him to the timber supporting the roof and leaned against it.

"Come on, Frank, let's have it!"

"We had a run in with Brandon. It wasn't my fault, not this time, Bill."

"What happened?"

Frank told him briefly, omitting nothing. Bill was rigid, his blood iced as Frank touched on Ruth's outburst.

"Ruth got mixed up in it then. She grabs hold of him and yells he's all wrong about everything. He just shook her off like you'd brush off a fly."

Bill hardly dared ask the question. "Frank … did he … touch her at all?"

"Do you think I'd be here now if he had?"

Bill flushed. "I'm sorry, fellow. Go on."

Frank completed the story and there was a prolonged silence. Bill walked across the floor. "Christ! It's a rotten business!"

Looking at his back, Frank was remembering the single incident which remained untold and would remain so. He had not mentioned the words that had sprung heavy and pointed from Brandon's lips. "If you're as smart as I give you credit for, Mrs. Randall, you'll be keeping your nose out of things that ain't your business. If you don't, you might be gettin' hurt one of these days!" There was no use bringing that up. There was enough for murder in each of them already. There was no use getting Bill all steamed up.

The door to the barn opened and Ruth came in. She looked perfectly all right now. She glanced at Frank, then she looked to Bill, standing with his back upon her.

"Bill … ?" she said tentatively.

He turned and held out his arms and she moved across the space to him. He stood, holding her tight, close and safe to him. Frank got to his feet and went out of the barn, pulling the door shut softly behind him.

Karl Brandon drove the big truck up to the porch steps. He climbed down and went stalking along the path round the house. He had not uttered a word since they had left town. Neither had she.

Mamie held her peace all through the evening meal. He went off into the big room after the meal and built up the fire. He slumped down in the chair and stared into the leaping flames. Mamie washed up the dishes and finally she joined him in the big room.

She did not sit down. Instead, she stood just behind him, looking over his head down into the flames in the grate. Suddenly she knew she could not hold it any longer; her voice burst forth, racketing out into the angry silence of the room.

"I guess, maybe, you been feeling pretty good!"

He stirred wearily. "There ain't no use talking about it."

She moved round the chair to a spot before the mantel so that she might see his dark, pinched face. "I kinda think there is."

"I don't want to talk about it no more," he sent his words out soft and definite.

"No…" she cried bitterly. "I don't guess you would. I sure wouldn't want to if I was you! Not if I'd made a damn fool of myself like you did!"

He made a slight, sharp motion as if he were going to get to his feet. She stayed him with a quick fling of her hand.

"Stay where you are, Mr. Brandon! I got things I want to say!"

He sank deep in his chair. She put her hands on her hips.

"So you got an idea you're pretty smart, pretty wise, ain't you? You know everything there is to know about everything, don't you? Sure… Well, just for the record, here's a tip! You don't know nothing about nothing!" She flung it at him defiantly. He let her go on; let her have her say. "You got all this figured out, ain't you? It sure must be swell, being able to get everything doped out ahead of time like that! I'd sure like to know how you done it! Only, when I do it, I want to do it right! Not get everything ass-back-wards!" She kept staring at him, the scorn in her face masking the hurt beneath. "For weeks I been wanting to get off this place for an hour or two. For weeks and weeks and weeks I been just wanting to go to town. I just been wanting to see some people, to see some other people. Well, I got to town! But I had to beg to go. I had to stall around until I figured you was in the right mood before I could even ask you. God! That's a laugh! Well, I asked you. All the time I was scared you was gonna say I couldn't go."

He had taken his eyes away from her face and sat staring into the fire.

"So I gets to town. What a big break that turns out to be!" She took a deep, steady breath and her voice was hard and metallic. "I met Ruth Randall right there on the sidewalk. Right out in the open. Jesus, you was there yourself!" She wondered suddenly if he were actually listening to her. "Listen to me, Mr. Brandon, I'm telling you how it happened—I'm explaining to you! I met Ruth out there on the sidewalk. She's a damn fine woman, Ruth Randall is. She's been damn nice to me. I like her lots. Ruth Randall's my friend, see? She's my very best friend in all the world, and she's gonna go on being my very best friend. She's the only real friend I got!"

He glanced up at her with annoyance. The look stung her.

"Go on, take a good long look at me! You don't like me getting friends, do you! You don't want nobody coming round here! Well, you ain't got nothing to worry about. There won't be nobody coming around here, not after to-day. You got all that fixed up this afternoon just fine!"

She looked away suddenly. Her tone was flat and limp.

"That Frank Parks, he don't mean nothing to me, nothing! He's a friend of Ruth's. He's her friend; he ain't nothing to me at all. He just happened to come up while we was talking. We was just walking along, just talking, that's all."

She lapsed into a crippled silence. He got up and faced her. She looked at him, the hurt crowding the anger a little.

"We ain't done nothing wrong! We wasn't ever together like you think!" Some of the shrillness returned. "We never did nothing! We wasn't together alone; she was there all the time, too. We was just walking along, minding our own business, and then you had to come out and make all that stink! What did you figure we was doing? What did you figure Frank was gonna do? Did you think he was gonna try and lay me right there on the sidewalk, for God's sake?"

There was deep pain in her voice, hurt that curdled into bitterness. The tears broke loose and spilled over her lids.

"You dumb, stupid fool! There wasn't nothing done, nothing said ever, between him and me. There wasn't nothing even thought about, not like that. Nothing's ever happened between him and me. I'm telling you God's truth, Mr. Brandon! Nothing's ever happened ... "

"And nothing's ever gonna happen, see?"

His voice cracked across the space between them like a whiplash. He moved swiftly and gripped her by the fleshy part of her arm, his fingers digging deep into her.

"Now you listen to me for a while. I got some things to say. You keep away from that there Frank Parks, see? I ain't kidding around. You keep away from that Parks. I ain't playing no games with nobody, see? You belong to me; what I say goes. You got plenty to do around here; you don't need to go traipsing off to town. It's what I want, not what you want, that goes around here!"

She was completely cut off, short-circuited, gone dead all over. The pain in her arm was dull, remote. She could hardly hear the things he was saying. All she felt was confusion, bewilderment.

"That's all I got to say. Now get to bed—get out of here!"

She lay in the big bed, staring up at the ceiling, thinking back, trying to reconstruct all that had taken place such a short time before. Dimly her ears picked up the sounds of him moving around the house. She realized he was getting ready to come to bed. She steeled herself for that moment when his hand would touch the door-knob. The key lay hard and cold, cupped in the palm of her hand.

He tried the door. She was tense in the silence that followed. He tried the knob once again. Suddenly he pounded on the panel.

"Mamie, open this goddam door!"

She lay rigid, motionless, the feel of the key sharp and reassuring in her hand. After a while he would give up, go away and let her alone. She could not bear the thought of him with her to-night. He pounded on the door again. The knob chattered angrily; and then, all of a sudden, a strange, ominous silence settled over the house. He must have gone away, she thought, with a little rise of triumph. He must have given up and gone away.

Wait! There was a different kind of sound out there in the hall. She heard the sound of metal dropping against the wood of the floor. And then the soft rustling of cloth dropped into a heap. Now a heavy thump, followed by another. Suddenly she realized what he was doing. He was undressing! He was taking off his clothes there in the hallway!

The pounding on the door resumed. She lay very still, stiff. Now there was a silence. She could hear him moving about. His feet were bare, she could tell. Then a sudden, rending crash split the stillness. The light from the passageway burst into the room, blinding her for the instant. The door hung crazily, snapped from the top hinge. He pushed through and stood at the bedside, looking down upon her, a deep black cruelty enthroned on his face. She stared at him with mounting horror. He was stark naked. His huge, powerful arms hung at his sides, the stubby fingers of his big hands withdrawn into the balls of his clenched fists. His lips, thin and white, spat his words at her.

"So you figured you'd be alone to-night, eh? Well, there's one thing we better get straight right off. My wife don't lock no doors on me, see? My wife and me, we sleep together like a man and his woman do. This here's my house—you remember that—and you're my wife!"

He loomed over her. She lay before him, straight and motionless, bringing her shocked sight up along the hairy trail from his stomach across his great chest to his face, dark and twisted with evil. He stayed that way for several moments, looking down on her, gloating with his conquest. Her eyes grew wide with the horror she saw approaching. Suddenly he reached down and seized the edge of the blanket, whipping it away from her with one powerful fling. She was before him, her nightgown hiked above her knees. He bent over her and she saw that he was grinning.

"You and me's gonna spend the night together like we should," he told her. "We're gonna be together, like a man and his woman ought to be!"

He raised his voice harshly on the last words, and, reaching forth his hand, he hooked his stubby fingers in the thin top of her gown. There was a sharp, quick ripping as he stripped the sheer garment from her body. She shut her eyes tight and a wrenching, agonizing pain came shooting, jagging through her. At first she raised her arms defensively, summoning all her strength, fighting bitterly, savagely, digging her nails into his thick hide, trying to bite, to kick, to free herself from him. But he was too strong for her. His arms came forward and pinned hers down behind her back. She was overpowered, held fast, unable to move, gripped as in a giant vise. He had trapped her in an inescapable snare. Suddenly her strength collapsed and fell away. His face came down and blotted out the light that came slanting through the broken door from the hallway.

CHAPTER EIGHT

FRANK had said he would pick her up at the lunchroom when she had finished. It was the usual Sunday night, the night of the dance. They had been going together now for some weeks. In fact, they had been steady ever since the day when Art had mentioned casually that he had to go on a job up in the mountains. He had wanted to know if Frank would mind taking her to the dance that week-end. She hated to miss out; he hated to have her miss out. Frank hated to miss out, too. From that time forward, even after Art had returned, it was Frank who escorted her. He arrived this night at the lunch-room, all slicked up, and sat waiting for her to wind up the day's business. She washed up the few cups and glasses that had accumulated during the evening and rubbed down the counter with quick, expert movements. His eyes trailed after her as she moved round the room, setting the boards into place against the screens. Her body was slim, well formed, lovely. Suddenly he knew, looking at her, that he wanted this Binnie very much. He wanted her for always, with tenderness, humility.

"I'll only be a minute more," she promised.

"That's okay. Take your time."

She went round behind the counter and disappeared in the little alcove by the back door. In a moment or so she came out. She had removed the white uniform and put on a flaring skirt with a tight-fitting blouse. He could see the shadow of the brassiere under the thin fabric, holding her small, rounded breasts firmly in place.

"Well, I'm ready, Frank," she announced.

She padlocked the doors and they climbed into the model A. They rode in silence to the dance hall. Somehow, the thought occurred to Frank, a guy didn't have to say very much when he was with her.

In front of the dance hall she linked her arm in his. "Arthur's going to be mad he missed to-night," she giggled.

Frank laughed. "He's been mad all week—in advance!"

She danced with the unthinking grace of the very young and the very content. With her in his arms Frank excelled himself. She relaxed close against him, letting the rhythm bear her along. She was very happy.

The big ape from Dutch Flat came and cut in on them later on. Frank yielded his place with an open show of displeasure and made his way to a vacant space at the wall to sweat out the finish of the number.

Frank leaned against the wall and took out a cigarette. A short, swarthy man stepped up to his side.

"No smoking in the hall, Frankie! You know that."

Frank grinned sheepishly. "Oh, yeah … sorry!"

He went out and stood on the little stoop just beyond the door. He gazed over the little cluster of automobiles and trucks tucked up into the trees. He took a deep drag on the cigarette and expelled the smoke in a long, thin line. He sure felt good. Inside the music raced at a faster tempo.

"Who's the dish with you?"

Frank twisted his head. "Hi, Corky! Just a gal I know."

Corky produced the bottle. "Want a shot?"

"No, thanks. Not right now."

Corky glanced at him in surprise. "What's the matter? On the wagon? You better take it easy, bud! Better have a short one now. There ain't liable to be much left later on!"

The thought came to Frank that he had not had a drink in a helluva long time! More than two weeks now, he thought. The music stopped; Frank stepped away.

"Be seeing you around, Corky," he said, heading back to the hall.

They were dancing again.

"I hate that bastard from the Flat!" he announced simply.

She smiled indulgently. "Oh, he's not really so bad, Frank."

"He's a louse for my money, a no-good louse! Any guy's a louse if he thinks he's gonna get you away from me!"

He drove her home after the dance. Binnie lived in Dutch Flat, off the main highway over a mile or so. He parked in front of the little frame building where she had her rooms. He switched off the lights. They sat close together, beside each other, saying nothing. Suddenly he slipped his arm around her and drew her, turning, to him. She gave her lips to him willingly, gladly, without reserve.

He released her finally, pressing her away from him slowly. "Oh, Binnie! Binnie, my darling!"

"When did you know?" she whispered.

"The first thing, the very first thing," he said. "I knew it was you from the very first."

She nodded quietly. "I knew before you," she said. "I knew when Arthur first told me about you. I knew then. I think I've been waiting for you, Frank, for a very long time."

"Will you ... you will marry me, Binnie?" he asked simply.

She brought her gaze back to him. "Yes. I'll marry you, Frank."

They fell silent for a long moment. Her words broke the stillness. "Only ... not right away, Frank, please. Not until later on. But I will marry you."

Frank was unusually talkative at breakfast the next morning. He jabbered along in an unending stream, without a break.

He related things about the dance, the music, the crowd, about Corky and his bottle. He told them almost everything.

"Who did you take?" Ruth asked finally.

"Why ... I took Binnie, of course!" he replied.

Bill looked at Ruth. Their eyes connected.

"That Binnie, she's a very nice girl," Ruth remarked.

"You bet she's a nice girl," Frank agreed vigorously. "She's a damned nice girl. You can say that again!"

CHAPTER NINE

MAMIE had gone to sleep that September night after their argument over the scene in town with bruises discoloring her arm and a deep, crushing hurt in her heart. She had awakened at his side the following morning with the grinding hurt gone, supplanted by a numbing indifference. Instinctively, as her consciousness had returned, she had moved her body away from the contact with his back, turned to her. As she had risen and dressed, she had gazed dispassionately upon his sleeping form and her eyes were empty, expressionless. He had exacted the last full measure of the bargain. He had crushed her resistance, and more tragically, her emotions, her responses. In the tempest of his victory, he had shattered her personality, stripped her individuality from her. When she walked, it was a listless, arrested movement, shorn of the old rhythm that had excited and stirred the blood. Only her fierce consuming passion for the house came through unscathed. The house remained the seal of her success, the immutable monument to her planning, her endeavor, the cornerstone of her future.

She moved into the kitchen and prepared his breakfast, as she had every morning. It was Sunday and the sky was clear. Mamie laid the breakfast things out on the table and paused, looking out of the window. She heard him enter and sit down. She remained mute, as if unaware of his presence. He glanced up at her sharply.

"Well ... ?"

The single word sank through her consciousness; she jerked her head and, blinking, looked down at him vacantly. Then without a word she went to the stove, took down a plate, scooped the bacon and eggs with a flat ladle. She brought the plate to him, retraced her steps, and got the coffee pot. She poured his cupful. She returned the pot to the stove and remained there.

"Ain't you gonna eat?" His eyes narrowed a trifle.

"I don't feel like nothing."

He hesitated, his lips drawn apart, as if he might be going to say something further. But he went back to his food without a word. She waited for him to finish, to go outside, to leave her.

When he had done, he got up and started for the back door. She had not moved from her place by the stove. He paused for a moment at the door, staring back at her curiously. But he made no further comment. He went on outside. Slowly, wearily, she drew her hand down across her face.

And so they entered into a new phase of living. Their meals became wordless, uncommunicative meetings. Each of them sat in the place opposite the other, across the table, wholly concentrated on the dishes. It was as if there were an unspoken truce of silence, a compromise of ignorance, between them. After the evening meal he would get up and go on to the big room, where he would set the fire and settle himself in the chair before the grate. And when her work had been accomplished, when her day was finally brought to an end, she would go on into the big room to sit in the chair across from him. She would sit like that, with her hands folded idly in her lap, simply waiting until it was time for them to go to bed. When that time came, she would get up and go quietly from the room. Later he would close the house for the night, and climb into the big bed at her side. When his need for her made itself manifest, he took her as he did everything else, routinely, according to a set pattern. She submitted without protest, closing her eyes without any direct emotion. It was a mutual need. The slanting rays of the morning sun would come again and the day would begin. It would be the unvarying copy of the day before.

Thus October came to the Brandon place. November skirted by. Mamie realized with surprise one afternoon that it was already December. She had no recollection of November at all!

On the Friday just before Christmas Mamie suddenly stepped over the line of their separation. She crossed with quiet deliberation. "I'd like…" She faltered when he glanced across the table top… "I'd kinda like to go to town with you, when you go tomorrow."

He made no answer at the moment. "If you want to," he said finally.

The next morning at breakfast he broke the silence again to ask her a question. His voice was casual.

"How come you want to go to town in weather like this?"

She bridled instantly. "You needn't be worrying."

His face darkened imperceptibly. He repeated his question: "How come you want to go to town to-day?"

She stole a wary glance at his face. "It's just I'd kinda like to get some things for Christmas," she explained.

"Oh… Christmas," he echoed, and said nothing more.

And so they made the trip to Colfax again. They met no one. Mamie spent most of her time in the five and ten. She bought him a muffler for a present. It was cheap—forty-nine cents—cheap cotton and gay with color. She bought a tiny bottle of perfume for Ruth. She managed to find a bit of silver tinsel, for a tree maybe. The store even had a couple of bright red balls left. She walked down the icy pavement with her few parcels and passed Charlie's Place. He had a holly wreath in the window. She hesitated, wondering if it would be all right to go in and say Merry Christmas to Pete. But she suddenly remembered what had started in there the other time. She went on back to the truck.

Back up on the place she got ready for her Christmas. She stamped through the woods searching for a tree that would be just right. She finally found it. It was a little tree, a silly little thing, with a gnarled twist near its top—as if the snows had come some other time and sat down too heavily on it. She hacked it free and dragged it back to the house. She set it up on the table in the big room and decorated it with the sparse silver strands she had ferreted out in town. She fastened the two red balls to the largest of the drooping branches. It looked real nice, she thought, viewing the completed job. Yeah, it looked real nice. Under the tree she put the muffler, now wrapped in some holly paper, and the little box with the bottle of perfume for Ruth. She gathered up some of the left-over branches and worked them into the shape of a wreath. She hung it outside on the door. Christmas had come, a furtive, uneasy stranger, to the Brandon place.

Brandon came into the room that night as usual after dinner. His eyes went to the tree, standing on the table-top.

"It's Christmas Eve," she reminded him almost apologetically.

"Yeah, so it is," he acknowledged gruffly. He made no comment one way or the other about the tree. He plumped himself down heavily in his chair and reached for a newspaper in the rack.

The next morning he went about his routine as usual. The breakfast had been laid out according to their set schedule. She glanced up from her place at the stove as he entered.

"Merry Christmas, Mr. Brandon!" It came out very softly, timidly.

"Huh?" He shot her a startled, uncomprehending look. "Uh, yeah! Merry Christmas!"

He was over at the back door staring out to the hard earth. A faint shadow shaded her eyes.

"You ain't planning to work outside to-day?"

"Why not?" He turned in surprise.

"But … this here's Christmas!" she exclaimed in protest.

He almost smiled. "Them cows gotta eat, Christmas or no Christmas," he countered bluntly.

"We're gonna have a real nice dinner to-night!" she announced proudly. "A real extra-special Christmas feed! I got turkey and the trimmings, remember?"

He grunted his approval and went on eating his everyday breakfast.

That night after the Christmas dinner they went on into the big room as usual. She bided her time until he had settled himself in his chair.

"Mr. Brandon, there's something I got for you."

He glanced at her with a brief flicker of curiosity. "What?"

She flushed with his unexpected, ready attention. She crossed over to the little barren tree and took his package in her hand. She handed it to him, smiling a trifle too eagerly.

"It ain't much," she lumbered along. "It's just something I got in town, something I kinda figured you could use, maybe."

She watched his strong, stubby fingers rip the thin paper into shreds. He dropped the litter on the floor beside his chair and the muffler unrolled itself until the end touched the floor. It was a bright little thing, a Scotch plaid mostly red and blue. For a moment something close to a look of pleasure threatened to seep into his eyes. She was waiting with a kind of breathless expectancy.

"It ain't very heavy," he remarked.

She could not have recoiled with greater swiftness had he raised his hand to strike her. Mamie was stung to the quick.

Brandon sat there, hefting the little strip of cloth in his hand. He was confused, ill-at-ease. He had no idea what she wanted him to do. All he finally did was grunt. He put the plaid on the arm of his chair and retreated behind his newspaper.

Christmas day at the Randalls' was always a gay, exciting time. They were five around the tree this Christmas day. There were Bill and Ruth, of course, and Frank too. Binnie and her brother, Arthur, were the honoured guests. Frank and Art, looking like a pair of oversized twins, a pair of twin dudes, as Ruth said, were garbed in the height of fashion for the occasion. Each of them wore a bright sports shirt and a new pair of gabardine slacks. Ruth thought they looked too handsome, the pair of them. Bill envied them a little. Binnie was just hopelessly proud.

They exchanged their gifts. Bill had a new portable radio for Ruth. That was so, he remarked scornfully, she could carry her soap operas from one place to another all over the house—she wouldn't lose a tear-jerk! They all laughed. In return she gave Bill an expensive leather jacket, similar to the ones Art and Frank wore. Art gave Frank a fifth of Seagrams. Frank gave Art a belt with a big silver buckle, just like the one he always wore. Art sat back, as the evening wore on, running his fingers over the metal square, and in his eyes, whenever he looked at his friend, there was deep affection.

Finally Frank got to his feet. He cleared his throat, a little for the effect, a little because he had to. For some reason it had become all tight, all bound up. Binnie gazed up at him with her love unmasked in her eyes. Ruth looked across the room at her and at Frank standing at her side. She took Bill's hand in hers and squeezed it hard.

"Folks...I got something here I gotta say." Frank sounded strangled. "So...I guess you better all listen."

Ruth clapped her hands. Frank colored.

"I guess everybody here knows how me and Binnie feels about each other." There was strict silence now. All eyes shifted to Binnie. Anyway..." Frank scratched his head "...what I gotta say is just this. Binnie and me is getting married...real soon, I hope!"

The smile broke out and went flooding across Ruth's face. She nodded very slightly as he finished. It was so slight a gesture that no one could have noticed it except Frank, for whom it had been intended. He turned to Binnie and looked down at her with new tenderness.

"Baby," he spoke softly, "I got here a little present for you. I hope you'll take it and be wearing it for me."

He held out a tiny package on extended fingertips. She reached up and took it. She opened the box and picked out the cheap, tiny ring and handed it back to him. He bent over and slipped the band, with its minute diamond, on her finger. Very simply and very quietly he cupped her face in his hands and kissed her lips gently. When he straightened there was the glint of tears in her eyes. She reached out and recaptured his hand. When she looked across at Ruth she could see there were tears in her eyes, as well.

Bill came across the room to him. "Congratulations, Frank!" He glanced at Binnie and grinned. "Well, I suppose I gotta go out and rustle me up another gal for the place!"

She laughed. "Not quite yet, Bill. We're not going to be married until spring, anyway."

"Well, that's good news! Good for me, at least!" he smirked.

Frank freed his clasp from Bill's and took Art's extended hand. "You know how I feel about you and Binnie." Art looked at him soberly. "I'm a lot gladder than I can tell you."

"Me too!"

Ruth took Binnie's hand. "I'm so glad it's to be you and Frank," she said sincerely. "I've hoped for this for a very long time, my dear. It will mean everything to Frank."

Binnie turned in his direction. "I love him very much."

Ruth pressed her hand firmly. "That's what I meant."

Bill's voice broke in above the rest of the conversation. "Hey, this calls for a drink! Frank, where's that great big bottle of yours!"

Frank held it aloft. "It's right here, and it sure ain't no great big bottle no more!"

They all laughed. The bottle passed into Bill's hand and he went over to pour out the drinks.

"Thanks, Art, for the Christmas present…for me!" Frank feigned his bitterness. Everybody laughed again. Bill passed the glasses round.

"Ladies and gents!" Bill began sonorously. "I give you the toast of the evening! To Frank Parks and his Binnie!" He glanced at Ruth. "May they be as happy as I have been, as we are." Ruth smiled.

Frank watched them both, and in his heart he devoutly hoped that this wish might be as it had been spoken. They all drank.

"Now I want to say something." Frank took Binnie's hand in his, and drew her to her feet beside him. "We want to drink to two swell people. That's you two there, Bill and Ruth. You been like our family, in a way. We want to drink to you."

The two of them raised their glasses and drank. In the corner, by himself, Art raised his. There was a silence in the room. It was the easy, welcome silence born of affection and understanding.

Art moved over and dropped down in the chair opposite the tree. He was the odd man in the party. He sighed very loudly.

"Gee whiz!" he murmured sadly. "I sure wish I had me a girl!"

The silence shattered and became a shimmering curtain of laughter.

CHAPTER TEN

AMIE and her husband, Karl Brandon, went on together in their place without any noticeable change, without any appreciable variation. After the fiasco of her Christmas, Mamie had fallen back into the old ways, withdrawn, shut within herself. She had come to realize gradually that Brandon was, in a manner of speaking, a bachelor, and that he would remain one. She lived with him, true; but the arrangement was more that of a housekeeper for him rather than a wife. In many ways she was quite content with this arrangement. She was as secure as she had meant to be. She needed nothing. And as the days of her existence under the plan spun themselves, she came to accept a certain satisfaction in the singleness of her life. Meanwhile, conversation had been re-established between them. They worked on an unspoken arrangement, comparable to the operation of the common water faucet. One could turn it on or off at pleasure.

One evening close to the end of January, they were sitting in their accustomed places before the fire. She was darning his socks, her fingers working steadily, automatically. He glanced at her, bent over slightly, the firelight flickering on her face.

"Heard something down in town to-day," he offered.

"Oh?" Her eyes never left the pattern of her work.

"Yeah. Something that might interest you. It's about Parks."

She went on working, her fingers never hesitating. Frank Parks! That name sounded so strange, so far away!

"Parks?" she echoed vaguely.

"Yeah, Frank Parks. Seems he's gonna get married!"

There was a deep, racing confusion spinning round within her for a moment. "Who's he marrying?"

"Some kid named Binnie. She works for Randall down at the place."

"Oh?" Her tone was quite even. "When's it gonna be?"

"Some time this spring. That's what I heard."

He was very pleased with the way she had taken this news. She was through with Parks, that was plain to see. There would not be any more trouble on that score, unless Parks came pussy-footing around! And it stood to reason, if he were hot after some younger, some prettier one... well, the odds were he had forgotten her as well. He closed his eyes and settled back against the chair. After a few moments a thin, low snore escaped from somewhere down in his throat. She glanced over at the sound, went on working.

So Frank Parks was gonna get married! Well, that was good! Or was it? She suddenly had a picture of him in her mind's eye, unbidden, unsought. She saw him as he had been, tall and lean, those long legs, the silver buckle like a square beacon hard against the flatness of his belly. There was a vivid remembering of long, thick forearms with curling, blonde hairs. She felt her cheeks flame and her fingers became damp, unwieldy. She laid the work to one side and got to her feet.

Brandon opened his eyes. "Where're you going?"

"I just felt like a drink of water." She manufactured the excuse and reinforced it with a wifely gesture. "Want some?"

"No." He was pleased. She was turning out to be a damn good wife.

February slipped into the picture, and a wet one it was. The rains pelted down and thick, clinging fog pushed up from the valley. Brandon complained that the early thaws were overtaxing the facilities of the ditch line; he would go off grumbling and cursing five and six times during the week, keeping a fearful, worried eye on the flooding stream that came roaring down through the wooden trough. She would stand on the porch and watch him go sloshing off down the red, muddy road in his big, rubber hip-boots, stamping along awkward and insecure. As the water-logged month wore on, her ears became attuned to the sounds of his coming and going, the thrumping scuffle of the boots against the earth marking his course.

One day, after she had seen him off on one of these all-day emergency jobs, she walked slowly back into the house. The prospect of another long, idle day before her was not pleasant. Suddenly she decided that she would clean house; she would go over everything with a fine-toothed comb. Almost eagerly, as if it were a release, she set to work. She went over the big room with precise, knowing care, easily, absorbed, and preoccupied. She did the big room, then the bathroom, and finally the bedroom. Suddenly she decided she would do the small room this time, as well. She was getting her spring-cleaning over early, she thought with amusement. Ordinarily she never bothered much with the little room. There was no need. Nobody ever used it.

The little room was furnished simply. There was the single cot, a bookcase with some very old, very dull-looking books; two pictures tacked on the walls; and an empty closet. She straightened the bedcover with a few well-directed pats. She swept the room and began to dust with more care than usual. The books in the case were loaded with dust. There was a heavy coat piled along the tops of them. She began to pull them from the shelf one by one, blowing on them lustily. She backed away slightly, away from the cloud of sifting particles. She coughed and blinked her eyes sharply. A book slipped from her hand and crashed to the floor. She bent over quickly and picked it up. The title was in gold letters on a hard, red cover. "The Mine with the Iron Door," she read; by some guy named Harold Bell Wright. She opened the book and riffled the pages. Something fell out and tumbled to the floor by her feet. She glanced down. It was a picture, a snapshot of someone. She stooped down and picked it up.

It was a picture of a woman. Just an ordinary kodak picture of a woman, and she was standing in front of the house here. Not a bad-looking woman either, Mamie thought; in fact, she was kind of pretty in a mousey sort of way. She judged her to be around thirty or so. She was standing right by the front steps; she was smiling. She looked very happy about something, Mamie thought. She studied the face of the stranger with rapt attention. She started to put the picture back between the pages of the book. Then she hesitated. She took another look at the woman's face. She was standing right there by the steps leading up to the front porch. Somehow, Mamie got the sudden feeling that this woman looked as if she belonged right there, as if she owned the place! She had a kind of "it's all mine" look in her face, Mamie thought. She slipped the picture in her apron pocket and set the book back on the shelf. She wondered who she was, what she was doing here, that woman.

Brandon hunched over the kitchen table eating his meal in the usual silence. She worked round the stove and finally came to the table. She put her hand in the pocket of her apron, waiting for him to finish, and her fingers touched on the sharp edge of the photograph. She had forgotten it! She drew it forth and gazed down on the picture of the woman on the steps. She slid on the chair across the table from him and shoved the picture, face up, to the front of his plate.

"I ran across that to-day while I was cleaning up."

He halted in his eating and stared down at the figure in the photo. She caught the open shock that came exploding in his eyes. He reached out slowly and with fingers that trembled, picked up the little rectangle. She waited quietly. He got up suddenly, and left the room. She followed him with startled eyes, her brows raised, as he disappeared into the hallway. She sat stunned with complete surprise at his action. In a little while he came back into the room. She peered at him curiously. He had a large magnifying glass in one hand and was holding the snapshot close to his face, the glass between it and his eyes. His breathing seemed to hang suspended, arrested, as he gazed at the picture. There was a stillness, taut with expectancy, in the room.

He remained in that position for a long time, holding the picture up close, examining it minutely under the glass. Finally he turned and left the room. He had made no comment. She listened to his footsteps as he went on down into the big room at the front of the house. Then everything was quiet.

When she had finished in the kitchen she came into the big room and took her usual place in the chair opposite him. He was just sitting there, still clutching the photo of that woman in his fingers, staring into the fire. After a while her curiosity got the better of her. She tried to make her voice sound casual.

"Who's the lady in the picture, Mr. Brandon?"

He freed his gaze from the hold of the fire and looked at her. It was as if he had suddenly returned from a very faraway place, and she were a stranger to him.

"The picture?" he echoed. "It's the picture of somebody I used to know…a long time ago."

His words were soft and gentle, and yet they seemed to bar her, to shut her out. She pressed for an explanation.

"Was she a good friend of yours?"

He let a full second slide past them. "She was the woman I was gonna marry once." There was something positive, final, ending in the way he said it. Mamie leaned forward slightly, studying the dance of the flames, pondering over the thing he had said. At first it made no sense to her. Then suddenly she saw the whole thing with shocking clarity. Their marriage bargain was suddenly stripped bare, naked and unashamed in the searching, revealing light this thing had caused to shine. The whole thing smote her with crushing force. The woman I was gonna marry, that's what he had said!

The truth thundered in on Mamie Brandon. Whoever this woman was, this house belonged to her! Mamie suddenly understood why everything had been ... as if a woman had planned it and seen that it was done. It hadn't been his handiwork at all. All these things that she herself had adored and held tightly to her were really not hers to adore at all! All the tiny give-away clues she had been too thickheaded to see paraded before her. The little brass dog moved from the mantelpiece—"I don't want nothing changed, ever!" The Christmas born dead and already forgotten. The impersonal intimacy of their bed. She was nothing! None of this was hers! The house ... the ring ... the name she had wanted so to possess ... none of them belonged to her! It had all belonged to the other one! Mamie staggered. All she was was a housekeeper ... for him and her! She had been taking care of somebody else's house and man!

He kept staring at her for a long time. She dampened her lips and asked the question that had suddenly become important.

"What was her name?" she whispered.

"Her name? Her name was Ellen," he said simply, softly.

The name cut deep. The initials stamped on the silver of the toilet set on the dressing table stood out ringed with fire. "E. B." That was for Ellen Brandon! "The woman I was gonna marry!" It came to her quite suddenly that, in his way, he had married this Ellen of his after all.

He got up and went out of the room, carrying the picture in his hand. She listened to his steps fading down the hallway. He did not return. After a very long time, when she was sure, she got up, put out the lights, and locked up for the night. She went down the hall to the bedroom. There was no familiar sound of him, no outline of his big body under the blankets. He was not there!

Suddenly the sound of his breathing reached her ears. She moved slowly to the door to the little room with the single bed, that same room where she had found that Ellen woman's picture. The sound of him was alive in that room, powerful and alone. She stood by the half-opened door for some time, listening to his steady breathing. Then, finally, with a vacant empty gesture, she turned and retraced her steps to the bedroom that had suddenly become hers alone.

CHAPTER ELEVEN

MARCH hung over the pine-covered hills, wrapped in the purloined garment of February's fog. Mamie went on living somehow. It was the same house, the same rooms, the same walls, the same building. Only now there was nothing that belonged to her within its frame. Feeling was gone; her fierce pride of possession had been shattered with the smash of her chance discovery. Mamie had, in an instant, lost her heart.

Brandon did not return to the bed he had forsaken. In the evenings, after he had spent the programmed hour or so in his chair before the fire, he sought out the privacy of the little room. It was she who sat before the fire later now; it was she who watched the flames die away. Only once did she mention his action. One night, some weeks after he had moved from the bedroom, she stopped him in the hall door.

"Mr. Brandon ... ain't you coming to bed to-night?"

He had made no answer. She went off to the big bed alone, irritable, an unfamiliar, empty gnawing within her.

It was while she was straightening her bedroom late one afternoon that she came across a little package wrapped in holly paper. It had been shoved behind a pile of handkerchiefs, out of sight. She frowned, not able to remember; then realization came with a shock. It was the little bottle of perfume she had picked up in town at Christmastime—Ruth's present never given. A slim ray of excited hope flickered in her heart. She had not seen Ruth since that day in town in September.

That night she put forth the subject across the dinner table.

"I'd kinda like to walk over to the Randall place to-morrow, if it ain't raining."

He glanced at her. "Over to the Randalls', you say?"

"Yeah … if it's all right with you."

He grunted and shrugged. "It's okay with me where you go."

When she woke the next morning she moved quickly. She got him fed, and while he was finishing, she made some sandwiches.

"I might not get back in time for lunch," she explained. "If I ain't, these here are for lunch."

"Where you going?"

She felt her heart go sinking. "You said it was all right if I went over to the Randall place to-day," she faltered. "Don't you remember?"

Her voice was tight, almost a cry. He just sat there gazing at her. The past moved a little to one side in his brain and allowed the present to peek through. His eyes narrowed slightly.

"Oh … yeah. I remember now," he said. His eyes narrowed.

"I don't like that there Ruth Randall," he grumbled, harking back to that day in town. "She goes around sticking her nose into things that ain't no concern of hers!"

He put his arms on the edge of the table and leaned his weight on them, his eyes sharp on her. He kept staring. He had become aware suddenly of her big thighs under the thin house dress, of her big, fleshy breasts as she bent over the stove. He rose to his feet.

She caught her breath. She felt his thought reaching across to her, felt the quick impulse of his returned desire. Suddenly, her own hunger, unappeased through these long weeks, slipped free. She wished fiercely that he would cross over and put his hands on her once again. For that she would give up the trip, for that she would put away the Randalls and the outside. The hot desire in her eyes was a naked, urgent signal fire. She threw back her head and let the message go forth to him boldly, unmistakably. Brandon's face was dark; his lips were parted. The fingers of his hard hands opened and closed at his sides like the nervous twitch of a cat's tail. The silence in the kitchen was electric.

Brandon remained standing at the table side, his eyes fixed on her for what seemed a very long time. She waited, tense, for what she was sure was to come. Here's one place where a ghost ain't much good, she reflected caustically; here's where some-body who's absent loses out! Her breasts rose and fell quickly with the pressured increase of her breathing. Brandon took a step forward; she stiffened. Then he turned suddenly and hurried through the back door. He went out across the clearing towards the barn, bareheaded, coatless, walking with rapid, jerky steps. Her body held taut and then broke and was limp and sagged. Her head throbbed; she raised her hand slowly and pressed her fingertips hard against her temples. After a few moments the feeling passed. She drew on her reserves. She was just over-tired, that was all. The whole thing had been pure imagination—nothing was changed; things were just as they had been. She was just tired, that was all.

She dressed and started over to the Randall place. Brandon, standing in the shadow of the barn watched her go. Her walk had a little of the old spring in it, a touch of that familiar, swaying lilt. His eyes were on her until she disappeared from view. Then he turned and came back to the house. He went through the kitchen to the little room and picked up his things from the top of the bookcase. He went to the bedroom. He put his things out beside her toilet articles on the dressing-table top. He stood for a long time, his eyes slitted, staring down at the big, empty bed with the expensive bedspread. The past stole up and nudged his memory, shoving itself forward again. He remembered how she had picked out that spread with her own hands. She had brought it up from the valley and put it on the bed herself. He had stood here, just as he did now, only she had been at his side. Slowly he reached forth and began to gather the toilet articles he had just brought from the little room. He took them back and laid them out along the top of the bookcase. Then he went outside and crossed slowly to the barn. The blood had come into his lips again; the past was reinstated; the present banished.

She came to the mailbox with the name "Randall" painted on its side. There was a newspaper in the catch; she reached up and pulled it free. Then she started off the road up the path leading into the woods.

The rains had been heavy all winter. Everything was damp; the carpet of dead needles was squishy underfoot. The earth was dark and soggy-looking; water gushed to the surface with each step she took. Now and then she came to a spot where the path dipped a trifle; the rains had filled the depressions, leaving large, clear puddles. She skirted the edge of one without mishap; the other she did not meet so luckily. She slid down its saucer-side, and the water, cold and unpleasant, slopped over her boot-tops and went trickling down inside. Mamie cursed softly. Her feet were wet now; she could feel them chilled. She finally came to the fence round the Randall clearing. She paused and glanced around. There was no sign of life. She hoisted herself to the top rail and swung her legs over, dropping heavily to the soft ground on the other side. She began climbing the gradual incline towards the house. From somewhere in the distance the sound of a dog barking came to her. The barking came a second time. Suddenly the dog came racing down at her from the corner of the house. He slid to within a few yards of her and barred her way, barking furiously. She was helpless, trapped before his defending stance. Someone came out on the porch up ahead and peered across the clearing.

"Keno, you come here!"

The barking trailed off into a sort of whine. The dog went trotting away up the path towards the house. Mamie started to move again.

Ruth stared across the clearing at the unfamiliar figure of the woman approaching. Keno came up. She stooped down and gathered him in her arms, stroking him behind the ears, her eyes on the woman. The dog stiffened again and Ruth put her hands over his eyes. He struggled violently and broke from her grasp, going out to the porch edge, bristling.

Ruth suddenly recognized the visitor. A quick smile broke on her face. She ran to the head of the path and held out her hands.

"Why … it's Mamie Brandon! Gee whiz, I'm glad to see you!" She hugged the big woman tightly. "My gosh, it's been a long time!"

Mamie smiled happily. "It sure has!"

Keno stared down at the scene of betrayal. Ruth glanced at him.

"Go on, now! Go mind your business!" she commanded gently.

He wagged his tail once or twice with an air of uncertainty and stole a speculative sniff at Mamie's dress. The women went on into the house and slammed the door in his face.

"Here, give me your coat!"

Mamie handed the newspaper to Ruth and then started to remove her raincoat. "It was stuck in your mailbox. I figured you might want it."

"Oh yes. It's the *Bee*." Ruth tossed it to the hall chair. She took Mamie's coat and hung it in the closet. "Your feet must be good and wet, too!" Ruth said disapprovingly.

"They are," Mamie grinned.

Ruth went ahead into the living-room and lit the already prepared fire.

"We'll get some heat in here," she called. "You'll be able to dry your feet off while we talk."

Mamie struggled to remove her boots; she set them in the corner of the hall. She walked with stockinged feet into the living room.

"Darned old wood is too wet, I think," Ruth grumbled between breaths. "It doesn't seem to want to catch." She took a can of lighter fluid from the mantel. "I'll give it a quick douse with this stuff." She bent forward and made a sharp darting motion with the can. A thin streak of liquid spat towards the grate and the flames came billowing forth with a rush. She set the can back on the mantel. "Bill gets furious when I do that," she said. "He's afraid one of these days I'll blow up the place! But ... it does get the fire going! Here, sit down, Mamie, sit down!" She pointed to the big chair.

Mamie sat, stretching her feet towards the roaring flames. Ruth left the room for a moment and then returned. She sat on the footstool opposite Mamie, her back to the fireplace. "You should have let me know you were coming over—we'd have put on the dog!" she grinned.

"This here's putting on the dog enough for me," Mamie said, "just being here like this."

"That's right!" Ruth realized suddenly. "You've never been here before!"

They were silent a moment.

"How's Bill doing?"

"Fine. Fine. He's down at the lunch-room right now. Binnie ... do you know Binnie?"

Mamie remembered what Brandon had told her about Frank and this Binnie some time ago. She shook her head.

"Well, Binnie is the girl who took your place. I guess, maybe, you've heard she and Frank are going to get married?"

Mamie nodded. "Yeah. I heard about it."

Ruth hurried on. "Well, with them getting married and all, Bill's got to start looking around for another girl. Naturally, she won't go on working." Ruth pushed her explanation. "You see, they're planning on living down in Colfax."

"Oh?"

"Frank's going back to work with the railroad, he thinks."

"That's what he used to do, ain't it?"

"Well, yes—that along with a couple of thousand other things!" Ruth looked at Mamie soberly. Their eyes held for an instant. "She's a very nice kid, Binnie is," Ruth said slowly. "It's the best thing that could have happened to Frank, Mamie. I think she's got what it takes."

"I wonder if it's gonna work." Mamie was impersonal in her speculation.

Ruth was intense. "I think it will. You see, Frank's really in love this time. You wouldn't know him, Mamie. He's got an aim now, a purpose. It's just like I told you once before you got married, remember? I said if he got the right person he'd snap out of it. Well, he has. He's completely different."

Mamie cleared her throat. "This Binnie... she's in love with him, too?"

Ruth's brows arched with surprise. "Why, of course!"

Mamie stared into the fire. Her feet were warm now. The conversation hung suspended for a few minutes. Then Ruth leaned over and put her hand on Mamie's big knee.

"How's everything been going with you?" she asked.

"Everything's all right, I guess."

Ruth looked pensively at Mamie's face. "Is everything all right? Or are you just saying that?"

Mamie brought her eyes to the cool, level gaze upon her. "Sure everything's all right. Why should I say it if it ain't so?"

"I was wondering that. Something's the matter—I can see it."

Mamie wet her lips slightly. "Nothing much's the matter. It ain't worked out like it ought, that's all."

Ruth was silent. She closed her eyes.

"I guess you got a pretty good idea what it's been like, after you seen what happened that day in town. After that happened and you didn't come round to visit no more, I figured I knew what the trouble was."

Ruth opened her eyes. "I didn't feel I could come again," she stated flatly. "I didn't dare take the chance."

"That's what I figured. I guess you was right at that!" Mamie glanced at her hands thoughtfully. "I was to Colfax once since. Otherwise I ain't been nowheres. This here's the first time I been anywheres since then." Ruth was sitting quietly, waiting. "I ain't been nowheres," Mamie repeated slowly. "I ain't seen no one but him all winter long. I been cooped up with him and the house and the sound of that goddam rain all the time. After that monkey-business in town, it just didn't seem any use to go out and maybe have another fuss somewheres. He still goes to town twice a week regular. He gets what I want."

There was a long silence. Ruth could see Mamie was thinking something out carefully. Suddenly she glanced at Ruth sharply.

"You ever hear of somebody named Ellen?"

Ruth shook her head. "Not that I know of."

"Him ... he knew an Ellen once."

Ruth's mind bolted back through the months. Why, of course! Now she remembered! She realized the things Bill had told her in the beginning were tied in with this Ellen in some way.

"Somewheres he used to know a woman whose name was Ellen." Mamie's voice was steady, controlled. "I guess it must have been a long time ago. He said he was gonna marry her once."

Ruth waited. So Mamie knew at last!

"I don't know nothing about her, that Ellen. He don't talk about her. I guess maybe I'd never have known about her at all, only I found a picture of her one day. That's how I come to know about her." Mamie hesitated. "That there house, it's hers—it ain't mine!" Her tone was almost without emotion. "Everything there is hers. Even him, he's hers. The pictures, the furniture, the whole damned place still belongs to her!" She fell silent for a brief moment. "I sure wish she'd come back and get all her stuff—him too!" she cried. "I sure as hell wish that there Ellen'd come back!"

"But she can't come back, Mamie," Ruth said softly.

Mamie looked up at her with a trace of surprise. "Then you do know something about her!" she exclaimed. "Tell me about this Ellen, Ruth!"

"She's dead," Ruth said flatly. Then she told her the things that Bill had told her a long time ago. Mamie sat very still, her eyes on Ruth's face, following her lips, her every expression. After she had done, Mamie was still for a long time.

"It's kinda funny when you get a good look, ain't it?" she commented at last. "In a way, Brandon and me ain't never been really married at all. All the time it's been like he was married to this here Ellen! We been kinda living together … that's all." She waited a long time before she spoke again, and when she did speak she uttered her simple truth directly, without embellishment. "I guess I made a helluva mistake," she said. "Just between you and me, I made a royal ass outta myself!"

Mamie raised her eyes. Ruth expected to see misery and anguish. What she saw was a sudden hardness, strange and sharp.

"You get what I mean, Ruth? Well, it's all over now! Here's something you can bank on for sure—I ain't doing it again." Her words were blade sharp. "I ain't about to do it again. I got a bellyful right now! From now on I'm gonna make sure I get what I want. I'm gonna play my way now."

Ruth felt a welling compassion. "You're just tired and upset. What you need is to get out more often, to see people! A person loses perspective now and then. Everything will come round in time, you'll see."

Mamie smiled sadly. "You ain't got no idea what I been talking about, have you, Ruth?" she asked unexpectedly, a trace of her wonder in her voice. "What I been saying all this time's gone right over your head, ain't it? Well, you can thank your stars that's the way it is!" she commented with a rush of feeling. "You got people to take care of you, I guess. I ain't been so lucky. Only, from now on, I'm gonna be on my own. I'm gonna take care of me! I ain't gonna worry about rules and stuff like that. If I see something I want, then ... I'm gonna take it!"

Ruth could think of nothing further to say. She got to her feet. Mamie looked up curiously.

"I've got lunch on the stove," Ruth explained. Mamie started to get up. "You stay right where you are!"

"But ... I ought to be getting back!"

"Why?"

"I don't know. There ain't no real reason," Mamie confessed.

"Well, you don't have to run off right away. Let him get his own lunch for once." She grinned. "You just relax and be a lady!"

Mamie watched her leave the room. Relax and be a lady, she thought grimly. There was a nice, wide space between her and any lady! She'd taken a flyer on that one; she'd tried to make the grade and look at her! Once was enough! She stretched out in the big chair, watching the flames nibbling along the sides of the logs. The sounds of Ruth's puttering around in the kitchen came muffled, an unreal, detached quality, to her ears.

She closed her eyes and listened to the varied, pulsing murmurs of the strange house. Suddenly her ears picked up a new sound. It was the opening of a door. She heard Ruth's voice, indistinct, and the voice of a man in answer. Then footsteps came down the hallway, approaching.

"Well! Hi, Mamie!"

Bill Randall pushed into the room, his hand outstretched. They shook like men, firmly, warmly. He plumped himself on the stool across the way and scanned her face with close interest.

"Gees, it's been an awfully long time, Mamie!"

"You can say that again!" There was a tiny pause. "You're looking swell, Bill! How's everything down at the sweat shop?"

"You've got a helluva gall, calling that little hole a sweat shop!" He laughed. "You don't happen to be looking for a job do you? Looks like I'm going to be that way again!"

"That's what Ruth's been telling me."

He glanced at her. "It's really a good deal, Mamie."

"How's everything with you folks?"

"Just fine," she said.

He nodded. They said nothing about Brandon one way or the other. She could hear the sounds of Ruth's voice again.

"We'd just about given you up," Bill was saying. "Sure glad you came over."

"I been meaning to come over for a long time. But ... you know how it is. I don't know where the time goes." She shrugged. "But it goes and there you are—nothing gets done."

"Yeah, I know what that's like. It's the same with the work round here."

Frank Parks came to the door and hesitated, looking across the room at her. She did not hear him nor see him at first. He looked at Bill; their eyes met and then broke.

"Mamie, here's an old friend of yours. Here's Frank," Bill announced quietly.

She twisted her head and glanced casually at him. She held her face under rigid control.

"Hello there, Frank," she said softly. "I hear you're in the market for congratulations, Frank." She looked straight into his eyes, the same old blue, steady, clear eyes. "I hope you'll be very happy."

"Thanks."

She got the instant impression he preferred to let it go at that. Well, it was okay by her!

Throughout the luncheon she and Frank kept outside the clutch of each other's wandering gaze. The luncheon finally came to an end. They got up, escaping from the close confinement of the table, and went on back into the living-room. The men lit cigarettes and sat together on the chesterfield. Ruth was in her old place, parked on the little footstool, sitting erect. They talked about everything under the sun. Everything, that is, but the one thing about which each of them was thinking.

Mamie stood at the window, filling in the proper phrases as the conversational cues were shoved at her, while all the time she was remembering the days before her marriage. She could recall very clearly the days when he used to come to her and put his arms about her, holding her tight against him. She could feel the hard cut of his lips on hers, the sharp press of his chest against her breasts. Her throat tightened with her remembering; she kept her face turned away from them, for fear that her very thinking would stand unveiled and open, stark upon her face for them to see.

Frank's eyes were on her steadily, constantly. He was doing some remembering, too. His mind went shooting back to the days when he had drawn her close against him, seeing again the flash of her eyes heavy with desire, tasting again the soft, gripping possession of her lips. He could remember the force of her full breasts on his chest. The unrewarded hunger, so long dormant and suppressed, came rearing unchecked. Suddenly all the want for her, put away and denied all these months, was unmasked within him. He was crowded with wild, frantic desire and there was a sharp, twisting fear in him.

Bill was watching Mamie at the window, forcing the titbits of talk, like an interlocutor at a theatrical performance. There was a touch of pathetic misery in her, he thought. He remembered the days before, the days when she had made her choice so surely, so confidently. He had known all along it would be like this. She need not say how she felt. He knew she was whipped, the loser; that now she knew her mistake. As for Ruth, she sat very still, her eyes not on Mamie but on Frank. She saw the way he was looking at her. She saw the old, hard tightness on his lips and the agitation growing in his eyes. Something inside Ruth turned over. She knew what was happening and yet she was powerless to check it. Suddenly she could hear Frank's voice, coming to her out of the distant past. "I'm scared of her," he had said. "There's nothing that's good for me in Mamie Brandon!"

Mamie listened to them talking in the room behind her. Her mind was truant, stalking along the corridors of the deserted months. She could remember him saying something once, a long time ago: "It's like this between me and you, baby. Sooner or later, it's gotta be you and me together, see?" She swung abruptly from the window and glanced across the room at Bill and Ruth sitting there, and then at him. He was remembering, too; she could see that in the instant. Her breathing became painful, laggard in her chest. She knew she must not stay here another moment, not like this.

"I gotta go!" she cried harshly. Ruth glanced at her with mingled surprise and sharp relief.

"Why don't you drive her part way, Bill?" she suggested.

Mamie shook her head sharply. "No. Honest, it's not too far! I kinda want the walk, anyway." All she wanted to do was get out of here. Go anywhere, just get off alone by herself, where she could try and think things out.

Frank rose to his feet. "I'll give you a lift, Mamie," he said pointedly.

She refused her striving eyes. There was a thick flush reddening her cheeks. Ruth found herself remembering the other time in Colfax. She opened her mouth to protest at his offer. But Mamie's mind was sharper to the danger.

"Oh no," she shook her head violently. "No, it could make trouble." Her voice was almost muffled. "God knows, I ain't looking for no more trouble!"

Ruth felt a quick stab of relief. Bill brought Mamie's boots from the hallway and she slipped them on. Ruth appeared with her coat. Mamie managed a steady smile.

"I sure had a real nice time," she said.

Ruth returned her smile in kind. "You come again, Mamie; come soon. It's probably better for you to come here ... " Mamie nodded, knowing full well what Ruth meant. Bill took her hand. "We sure mean that, both of us. Come back real soon."

She had not been sure of Ruth; she knew Bill asked her because he really meant it. She felt a sudden rush of friendship.

"I'll try, honest, Bill."

Frank had gone on ahead and stood waiting on the porch. He had put on a leather jacket. Ruth's eyes were on him.

"Coming in, Frank?" she asked lightly.

"I think I'll walk as far as the fence with Mamie," Frank answered.

The fence at the edge of the area barred their way. He made no attempt to assist her over the rail. She climbed up by herself and, perching there, swung her legs over the top. As she did, she nearly lost her balance. She teetered on the edge and he reached up suddenly and put his steadying hands on her body, his fingertips firm near her breasts. But he snatched them away as suddenly as he had placed them there. He stepped back, his eyes on her intently, as she jumped down to the other side.

There had been no word between them during the walk from the house. They stood now, facing each other, the safety of the barrier fence between them.

"Well ... " she shifted nervously, "thanks for walking down with me."

"That's all right," he returned flatly.

Her breath began to race, whipped before the storm of the conflict. Her eyes fastened on the dark, knotted welt in his forehead. The dam within her broke; the hoarded emotions, stifled so long, came spilling, swirling in an overwhelming rush. The terrible, racking want for him crushed down on her and she heard her own voice, strange and alien, ringing out.

"There ain't nobody there Tuesday or Friday night. You could come then!"

She felt the shock of her own action jab through the need for him; she spun away and went stumbling down the path into the chill midday twilight of the pines. To him, rooted by the fence, fingers gripping the edge of the top rail, watching her go, she looked like a drunken woman, staggering a little, running blindly down the path that led to the highway.

CHAPTER TWELVE

B INNIE walked over and dropped a coin in the juke box. She waited pensively for the music to come. Her gaze drifted out through the windows over the gravel strip towards the highway. Lord, business was sure slow! Slower than molasses! She had had exactly three customers since early morning. And they were regulars. Three cups of coffee, six doughnuts—no more, no less!

She peered down through the glass front of the machine at the elaborate mechanism inside. The record slid out from the cylindrical pile on the left and settled down on the spinning turntable. In a moment the arm moved forward and dropped into place. The music came blaring out into the room. She moved away and began to dance, gliding round and round the empty room, her eyes closed, her arms held out, embracing an unseen partner. Suddenly she stopped short, grinned, and muttered to herself aloud. "You're nuts, sister!"

She retreated behind the counter and began to straighten up. She hummed along with the music as she worked. She heard the rattle and clash of the model A, heard the scrunch of rubber against the pebbles outside. She glanced up curiously. Frank jumped down and came hurriedly to the door, almost on a run. He pulled it open, stepped inside and came directly towards her, forgetting to let the door slam against his heels as he always did. The winter window rattled loudly in its frame. "Well, hello, sunshine!" she greeted, concealing her surprise. "What brings you round these parts in the middle of the day?"

He was in front of her now. He leaned over the counter and, taking her chin in his hand, he pulled her face up to his and kissed her roughly, harshly. She stepped back with a squeal.

"Frank! You hurt!" She frowned, sucking the inside of her lip where it had been pressed against her teeth. "Whatever's the matter with you, anyway? You look all up in the air about something."

His breath was short and gratey, as if he might have been running for a long time. He said nothing at first; she could see he was trying to regain control of his breathing. When he finally spoke his words burst forth in a rush.

"Binnie! Darling! You gotta marry me right away!"

She blinked with surprise. "But … why? Why right away? All of a sudden you mean?"

"I can't explain. You just gotta, Binnie, you just gotta marry me! To-night! You and me'll go to Reno and get it done right away!"

She took another step back, apprehension crowding into her eyes. The icebox came hard against her buttocks, blocking her further retreat.

"I'm afraid I don't understand, Frank."

"I ain't asking you to understand. The only thing I want is for you to marry me right away, now—to-night! No questions!"

She said nothing for a few moments. She made no motion, said nothing. Finally she shook her head slowly.

"No," she said. "No … not like that, Frank. Not all hurried-up and confused like that. It isn't how we planned."

He became exasperated. "What difference does it make whether it's like we planned or not? You are gonna marry me, ain't you? Then what difference does it make if it's tonight or next month?"

"No," she repeated stubbornly. "I am going to marry you, Frank, yes. But I'm not going rushing off like this. It has to be my way, Frank. You've got to let me have this my way."

His voice became urgent, pleading: "You gotta, Binnie, you just gotta!"

She stared at him, suspicion darkening her eyes. "You've gotten into some kind of trouble! What is it, Frank? What kind of trouble are you in now?"

"No. No, I ain't in no trouble! Believe me, Binnie, it ain't that! Honest, I ain't in no trouble!"

She kept staring at him intently, trying to fathom the reason for this turn of events. But he kept his eyes averted, away from her. There was some kind of trouble, she was sure of it.

"I ain't in no trouble. None at all, honest!" he repeated.

"But I don't understand, Frank."

"I can't explain it to you, darling."

"But…why?"

"Oh, Jesus! Stop standing there saying 'but why' over and over like that!"

"Well, really, Frank! You come bursting in here like a cyclone and tell me I've got to marry you to-night, right away, and then you say you can't tell me why. I think I've got a right to know!"

"There ain't nothing for you to know," he said sullenly.

She moved slowly from behind the counter and sat down on one of the stools, looking up at him, bewilderment deep set in her eyes.

"I don't understand you at all, Frank. You come in like a storm and say we've got to get married right away, but that you aren't in any kind of trouble or anything like that. Has the railroad called you?"

"No."

"I don't understand. Why all the rush, then? You were content to wait before."

Frank went down on his knees beside her. He took hold of her firmly round the waist. She stared down into his eyes, those vivid, blue eyes she had come to know so well. She could see them clouded and wild with a look strange and foreign to her.

"Look, baby! I'm just asking you! Please let's get married to-night! Please let's go get it done now—let's do it right away! Let's go to Reno to-night and get it done once and for all!"

She parted her lips to reply. But he reached up and put his fingers over them.

"Don't say nothing right now. Just sit there and listen to what I gotta say."

He swallowed. She had to see this was important! She had to feel, to know the need for getting it over right away, right now! And, yet, there was no real way he could tell her the why of it. There were no words, no way of putting it into words if there were, so that she would see it as he did, so that she would understand. There was no way he could tell her how he felt inside. He kept seeing Mamie staggering down the path towards the highway, feeling once again that powerful tug at his insides that had come when she had said that about Tuesday and Friday nights. Binnie had to understand!

"Honey..." He gripped her tight. She winced a little under the cut of his fingers on her body. "You just got to trust me! You just got to believe in me! You got to know I'm asking you to marry now because there is a good reason!"

"You're in trouble of some kind," she persisted dully.

"Stop saying that! I ain't in no trouble! There ain't no trouble!"

"I just don't understand..." she kept going round in circles, unable to follow him.

"Baby, I'm trying as hard as I can to make you understand a little. It's just that you and me, we can't wait no longer, Binnie. We gotta do it now! There's reasons I can't tell you. I can't put them into words. I couldn't make you see why even if I was to get them into words. You don't know nothing like this. There ain't no way I can show you why. The only thing I'm asking, please... do what I want now, trust in me this once!"

She sat quietly for a long time without saying a word, just sit-ting, looking down into his face. The vein on his brow was near to bursting; something had taken hold of him. It was as if he were tormented, seared by some inner fire. He wasn't himself, not the Frank she knew! She pulled away from him and, rising to her feet, went to the window across the room.

"I don't want it like that," she said slowly. "It's ugly when it's like that. That's not the way I want it."

He remained behind, kneeling beside the empty stool, his eyes wide, stunned at her insistent refusal, so outright, so final. She was still talking.

"You say you're not in any trouble. The railroad company hasn't called you. You just want to get married in a hurry like this—to-night. Now. As if we were running away from something!" She hesitated. She turned from the window and looked at him with sharp realization suddenly softening her eyes. "This thing'll pass, Frank; you'll feel better later."

He ran his tongue over his lips quickly. It hit him with a wallop! She thought he … She thought … She thought what ailed him could be cured with a long walk or a cold shower or something like that! She thought that was all that was the matter with him. For an instant he had a wild impulse to laugh right out loud. It came racing up, pressing inside him, almost strangling him with its struggle to escape into the room. Then it died, choked in his throat, stifled, cut off.

"It ain't sex!" he said bluntly. "It ain't got nothing to do with climbing into bed!"

She flushed deeply and bit her lips in embarrassment. "I didn't mean that," she lied, trying to cover her confusion.

He crossed the room and pulled her to him. Her cheek was smooth and cool against his fevered skin. He pressed his face hard against hers. There was a soothing, gentle fragrance about her, a soft-scented protection held within her hair. He closed his eyes as if he could shut out the churning within him.

"Darling … " he tried once again, his words low and steady in her ear. "This here's not just an idea I got. It's something there ain't no way of putting into words. It wouldn't sound like it is even if I was able to tell you. All I'm asking you to do is just trust me. I need you now. I need you now more than, maybe, I'll ever need you again. I need you more than I ever needed anybody before. You're the only one who can help me. It's right now I need you, now, like this. It ain't tomorrow, it ain't next month. It's now to-night. Binnie, you gotta listen to what I'm saying. You gotta listen and believe in me this once!"

She stared up over his shoulder into the faded yellow of the lunch-room ceiling. She knew she couldn't do it, not the way he wanted. She couldn't do it quick and rushed, all over in a minute. He knew that. They had been all over this before. Not like this, exactly, but they had discussed it over and over; he knew what she wanted. She wanted it to be right when it happened. And now he was forcing her, taking an unfair advantage. To-day he felt like this. To-morrow was different; to-morrow he would be willing to wait. In the long run she knew he would know she had been right. It was better to wait a little longer. Better to wait until everything was settled, until they had their own place, until everything was in order. If he would only stop and think for a moment, he would see. He didn't, he couldn't really want it this way!

She pulled away from him and smiled tenderly. A great shining hope burst through him. He searched her face for the answer. His eyes were dark, shadowed with his intensity.

"Not this way, honey … not all rushed!" She reached up and put her fingers on his lips as he sucked in his breath with sharp disappointment. "You'll see. It'll be better the other way. It'll be better if we can put it off just a little while longer. It's only for a little while longer, Frank, that's all!"

He looked at her quietly now. There was a solid, determined finality in her soft words; he knew quite suddenly that it was over, that he was beaten. The whole thing had been useless. She would never consent. He turned and walked away from her. He sat down heavily at the counter. He swung round and glanced back across the room to where she stood.

"Okay, honey..." His resistance collapsed. "Whatever you want."

She smiled her strong, positive smile. She came over to him and stood at his side, pushing her long fingers through the waves of his hair.

"That's right—you'll see. You'll see that I'm right, Frank. It's better this way. It's better to wait just a little while longer."

He could hear her words floating down to him, wafting down from above, a gentle, fluted cadence in the stillness of the room. He could hear what she was saying, but it had no meaning; it was empty, severed from him, somehow. There was a heavy fear frosting his heart. He looked up into her face suddenly with deep sadness in his eyes.

She stopped running her fingers through his hair. He was so like a stranger, so different. She frowned with annoyance, looking down at him and finding herself unable to read what was there. He got up, took her in his arms, drawing her to him tight, and bent his head, burying his face in the soft curve of her neck. Then he pulled his head back, leaned down and kissed her long and steady, without passion. He broke away and went to the door. He turned and glanced back to where she was standing, puzzled and a little uneasy.

"Coming by for me to-night?" she ventured lightly.

"Sure... sure thing, kiddo," he replied, wrinkling his nose and grinning. "Be seeing you then."

He closed the door quietly behind him and she moved over to the window. She watched the truck move out to the highway and the bewilderment and uneasiness in her was gone now. So she had been right all along! There was a confident smile on her face as she watched him go.

CHAPTER THIRTEEN

Mamie ran blindly, unevenly down the soggy, rain-soaked path. She ran as hard and as fast as she could. After a few moments she was forced to slow down, and finally she came to an abrupt halt in the middle of the path. Her breath was sharp and restricted, and instinctively she grabbed at her heaving breasts as if she could halt their fluttering movement, as if by seizing them she could pull the tenor of her breathing back to normal. There was a pointed, pinprick pain in her right side. She shook her head once or twice, attempting to clear it, trying to regain her old perspective. The woods were silent, ringed about her with suspicion and accusation. Slowly her body relaxed; her breathing became smooth. She ran her hand over her face, pressing her fingertips against her lids, massaging her eyeballs. The pain in her side seemed to lessen, and at length faded out entirely.

Mamie shoved her hands down deep in her raincoat pockets and started to walk again. Her fingers touched something small and hard in the bottom of one of the pockets and she paused. She drew forth the tiny perfume package and looked down at it cupped in the flat of her palm. She had forgotten, what with everything else that had happened—Ruth's Christmas gift! The one reason she had gone to the Randalls' in the first place. Certainly it had not been on the slim chance of seeing him again. Why, the thought of Frank Parks had never crossed her mind. Annoyed, she shoved the parcel back and started to move down the path once more. Her feet were good and wet. The blind dash down through the woods, the flight from him, from herself, had taken her through all the pools and puddles without knowing. Her feet sloshed round inside the boots, uncomfortable and cold. She stamped on down towards the highway.

It had clouded over again; the woods were dark and chilled with a dankish feel. As she made her way, a thick, curdled fog came dripping from the branches of the trees, touching her garments and her hair, clinging to everything. She raised her hands tentatively. Her hair was wet and stringy. She shot a quick glance round her. Through the woods on her right, almost obscured by the screening trees, was a small shed of some sort. She hesitated, then left the path and made her way over to it. The warped door hung half-open. She poked her head inside and peered round. It was almost dark in the little hut; it took a moment or so until her eyes were adjusted to the gloom. The interior was in fair condition. It was dry, for one thing. The roof had broken through—a noticeable hole gaped here and there. Still, all in all the shed was still in fairly good condition. She stepped inside gingerly. There was a plank flooring, the twisted remains of an old rusty iron stove piled up against the far wall, and a battered, broken-down rocking chair listing in the corner. That was all. A few old newspapers, yellowed and dusty, lay heaped over the floor. The walls had been papered with newspapers, too. She crossed over and glanced at the headlines. They were uninteresting, half-forgotten news of years gone by. Absently she fluffed out her damp hair and moved over to the small rectangular slot in the wall. This must have been the window. The mist was thinning outside. She decided she had better go on ahead rather than wait here for the weather to clear. She made her way back to the path and stepped up her pace, hurrying down towards the road.

As she came to the Brandon clearing she could see the lights already on inside the house. They tinted the shadeless windows, giving the place a warm, cheery look even from the distance across the open space. She plodded up the road towards the house. On the porch she leaned over and kicked off her boots and removed her wet raincoat. She shook her head sharply, flicking droplets in all directions, fluffing out her hair with her fingertips. It was no use! It was thoroughly drenched now. The hairs hung in matted strings, framing her face like seaweed. She wiped the wet from her face with the back of her hand and pushed open the front door.

She was a little late getting the dinner on. Brandon had come in from the outside a little early as well. The deviation from his set routine made her nervous. He sat in the big room before the fire, waiting for the call to come for his meal. She set the dinner on the stove hurriedly and then went to her room and got out of her wet things. Bending over, she gazed at herself in the mirror over the dressing table. The color sat high in her cheeks; there was an uncommon sparkle in her eyes. She parted her lips slightly; she felt good, revitalized, strong once more. She backed away and picked up the raincoat from the bed to shake it out. She put her hand in the pocket and took out the little package in the Christmas wrapping. She laid it on the dresser top with an annoyed grunt. She returned to the kitchen and finished preparing the evening meal.

They sat across from each other as they always did. He had eaten silently, as usual, though to-night, as he ate, she got the impression that he was watching her steadily, his eyes screened from her glances by the thick veil of his lashes. She had made none of the usual attempts towards opening any conversation. It was he who finally broke the silence.

"Well, did you have a good time?"

She glanced at him for a moment with a trace of caution before she answered. "Yeah. Yeah, I had a real nice time." He made no comment. He held his head high, his eyes steady on her. His fork was arrested, the prongs pointing on an angle towards the ceiling, a small bit of meat speared on the tips. She attempted to concentrate on her plate before her, to try and ignore his close inspection. But it was impossible. He continued to sit like that, staring directly, obviously at her. She flushed and returned his look.

"What're you staring at?" she demanded sharply.

"You," he said simply.

"Well ... what's the matter with me?"

"I don't know. You look kinda different, somehow."

She became acutely aware of herself. She was a little flustered, remembering how she had looked to herself in the mirror a short time before.

"I look just the same as I did the last time you seen me."

He shook his head briefly. "No ... no, you don't." He wet his lips. "You look kinda different." He peered at her, trying to think back, to remember when she had looked like that before. There had been a time somewhere, some place in the past, when he could remember her looking as she did now. There was a sudden, quick twist in his memory and he had it. His eyes narrowed a trifle. His gaze never left her face. With the passing of the silent minute she grew a little resentful of his rude, open surveillance.

"Do you have to sit there staring at me all the time?" she demanded.

He waved the meat-laden fork to cut her short. "Wait! I remember. You look like you looked that morning after Reno!" he crowed triumphantly. "You look like you did the morning after we was married!"

The flush deepened on her face. Reno! She could hardly remember what she looked like then. Reno was a way back, buried deep in the debris and cobwebs of the dead months. She looked at him curiously. It was as if she suspected him of having gone a little mad during her absence. There was neither fear nor apprehension in her eyes. Only a curiosity, coupled with a light indifference. She did not press the subject further. She got up and started to remove the dishes from the table. He kept watching her closely, resuming his eating but never taking his eyes from her.

He followed her movements without a break. They said nothing more about the day's visit, for which she was grateful.

But that night, in their accustomed places before the fire, he brought the thing up all over again. She was sitting, her hands idle, looking into the fire, thinking back over all the things that had happened over there on the other place, when his voice interrupted her, scattering her thoughts before the breeze of his words.

"How are all your friends?" There was only a faint suggestion of an accent on the last word.

She turned her head and looked at him a trifle warily. "They're all right."

"The Randalls all okay?"

"Yeah. They're all right."

He hesitated. Suddenly she got an inkling of what was coming; she held herself steeled, ready for him.

"And … Frank Parks. How is he?"

There was an odd, funny glint in his eyes. It might have been the reflection of the firelight.

"Frank Parks? Uh … he's all right, too."

He said nothing for a moment. She glanced at him curiously, thinking he had finished.

"Did you see him?" His voice held steady, putting the question to her shrewdly.

She looked him straight in the eye. "Yeah," she said calmly; "I seen him."

She had an idea he had nodded to himself as she spoke, as if he were confirming something already in his mind. It was an "I-thought-so" gesture. She became slightly angered with herself. She was deliberately trying to start something tonight, trying to bait herself, by putting things into what he said and did. After all, he had been asking plain, everyday questions. They were perfectly natural, perfectly harmless questions. They helped to take up the slack in the evening.

"He get married yet?"

147

She became the unwilling tool in his hands. Desperately she wanted to drop the whole conversation. He wasn't interested in these people, any of them! She knew that. Then why was he driving her now? What was he getting at? What was he trying to find out? She became sharply aware of a possible trap, a hidden snare that might be concealed beneath this casualness of his. She volunteered nothing. What he would ask, she would answer. Nothing more.

"No, he ain't married yet."

"I thought he was getting married soon?"

"He is. It's gonna be sometime this spring."

"Oh?" His eyes never left her face. "And that special friend of yours, that Randall woman. How's she doing these days?"

"She's all right!"

"Busy, I guess, huh?" He led her along slowly.

"Busy? As far as I know."

"And Randall...Bill, I think you call him?"

She felt the gorge of her resentment rising slowly. She fought to control her sparking anger, to keep the annoyance away from her. His slow, insistent questions kept scraping her raw and tender.

"He's all right, too. I told you once before, everybody's all right!"

He seemed to smile faintly at her open irritation. It was a thin, mirthless grimace that came poking out from round the corners of his mouth. It reminded her of the way lizards come poking out from under rocks.

"I just like to hear all the news," he said with oily ease.

She shot him a quick glance. Her anger boiled over suddenly and ran down the sides of her face, leaving it pulled and drawn.

"What are you getting at?" she rasped harshly.

"I don't know what you mean."

"You know what I mean all right! How come you're needling me to-night?"

"Needling?" His voice swung up in mock bewilderment.

"Yeah, needling, that's it! What are you trying to make up now?" her voice was shrill, rising in pitch.

His was as cool and unruffled as before. "I'm sure I ain't trying to make nothing up!"

"The hell you ain't!" She pushed herself up out of the chair and stepped to the fireplace. She put her hands on the mantel-edge and stared down into the fiery grate, trying to quash her aroused anger.

He came up behind her stealthily. "You think I'm blind or something!" His words hissed through his set teeth. "You think I ain't seeing what's in your eyes, in the way you look, in every move you been making round the house to-night?"

She spun round and faced him, her eyes blazing. "So what's with the way I look? What's it you're trying so damned hard to find out, Mr. Brandon!"

He was standing solidly, a little too close to her, that same unpleasant, thin smile stitched into place. Her words came spilling swiftly, half-defiant, half-defensive. "I ain't on to what you're after! You're kind of a devil, you are! You ain't after me—I know that. If it's me you want, then take it; it's yours! You got the right any time you feel like it. Everything round here's your way. If it ain't me … what is it you want? Jesus, I can't even go off the place for a day without we have to go all through this again! What do you want me to do? Do you want me to go on sitting around here on my tokas, day after day, cooped up like I been … forever! Is that what you want? Do I have to be locked up here all the time, never seeing nobody, never going nowhere?"

His words blocked her; they came clipped and strident, turned black and galled with the hot poison of jealousy. "I know what you been after! I'm on to what you want! You had your eye on that Parks before you ever came out here. I been waiting for something to happen. I been knowing ever since the start it was gonna happen like this." His voice was a low-pointed dagger of bitterness. "That's where you spent the day, maybe—in some goddam hay pile with Parks, hey? That's why you got them lights in your eyes to-night! That's why you been swishing round here like you used to in the old days! That's what's thawed you out all of a sudden-like!" He reached out and his fingers locked on the flesh of her arm where he had gripped her twice before. Her face contorted sharply with the quickening pain. Her mind went spinning before his charge, seeking a sanctuary in which to hide, a cover to shield the half-truth she felt shining in her eyes. She put out one hand towards him instinctively. The key to the gate of her escape fell into her palm! Suddenly that morning in the kitchen came back to her vivid and brilliant. She could remember the way he had looked at her, the desire, the return of his old hunger so plain in his eyes. She could remember how the want had come to her by the stove. She clenched her fists round that key. She had the weapon to beat him away from the truth. She moved quickly, throwing the lure before his flaming mind.

"You got me all wrong, Mr. Brandon," she said silkily. "For once you been barking up the wrong tree. You don't know very much about women, do you, Mr. Brandon?"

She was leaning just a little in his direction now. She had him blocked completely. He stood confused, motionless, silent, still holding her arm in that painful grip, as if he had forgotten to release her. He was staring at her, trying to peer through the veiled defences shrouding her eyes. She could see the wild fire in his look failing in its strength. She shoved her words across at him carefully, measuring her time, her purpose.

"Ain't you got the truth yet, Mr. Brandon?" she asked slowly. "Ain't you seen what makes me look like this? You said you could remember how I looked then, after Reno. It wasn't no Frank Parks what done that!"

She edged away from him as she spoke. She pulled her arm free from the bite of his fingers. He let his hand drop limply to his side, following her with a startled, bewildered gaze. The gleam of suspicion wavered slightly and hung. She moved round him carefully, away from him, away from in front of the fire. She went to the long, low table in front of the double windows and turned, facing him, placing her hands behind her, touching the edge of the table with the tips of her fingers. Her body was tilted, her back arched just a little. Her glance went back across the space between them; there was a steady, determined fire kindled in her eyes.

"Ain't you got it yet, Mr. Brandon?"

He had pivoted as she moved from him. Slowly, as surely as she had planned it, the snaring skeins of her manœuvre caught him in their binding traces. She had walked with all the old swing and excitement. His blood pounded inside him; his temples ached dully. His tongue was thick in his mouth; his eyes hot and blood-smeared. He looked at her standing like that, bent back, her rich body tempting, ready for him to come and take. She swept his doubts away with one fell swoop, blacked-out the memories of the past, whipped the present into a whirling, blinding maelstrom.

He came over and took her roughly in his short, powerful arms. His voice, forcing up from his tightened throat, was strangled and hoarse, strange sounding to her, trembling a little.

"You mean … all the time it's been me you been wanting! It's been me all along? And all the time I been thinking it was him, and it's been me all the time!"

She looked over his shoulder, up towards the place where the ceiling met the wall. She could see the reflection of the firelight as the flames rose and fell with uneven, jerky motions. She was smiling now, a hard, cold, winning smile, brittle and sharp on her face.

"Why … sure, Mr. Brandon. Sure thing," she said easily. She permitted her fingers to raise, to stroke his iron-grey hair once or twice with loving care.

"Why, sure, Mr. Brandon. Ain't you got wise to that yet?"

CHAPTER FOURTEEN

WHATEVER suspicions Brandon may have entertained regarding Mamie's visit to the Randall place were completely dissipated now. She established her possession of him as completely as he had held her previously. She held him locked firm, inescapable with the vise of her physical grasp. She catered to his needs and his desires at his supposed will, and yet, all the while, she was deliberately and elaborately weaving round him her binding wall of purpose. The little room was tenantless; the clock unravelled its hours by day and she carefully, methodically rewound them by night.

The first Tuesday finally came. For the first time since their marriage Brandon, drunk with his new-found favour, was reluctant to go out on his inspection of the ditch line. This was unexpected and disturbing. She was instantly fearful that she might have over-exerted her advantage. But, aside from the momentary wavering in his course, the routine demand of the chore was stronger than his personal wants. He took the lunch she had prepared and went plodding off into the late afternoon. She sent him off, playing out her hand carefully, enacting a tender farewell on the front porch. He turned and looked back when he had got to the edge of the clearing. She was still standing as he had left her, holding the column support in her right hand. He thought he saw her wave once, and he almost returned it. She watched him disappear into the trees. She sighed with relief. Thank God he had finally gone! At last she was alone!

She went back into the house. Her gaze flashed round the big room. Everything was in order. She pulled down the blind on the double window and went through to the kitchen.

Her mind seemed extra-brilliant and steady. Her emotions were in close check, well under control. She wondered if he would come to-night. She screwed the lid on her patience tightly. It was still early, not completely dark yet.

Generally she never bothered to go into the big room when she was left alone. Instead she did her sewing or reading or thinking, sitting at the window in the breakfast nook. To-night, for some reason, she did not feel much like reading or sewing. She did not feel as if she could concentrate. She felt calm enough ... but there was a kind of restlessness in her. She went into the big room and switched on the light. From the drawer in the table she got a deck of playing cards. She turned off the light and came back into the kitchen and sat down at the table. She shoved the sugar-bowl and the salt and pepper things out of the way and started to lay out the cards for a game of solitaire. They made a sharp, snapping sound as she set them out in the prescribed row, seven across the face of the table. Automatically she played. Draw, play, discard. The game hung itself. She reshuffled the deck and began all over again. She grew tired of the subterfuge. It was hard to follow the cards when all the time your mind was out there, listening, waiting. She strewed the cards out across the table and sat, chin in hand, staring into the anonymous blackness outside. There was no sound anywhere. There was no hint of a quickening step on the walk. She played the cards again. The game never worked out. She sat there at the window until quite late.

Finally she got to her feet wearily, crossed the kitchen and snapped off the light. She went to bed alone, not quite according to plan.

For the next two weeks the pattern was unbroken. She played at her games, the three of them. The one with Brandon, in which she knew she now held the trump card. That was a one-sided game, no challenge any longer. The other, solitaire, each Tuesday and Friday night. She alternated her winning here. Sometimes she won; sometimes she lost. There was the other game, too, the game of waiting, at which she lost consistently. At first she had expected to lose, more or less. At least she had been prepared to lose the first few hands. But she had been confident of the finish. At the end of the second week when there had been no sign, no word of him, she had begun to wonder, had begun to have the first misgivings about the outcome; the shadow of doubt fell across her confidence.

She sat in front of the dressing-table in the bedroom, studying her face objectively. There were more lines of fatigue shadowing her eyes again. The little obstinate roll of fat under her chin had become a little more pronounced. Her eyes had become sharper, a little more glittering, sparkling in the weeks that had passed. They were the old, familiar eyes, fairly clear, fairly steady. The lashes were unchanged, still too short. Her gaze dropped away from the reflection and she shrugged faintly with impotence to change what she had seen. Her eyes fell on the tiny package in the holly paper. She picked it up and turned it in her hand. Ruth's perfume still here! She had to take it over sooner or later. Well … later, she decided. She was unwilling to go through all the after-tension that always came in the wake of her trips. She held it tightly. This was the second Friday since that other time. She listened intently.

What was that! There had been a sound somewhere out there, outside! She got up and stood very straight, the tips of her fingers resting on the edge of the dressing-table. There was the sound of a footstep outside—it was unmistakable! It sounded like a feeling, cautious step. She tried to crush down the tidal wave of anticipation that came towering within her. The glitter in her eyes heightened. She took a deep breath to steady her quaking heart. Her palms were oily with nervous sweat. She turned and went out of the room, trying not to hurry.

Mamie paused in the doorway to the dark kitchen. The sound came again, out there, behind the house, somewhere near the back door! Her being seemed to have gone numb, frozen. Trembling she crossed the floor and unlocked the door gently. She moved through the wash-room and pushed open the back screen. Her eyes could make nothing of the night blackness. Suddenly she saw the figure of a man standing in the dark. He was standing a little to the left, off from the house, as if he were uncertain which way to turn. She shoved the door open a little further. He was almost hidden in the darker shadow cast from the house; she could not quite make out the form. He had come to her! she thought triumphantly. At last, he had come as she had known all along he would! She opened her mouth to speak his name, to reveal herself to him, ready, waiting. But before the sound could come from her throat, the light came blinding out of the dark. She stepped back, the painful brilliance dazzling white in her eyes.

"You still up?"

Brandon moved towards her, the light held against her face.

She caught herself violently. She could feel the perspiration released, oozing from her body, soaking her clothing. She took a sharp, wobbling breath. "Oh … it … it's you? How come you're back so soon?"

He had come close and stood at the foot of the few steps before her. He extinguished the torch and made a half-gesture towards the shed.

"There's a break on the line up aways. I gotta have some tools."

Her breath began to level out, to come a little freer. She scanned his face closely. He suspects nothing, she thought, with a tiny prickle of relief. "I was just going to bed when I heard you," she remarked truthfully.

He glanced at her. "I was wondering. It's getting kinda late."

She forced her voice up a notch, made it light and casual. "I ain't sleepy. I ain't felt much like going to bed yet."

"Maybe you been missing me a little." He supplied the obvious reason.

She said nothing.

His mind went back to the break in the line. "Well, I best get going."

"Is it bad—the break, I mean?"

"Ain't too bad. Kinda small. Won't take me long to patch it up."

The April night was lush and warm. She looked out beyond him over the clearing. Everything was still. From over in the direction of the barn she caught the sound of the stock shifting around restlessly. Overhead the stars speckled the dark of the sky with white-studded brilliance.

"Gees, it's sure a swell night!" she breathed.

"Yeah. Kinda looks like maybe we're gonna have an early summer round here."

He had moved away, going down the path towards the shed. She remained in the doorway until he had returned with his sack of tools in his hand. He had them wrapped in sackcloth. He was a great one for sackcloth, she thought suddenly. Everything he had out there was wrapped tight and secure that way. All his tools and that big double-barrelled shot-gun hanging on the wall of the shed. That was wrapped in sackcloth, too. It kept the oil in and the dirt out, she recalled him saying once. He pushed on past her, down the path that led round the house. He said nothing further. She waited until the sounds of his footsteps had been swallowed up in the stillness of the place before she closed and locked the door. She went back into the bedroom.

A brush of apprehension passed over her. Suppose Frank had come to-night! And, suppose he had come back like that when Frank was here! She knew instinctively what that would mean, what would happen. She stopped in her tracks, going a little sick at her stomach at the realization of her own stupidity. She reached out and seized the bedpost to steady herself. Suddenly she knew

Frank must never, never come here, not to this place, not here. There was too much risk. They must change the arrangement somehow. She must get to him right away, see him, tell him before he did come. But how? How could she see him...without stirring up Brandon or even the Randalls for that matter? How could she see him private-like? Her eyes strayed round the room as if to find the answer in some obscure corner; they came to the tiny package on the dressing-table. She brightened instantly. The perfume—that would do it! She would go over to-morrow and take that bottle to Ruth again. Her eyes widened; she saw the whole thing work out smoothly. That way, maybe, she would run across him. It could work like the last time.

She put out the light and climbed into the big, lonely bed. She lay there for a long time, staring up into the darkness, trying to shut away the crowding implications born of Brandon's unexpected, unanticipated return. Suppose Frank had been here, at her side, when he had come back like that! O, my God! She twisted sharply and buried her face in the pillow. She finally fell into a fitful, restless sleep. She slept uneasily, tossing, turning, strange and frightening shadows shifting along the walls of her subconscious.

She dreamed of herself waiting for Frank at the window of the kitchen. The cards were laid out before her. In her hand she held the ace of spades. Somebody, she could remember suddenly, had told her once the ace of spades was death. Maybe she had read it somewhere. Or seen it somewhere, sometime. It made no difference. There it was in her own hand, very clear, without question. The ace of spades was death and there it was, in her own hand. Just as she was about to play the card, there came a light tapping on the pane, and when she looked up there was Frank! The light from the kitchen was caught in his eyes; she could see them blue and vivid, set on fire with his need for her. She got up and let him in; they locked themselves together in the brilliant light of the room, holding each other tight and close, pressing their bodies together, letting the hot breakers of their desire come rolling over them. Their roaring seemed to drown out the world and she broke away and led him down the hallway. He closed the door behind them and reached out to seize her again. His trembling fingers fumbled at her clothing, and she stood, breathing heavily, waiting for him. She put forth her arms, striving for him, reaching out…

There was a terrible deafening, obliterating crash; the room became a single gigantic, blue-white flame for an instant; she was hurled back, staggered, shocked. Her eyes fled down over the white softness of her body. It was white no longer. There was blood on her, blood splashed scarlet, smeared upon her body. She rubbed frantically, trying to erase it, and when she took her hands away there was blood red and thick upon the palms. She looked back to where he had been and horror gripped her heart. She choked with terror. His eyes were on her and there was a sad, bewildered, pleading look in them. Suddenly the horror abandoned her. His knees buckled and he started to pitch forward. She ran and seized him. She stood in the centre of the room, clasping him up against her, holding him slumped, hanging outward from her arms, feeling the warmth of his life's blood gushing forth, washing against her. Her eyes went out past his bowed head, out across the room to the open door, and she looked into the cold, cruel eyes of Brandon.

In his hands, the barrel pointed at them still, was the double-barrelled shotgun, wrapped even now in the sackcloth. And as she stared in horror and revulsion, she saw his finger tighten a little. There was a smile on his thin lips, broad and wide and full of hate. He pressed the trigger. She could not see him any longer for the shocking flash that burst about her. There was a single, zagging, terrible pain in the whole of her chest and she could feel Frank's torn and blasted body sliding from her grasp. The darkness came crashing, thundering down upon her.

Mamie woke with a start. The bedclothes were pushed away from her body; her nightgown was high, painfully tight across her chest. Her body lay twisted, distorted, naked against the sheet. The window shades were up and the brilliant sunlight from the outside filled the room with glaring brightness. She remained as she was for a moment or so, collecting her wits, her eyes wide and staring, the sleep jogged and stripped from them. Then she began to relax gradually; her breathing lapsed into a quiet, even cadence. She rolled over and glanced at the dresser top. The little bottle was propped against the mirror. She knew what she had to do and do it right away!

She rose and went through the house, raising all the curtains, admitting the safe, secure sunlight. The more light she could get into the house, the better she would feel. The horror of the night was vivid in her mind. She tried to throw it off. But each time she closed her eyes and held them shut tight, the whole dreadful scene came back fresh and full of horror. She ran into the bathroom and let the cold water run for a time. Then she slapped it briskly into her face. After a moment or so she felt a little better, a little more controlled, a little more herself. She moved down the hallway to the kitchen and put the coffee on. She fidgeted impatiently until it was done. At the stove she poured a cup. She had a good case of the jumps! She raised the cup, swallowing the hot, black liquid in quick, painful gulps. After it had got down and started to warm her insides, she felt a little strength start to come back. The night began to fade, to assume the unreal cloak of a dream rendered negligible in the bright light of day.

He was due back any time now. She waited for him, standing before the double windows in the big room. The time dragged. She roamed through the house distractedly. Her mind insisted on trying to return to the pictures of the night. And, yet, it was not only the dream and its remembered terrors that kept her on edge—there was the warning that had been sounded with his unexpected return; she kept thinking of what might have happened had her foolish plan succeeded.

He was late coming back. She stood helplessly in the kitchen. All her activities were suspended, dependent on his return. She wished fervently he would come. She wanted to get over there as soon as possible. Each minute held its own importance. It was as if she were afraid that Frank might attempt to come now, in the middle of the day. She had to get to him, to block him, before he blundered in, before she saw him coming across the clearing hand in hand with disaster. She was tense and stiff, agitated and upset. Her eyes kept going to the clock on the stove. Brandon was more than an hour behind his usual time. Anger flicked at her. Damn him! Every time she wanted something for herself, he managed somehow to stand in her way! She resumed her idle wandering round the house. She opened the front door and went out on the porch to peer out over the clearing, searching for the sight of him down along the road leading in from the highway. That was the way he had gone; that would be the way of his return. She went down the steps into the bright, warming April sunshine. She stooped and picked a slim freesia, holding it to her nostrils to sample its fragrance. She idled along, moving down the road towards the pines. She had walked almost to the beginnings of the woods before she snapped out of her reverie. She glanced down through the green tunnel. There was no sign of him. She turned and made her way back to the house. She came through the living-room to the kitchen. Her eye fell on him, sitting at his customary place at the table.

"Oh!" she cried. "I didn't know you was back yet."

"I came up through the back, up from the crick."

"I was out front. I kinda figured you'd come that way."

She worked swiftly, pouring his coffee, setting his breakfast before him. He watched her, pleased at her admission that she had been waiting for him, noting the breathless manner in which she performed her chores.

"You look like you was going somewheres," he commented.

"Yeah; I figured maybe I'd go over to the Randalls' for a little bit." She made the statement easily, as matter-of-fact as she could. She turned from the stove and their eyes met briefly. She forced a shallow smile and cleared her throat. "You see...I done the damnedest thing!"

"What?"

"Remember that time I was over a couple of weeks back?"

"Yeah, I remember."

She skidded past the dragging up of old remembrances. "Well...I went over there in the first place to give Ruth that there perfume I got her for Christmas, and then, like a dope, I forgot all about giving it to her!"

"You sure don't have to hurry now. You're just in time for Easter."

She flushed slightly. Well, anyway, she had an excuse for the trip now. Easter present for a Christmas present!

"My, my—is it Easter already?" she said vaguely.

He had started eating. She came over with more coffee and stood close at his side. The nearness of her flowed out and engulfed him. He reached up and took her bare arm in his fingers, stroking her flesh gently.

"I been kinda hoping maybe we'd get together this morning..."

She flashed a synthetic smile down at him. "I ain't gonna be very long." She twisted it slightly, so that it carried the weight of a half-promise.

He latched on, precisely as she had meant him to. Then he remembered it was Saturday. "You'd better leave me a list before you go."

She paused, momentarily blocked again. Damn! She had forgotten this was the day he went to town.

"Oh, yeah. I guess I'd better." She rummaged round and dug up a pencil and paper. While he finished his breakfast she scribbled her needs and wants for the coming week. She brought it over and laid it on the table by his plate.

"That's about it, I guess." She tried to think past her own immediate problem. "As far as I know, that's all I want."

She seemed sort of high-strung and flighty this morning, he thought. She moved round on pins and needles, as if she were tied down and, yet, if the strings that held her were cut, she would go floating off the ground. He got up and stretched.

"I guess maybe I'll grab me a little shut-eye before I go." He stood in the middle of the kitchen, scratching his ribs, his nails noisy on the fabric of his shirt. He yawned loudly, his eyes pinched into two little slits by the crowding flesh of his cheeks. He moved over to where she was standing by the stove and took hold of her. "You got a little time before you gotta go." The suggestion was strong and urgent in her ear. She edged away from him a trifle, carefully.

"No … no, not right now." She put a little protective distance between them. "I gotta go quick. So … so's I can get back to start dinner." Her mind had selected the first feeble excuse from the discard pile. "I was pretty late last time."

He shrugged, yawned again, and withdrew his suit. He was tired, working all night like that. She went ahead of him into the bedroom and slipped on the tan raincoat over her house dress. She picked up the perfume package from the dresser and shoved it in her pocket. He was standing in the doorway, watching her. She caught sight of his reflection in the mirror as she bent forward. There was nothing she could see in his face other than casual interest, everyday curiosity. That was the way she wanted it.

"It ain't gonna rain," he commented.

"I know," she said, glancing down at the coat. "But this here's light; you don't have to be careful with it. The other snags on bushes and things."

She crossed the room, going round the foot of the bed, and came past him at the door. He stepped to one side to let her pass.

"Well..." she turned and looked at him. The formalities of their partings were always a little awkward for some reason. This one was no exception. "I...I guess I'll be on my way," she said superficially.

He nodded. He watched her cross the big room and open the door to the porch. She stepped out, pulling the door shut behind her. The winter had warped it slightly and it caught, not closing tight. She ran down the porch steps and struck out along the hard-packed, red road. He followed her through the house and jerked the door open, standing in its frame, watching her. She seemed all tensed-up, in a hurry about something. He shrugged, yawned loudly, widely, and stepped back into the room. He shoved the door tight, forcing it over the sticking point with the pressure of his knee on the panel. He turned and went down the hall to the bedroom.

She came to the highway at last. She hurried down along the shoulder of the highway to the other mailbox and then made her way rapidly along the path into the woods. The winter wet had seeped into the earth already; the carpeting needles were soft and fairly dry, full of pungent fragrance. She went along past the little abandoned shed in the screening clump of redwoods. She glanced briefly in its direction; she noticed the roof was green with vagrant weeds sprouting from the cracks in the spring sunshine. She hurried on and came to the fence round the Randall place. She climbed over and started across the clearing.

The house, everything about the place seemed quite deserted. Keno was absent as well—for which she was dimly grateful.

She came up on the porch and knocked at the solid door. There was no bell. There was no answer, either. No movement, no sound came to her ears. She knocked again, a trifle sharper this time. The third time she kicked against the door with the toe of her shoe. She made an awful racket, but no one answered. Frustrated at this unforeseen development she stood uncertain for a moment. She stared out over the vacant clearing and frowned. She moved down the steps slowly and hesitated on the path, trying to think what to do. Then she turned and followed the path round the house. In the space near the back door she came upon the model A. Frank was around here somewhere, she realized with a sudden lift. She tried the back door, but it was locked, too. She knocked tentatively once more. There was no response, just as she had expected. She stood on the back steps, perplexed. Her gaze drifted round the empty yard, shifting out over the clearing towards the trees, over to the big red barn. Maybe someone, maybe Frank even, was over there. She stepped down from the porch and headed along the path.

She came to the door at the side of the barn. There was a latch fastening on it. She put her fingers forth and pressed down on the handle gingerly. The door swung open. She stuck her head through and peered round the interior. Joe, Ruth's old sway-backed horse, was standing over in the corner in his stall. As she scanned the place he moved his head and eyed her coldly. She could see the billiard-ball blacks of his eyes, the generous flash of whites as well as he strained to see her. She shoved the door wider and stepped inside. Joe stamped, shifting himself uneasily. She listened intently. There was no sound save his moving around. No one seemed to be here, either. She gazed around. Over to her right there was a small door cut in the back wall of the building.

She went over and tried it. It was unlocked. She pushed it clear and stepped into the little room.

Her eyes took a rapid, complete inventory. There was a single cot with a small table at its side, on which there was a pitcher and a basin. A shirt was pinned to a line strung across the room. It was a familiar item, that shirt. She moved cautiously into the room and glanced around with growing interest. There was a chest of drawers with a mirror tacked to the wall above it. There were a few loose masculine toilet articles strewn over the face of the chest. She saw the razor, the bent and twisted tube of shaving cream, the comb, and the brush with some blonde hairs clinging to its fibres. Someone had stuck a snapshot in the lower right-hand corner of the mirror.

She crossed to the chest and, bending forward, examined the photograph closely. There were two men and a girl. One of the men was Frank; the other guy was tall, younger, good-looking too. He looked a lot like Frank, she thought. Then she remembered what Ruth had said about Frank's friend, how he looked and acted and dressed like him. This must be him. The girl was very attractive and very young. She had her hand on Frank's arm, the way a woman has when she's pretty sure about her man. Mamie gazed absorbed at the picture. She was so engrossed she did not hear his footsteps.

"Where'd you come from?"

His voice was easy, more curious than anything. She straightened with a start and twisted her head towards the sound. He was standing in the doorway, one hand against the frame, the other shoved down in the rear pocket of his jeans. His eyes were on her, but there was nothing in his voice to give a clue to his thinking.

"You scared me!" she cried. She caught her breath. "I was up at the house, only there was nobody there."

"Bill and Ruth've gone down to Colfax," he supplied. "They always go Saturdays."

"Oh?"

He came on into the room and busied himself, ignoring her. He unpinned the shirt from the line, tossing the clothes-pegs on to the couch.

"I been doing a little washing," he remarked absently.

"Yeah ... I can see."

She kept her eyes on him as he folded the shirt carefully and came past her to the chest of drawers. She moved slightly, stepping out of his way. He pulled open the drawer and bent over, laying the garment on the bottom. She looked down on his back, at the muscles working whenever he moved a finger. His back was a smooth, unbroken expanse of cotton cloth, with the little line of knobs ridging down the centre, marking his spine. She turned her head slowly until her eyes were away from him, on the little white-edged square stuck in the mirror. She pointed her finger at the snapshot.

"I suppose that there's your Binnie," she said levelly.

He straightened; his eyes followed the line of her finger. "Yeah, that's Binnie," he remarked soberly. He reached over and pulled the picture free. He bent forward, peering at it closely, as if he were the one who was seeing it for the first time, not she.

"That there's her brother, Art," he added. He handed the picture to her.

She took it and stared at the three of them. "They're a nice-looking couple of kids," she said.

"Yeah; they're swell."

The silence moved in on them. Looking at the picture Mamie suddenly wanted to go, to get out. The whole set-up was wrong, wrong, wrong! She had no right here—it was wrong. She had to go right away. It had been right when he had not come to the Brandon place. He must not come, ever! She remembered how they had been at the fence together, the last time she had been here. She could remember the sound of her own words striking loudly in her ears, telling him to come to her. Whatever had made her say that? Whatever had made her forget? Whatever had made her go on and on all these weeks expecting him to come, waiting for him like that—when all the time it was wrong? She moved away from him slowly, going towards the door. She caught herself and turned back, handing him the picture. He stuck it back in the crack between the glass and its frame. She went on to the door. Suddenly a vagrant thought came to her. Her curiosity stirred and she swung round, gazing at him quizzically.

"Frank…?"

He glanced at her coolly. "Yeah?"

She took a deep breath. "There's something … how come you didn't show up, Frank?"

He swallowed hard and glanced in confusion at the dresser top for a moment, shoving the razor around with the point of his finger. "I was scared to," he confessed flatly.

She raised her brows. "Scared? Of Brandon?"

"No; I wasn't scared of him." He moved from in front of the dresser and went over to the window, his back to her. "I was scared of you."

She said nothing. She had no idea what he meant. Something made her cross over and she took her place just behind him, looking out past his shoulder to the trees lined up outside.

"I guess I'm always gonna be scared of you a little," he was saying. "Only now it don't matter."

"What don't matter no more?"

"Me being scared of you," he repeated dully. "Nothing much matters any more, does it, Mamie?" He turned and she saw the flash of the old feeling in his eyes. "Nothing matters much except you and me, Mamie."

She backed away from him, her eyes wide. It was the degree of his intensity, spurred quick and sharp, that threw her off for the moment. The thought kept nagging at her that she had better go, that she ought to get away from here, from him. She moved slowly, backing towards the door. But something about him, something in his manner, arrested her. She stopped, her eyes on him. Suddenly she laughed a trifle bitterly.

"What's so funny?" He took a step towards her.

"Oh, nothing much. Only, for some time now I been kinda sorry I didn't take the chance and marry you instead of Brandon!"

"I don't get it. What's so funny about that?"

"Oh, I don't know. Maybe it ain't really funny, after all. Only I remember you telling me once you didn't figure as how you was the marrying kind!"

"Yeah … that's right. So what?"

She waved a finger in the direction of the mirror, at the photo stuck in that crazy angle at the bottom of the glass.

"How about that, about her?"

He started towards her. "I told you already. Nothing matters any more but me and you!"

She shook her head sharply. "Stay there!" she cried. "Right now it ain't just you and me. It's her, too. I been doing a helluva lot of thinking, Frank. I kinda figure it ain't right, us getting together, after all. Not when there's her around to get hurt. I ain't wanting to hurt nobody like that!"

Frank spun around and sent his gaze through the window. "You ain't got nothing to worry about," he said flatly.

She stared at his back, uncomprehending. "I don't get what you mean."

He was silent for a split second. Then he swung round and crossed the short space between them, sweeping her into his arms, crushing her harshly against him, seizing her lips roughly, painfully with his. Mamie struggled and fought against him; she dug her fingers into his chest, curving them like talons, pressing deep into his flesh. She twisted her head from side to side, trying to break the hold he had upon her. After a savage moment she wrested free and stumbled back, gasping, her hand clutching her breast, her eyes wide and shocked.

"No ... Frank, no! You shouldn't have done that. It ain't right. It can't be this way!"

He grinned sharply. "Why not? Why ain't it right? There ain't nothing that's changed between me and you. You and me's the same as ever, Mamie!"

She felt the overwhelming force of her desire for him seeping out from under her pressing will. She backed to the door and the frame came pressing sharp against her shoulder-blades. She shook her head violently.

"No!" she cried breathlessly. "No, Frank ... I ain't sure. I ain't sure it's right."

He followed her across the room and pulled her to him. The mad tide of wanting him beat against the storm-gates she was striving to hold within her; she felt them strain and start to yield. All the months of deprivation, of loneliness, of starving for someone at her side returned with overpowering strength; she fought bitterly to quell their demands, to step from the path of their onrushing torrent.

"Frank...no!"

His lips covered hers and the words were smothered in her throat. She struggled fiercely. Suddenly she went limp, whipped by the thing that was stronger than her will. He released her shortly and stepped back. There was a hard smile on his lips.

"You ain't changed so much, baby!" he said abruptly. "You ain't changed a damn bit, as far as I can see!"

Mamie stood rigid, ramrod straight against the door frame. Her eyes were closed tight. She heard his words and she knew them for the truth they were. She had not changed; in spite of all the months that had piled themselves between them, she had no more changed than he had. She opened her eyes, not altering her position and stared at him. She sent her eyes out past him through the little window to the green backdrop of the trees. They both stood silent, facing each other. He saw she had run aground, her thinking stranded. He moved towards her.

"It's gonna be you and me, Mamie. I gotta have you, that's all I know. I gotta have you, Mamie!"

She brought her gaze back and looked at him. "More'n you gotta have her?" she asked quietly. "You want me more'n you want her?"

His gaze shifted vaguely. "Why don't you leave her out of it?" he cried sharply. "Why keep bringing her back into it? It ain't got nothing to do with you and me!"

"There's one thing you better get straight now, Frank. I ain't bustin' up nobody's wedding, see? I ain't doing that to nobody, not me!"

His eyes bored into her. "There's times I hate you! You're like a devil! You got devil ways in you! You keep on pushing and pushing and pushing—you keep in front of me all the time! Night and day, day and night! I been trying to forget you, trying to push you out of my brain, out of my body, out of my life. And all the time you been sitting around waiting, knowing I ain't gonna get rid of you! You been knowing it all along. You been sure how it was gonna come out sooner or later. You been knowing all you had to do was reach out and take." His words ground through his teeth, choked and hoarse. His face was dark and the vein was a thick daub on his brow. "There's times I hate you, Mamie Brandon! There's times when I want to kill you with my hands!" He held them up before her, the fingers long and hard, straight and powerful. "Sometimes I dream I kill you. I see myself, feel my fingers round your throat, pressing tighter and tighter. I can hear your breathing whistle down there and stop. I can feel your throat in my hands, your neck with my fingers round it. I could like doing that! I could almost have fun killing you off!" His voice shattered and he spun away from her shocked, startled eyes. "There's times when I figure you'd be better off dead, out of the way! I'd be better off! Only I can't do it; I ain't strong enough! Goddamit, I ain't been strong enough!" His head tilted forward as he buried his face in his hands.

His emotion caught her; she knew she had what she wanted now. Brandon, Ruth, Bill, Binnie ... none of them mattered to her any more, in this moment! She had him, at last! Her breath came quick, tight in her chest. She wanted to run across the room, to fling her arms about him, to hold him to her hard.

He suddenly wheeled and threw himself at her feet, his arms tight round her legs. She held herself rigid, taut, resistant. This was not the time; this was not the place.

"I gotta have you, Mamie! I gotta have you! I gotta have you!"

She was erect, her eyes bright and shining, staring down at him, at the top of his head hard against her knees. Her blood was thick, throbbing in her head like the old time birds' wings beating. She looked down at his trembling body, at the brown arms round her legs, at the set of his jaw with the dent cut below the ear. His hands were clenched together, locked behind her knees, the muscles of his arms strained and firm in the swamping flood of his passion. She smiled slowly, her face flushed and hot. To hell with Brandon and his make-believe Ellen, with bargains, with all the rest! She leaned forward and her words were barely audible. "Frank... you know that little shed just off the path—the one in the bunch of trees?"

He did not lift his head but she knew he had nodded slightly.

"Tuesday night... there. I'll be waiting."

She was hoarse. She had to get away instantly, get away now, before it was too late, before her thin defence collapsed entirely. Her resistance was failing, weakened with the urgent nearness of him. She pulled her body free from his imprisoning grasp and hurried from the room.

He remained kneeling, staring at the open door for a long time after she had gone. Suddenly he pitched forward and threw himself full-length on the floor of the little room, his face hard against the boards. His shoulders shook violently as he wept.

Mamie felt new, a completely different woman. She walked with strength and majesty up the path from the barn. She felt magnificent, full of confidence. She felt great and omnipotent. She dwarfed the trees, the very distant mountains themselves. The world had shrunk and become a bauble for her to wear.

She drew herself straight and hard and walked up the path towards the house. She came to the back door and rapped on it with her knuckles. Ruth came from the kitchen, wiping her hands on her apron, a curious look on her face.

"Why... it's Mamie! Welcome!"

Her voice carried a note of tempered pleasure. She glanced at Mamie oddly. There was almost a radiance of some sort surrounding her. She seemed filled with a remarkable, animal-like vigour. Ruth held the door open and Mamie swept past her into the kitchen.

"Mamie! You look positively marvellous this morning! What is it? A new diet or … just plain spring?" she grinned.

Mamie smiled loftily. "Maybe it's a combination of both!" she laughed loudly. She reached down in the raincoat pocket and brought forth the tiny package. The holly wrapping looked so silly in the April sunlight. "Here—Happy Easter!" She held it towards Ruth.

"Well, what on earth?" Ruth took the parcel and glanced at Mamie in surprise.

Mamie laughed again. "It's my Christmas present to you! I carried it over the other time and then forgot all about it. Ain't I the nut?"

Ruth's fingers went to work. She tore off the wrapping and took out the tiny bottle. She held it appreciatively to her nose and sniffed.

"Mamie, you shouldn't have!" She held the bottle in place. "Ummmm! It smells so good!" She turned and led the way into the living-room, pausing to give an extra stir to the pot on the stove.

Ruth pointed to the big chair. "Sit there, Mamie!"

Mamie dropped to the chair with a lusty sigh. "I ain't gonna stay," she remarked. "I just took the walk over to … give that to you before it was Christmas again!"

"You really shouldn't have done it. But I'm crazy about it!" Ruth smiled. "Bill's around somewhere—out in the woods, I think. Frank's around too."

Mamie glanced at her briefly. "Yeah, I know," she said quietly. "I been talking with him."

Ruth shot her a sharp look. "Oh, have you?" was all she said. Ruth remembered the last time Mamie had dropped by. She remembered all the agitation and the turmoil she caused in

Frank and the rest of them. Suddenly, with a jag of surprise, she found herself wishing Mamie wouldn't come round any more! If that was the way it was going to be every time she came, then she wished Mamie wouldn't come. Ruth flushed, a little guilty harboring a thought like that. Impulsively she reached over and patted Mamie on the arm without reason. Mamie raised her eyebrows in surprise.

"What's the matter?"

Ruth colored deeper. "Nothing. Just glad to see you," she lied. "Take off your coat."

"No, I can't. I gotta go right back." Mamie rose.

Mamie had suddenly found the conversation too silly to keep on with it. She knew Ruth was awfully sweet and all that. But there were times when Ruth seemed kind of stupid, kind of dull, simpering along in that "I'm so happy" way of hers! Ruth was like milk and water mixed, Mamie thought sharply. She covered her thinking with a bland smile. Ruth followed her to the door, a little trouble cloud in her eyes. She was wondering if Mamie had sensed what she had been thinking.

Mamie went out on the porch and turned, shoving her hands man-like deep in her coat pockets. "Well ... " she said, hoping the good-bye would be short and sweet.

"Thanks awfully for the perfume. It's lovely," Ruth said.

Ruth always said the right thing at the right time in the right way, Mamie thought. "Sure ... sure thing," she said and moved down off the porch.

"Maybe you'll see Bill out there somewhere!" Ruth called. "I know he'd like to see you."

"Yeah ... maybe I will," Mamie shouted over her shoulder. "So long!"

Ruth made no answer. Her wave of good-bye was lost as Mamie went off across the clearing. Ruth stood on the porch, her hand upraised, feeling the nibble of an unknown, undefined fear round her heart. For the first time she realized quite clearly that she had never really cared for Mamie Brandon, not much, ever. She had no idea why; she just did not. Further, she hoped Mamie would not come again.

Mamie headed quickly for the fence at the end of the clearing. Her eyes kept sweeping back and forth before her like the searching beam of a light. She kept hoping she would not meet Bill. "I hope I don't meet Bill, I hope I don't meet Bill," her mind kept chanting. She kept an alert watch for him along the path. But there was no one in sight. Thinking back, she realized that Ruth had not said her usual "Come again." Mamie sniffed, dismissing the rebuff. Nuts to Ruth Randall, she thought. She climbed the fence easily and dropped to her feet on the other side.

She started down the path, drawing a deep breath as if she were cleansing her system of the entire past to this moment. Here was relief in the cool fragrance of the pines. It was good to be alone again. She was as before, strong, sure, rock-like.

"Hey, there! Where you off to so fast?"

She stopped dead in her tracks. She spun round and looked in the direction from which the voice had come. Bill Randall stood resting against the axe-handle. The half-felled tree rose up before him, a chewed yellow gash indented at his knees. He gestured at it with a grin.

"I'm making firewood, I think. What a mess!"

She shrugged to herself. He expected her to come over there, she knew that. She had no choice. Reluctantly she stepped off the path and trod over the pine-needle carpet. The ground by his feet was strewn with chips.

"What's up, Mamie?"

"Nothing much, Bill. I just brought something over to Ruth."

"Lucky you caught her at home. We've been in town all morning."

"Yeah; so I heard."

"Ruth been telling you about it?"

She hesitated a moment and then said it. "No; Frank told me where you were."

An open, ill-concealed flicker of apprehension shadowed his face. She saw it come and her annoyance whipped up within her.

"Yeah, Frank told me. You needn't worry, Bill. He's a virgin as far as I'm concerned."

Bill was shocked by her bluntness, visibly startled. "You got me wrong! I don't know what you mean, Mamie!"

She felt a surge of weariness for all this fencing around. "Oh, let's not kid around, Bill. All of you have been fretting and stewing around for months for fear I'm gonna get my hands on your precious Frank!"

Bill could say nothing. She had opened the attack and she had hit the nail squarely on the head.

She fell into a confused silence. From the way he had taken her crack she knew he had been thinking just that. She said nothing for a moment or so. But as the silence lengthened, she spoke again.

"I ain't had my hands on him, Bill. Not yet!" She could not resist the sudden unpremeditated thrust. She had not meant to say that; the temptation was too strong. She saw his hands tighten imperceptibly on the axe-handle. She wondered suddenly if he were thinking about taking a whack at her with the axe. Frank had said he wanted to kill her too! She was getting damn popular! Well, one thing, she knew. Neither of them had the guts to do it. You had to have guts to do the things you wanted to do in this world.

"Why don't you let the kid alone, Mamie?"

She stared at him with open astonishment. "Me? Let the kid alone? Hey, wait a minute, I don't get it!" She laughed a little shrilly. "My God, you people make me sick! He ain't exactly what I'd call a kid. He's a grown man and a damn good-looking one at that! I ain't been on the make for him—it's him that's been on the make for me. You got things ass-backwards! 'Course, I know there's other opinions around here; but that's the way it is, whether you think so or not."

"Sure ... I know he's been hot for you, Mamie. Only that's the wrong way."

"I ain't so sure what's right and what's wrong no more," she said sullenly.

"You know right from wrong, Mamie; you're no fool!"

She grunted. "Well ... come on, what's the sermon? Let's have it!" she made her tone heavy and bored.

He looked at her seriously, concern in his eyes. She avoided looking at him.

"What's come over you, Mamie? I noticed it the other time you were here. You've changed in a way. You've become different. You look swell; you look better than you ever have. Only ... you've changed somehow. I get a funny feeling when I'm around you!"

She grinned savagely at him. "Don't you worry, honey!" She put her hand on his arm reassuringly. "You're safe! I ain't on the make for you, too!" She laughed sharply. Bill flushed deeply. Instantly she wished that she had not said that last. Bill was, after all, only trying to do what he thought was right. She sobered. "Sure ... sure, Bill, I guess I've changed. I know it!"

For a moment he thought she was going to break down and tell him what was behind all this, what was troubling her. But she tightened up and the glazed look fitted into place in her eyes.

"You know what it is, Bill? Just lately I been having a helluva appetite! Maybe it's spring!"

She laughed as she said it, and the brittle tone went ringing off into the quiet of the woods. Bill averted his eyes, staring down at his feet, his face flushed. He toyed with the axe-handle, pressing it down, pushing the steel head against the needles, making little oblong dents in the smooth carpet. "You're making a damn fool out of me," he observed quietly.

She was sorry. This Randall, he's always been on the square with me, she thought. She was silent, trying to purge her heart of resentment. When she finally spoke once more her voice was level and secure.

"I'm sorry, Bill. I got the jitters to-day."

He thought he detected a weakening in her defences. He moved quickly to take advantage of her change of front. "Mamie..." he said urgently. "Take it easy, Mamie. Keep away from the kid. That's all...just keep away from him. Give him a break. Give him and Binnie a break. They're going to need all of them they can get, God knows!"

She glanced at him and there was a little edging pity in her eyes. "You're still trying, still in there pitching, ain't you, Bill? You're still trying to save something that ain't worth the powder to blow it to hell!"

"I'm trying to help Frank over the rough spots, if that's what you mean!"

"Give up, Bill, you ain't gonna do him no good. You ain't gonna do no good. Even that Binnie... she can't do him no good. Look at Ruth. She's been at it for years and she ain't got no-wheres. There's lots in Frank that's like me, Bill. Him and me, we're kinda like each other, I guess. We ain't much good to nobody, really. One of these fine days, you people're gonna find that out!"

"Just keep away from him, Mamie," Bill persisted. "Just give him a break!"

She stepped back suddenly, pulling into her shell again. She fixed him with a cold, hard gaze.

"I ain't making no promises, Bill. I ain't about to lead with my chin no more. Every time I made promises I'd do something, what happens? I get kicked in the teeth. From here on they don't get no promises from Mamie Brandon! Things work out like they work out, see? Me..." she shrugged... "I'm just going along for the ride!"

"Will you lay off, Mamie?" He kept hitting at her, kept persisting.

She shook her head sharply. "I ain't making no promises to anybody. When you got no promises, you don't get no disappointments!"

She wheeled and left him, returning to the path. When she turned to glance back he was still standing as she left him, gripping the axe-handle tight in his hands, his eyes on her.

"So long, Guardian Angel!" she called out. She laughed, a crack of a laugh that went out like a dry twig snapped somewhere in the woods. She went off down the path towards the highway.

She had been right. Even though she had not realized it, she had been very close to the truth. His hands were tight on the axe-handle and for a few brief seconds, for the only time in his life, Bill Randall could have murdered a human being.

CHAPTER FIFTEEN

TUESDAY was born brilliant to the hills, haloed with a sun warm and penetrating. That morning when her work was done, Mamie went out across the clearing, down the trail to the creek-bed for the first time since that autumn long since gone. She scrambled down around the big rocks to the boiling, churning waters of the swollen rivulet and sought out a perch on the old, familiar flat rock where she could sit for a while and watch the white-frothed angry stream beat vainly against the stubborn barriers in its course. She lay back, cat-like, luxuriously, stretching herself full-length, relinquishing her body to the healing embrace of the new sun's strength. She was immobile, sometimes with her eyes closed, sometimes with them open, staring up into the empty, cobalt sky. The sounds of the stirring, awakening forest were a dreamy serenade in her ears. She felt supreme, complete, mistress of her world. The hours tantalized her, teasing, dragging their minutes past her consciousness with lazy unconcern.

She was waiting for night to come. In brief little moments she mulled her plans, her rendezvous with objective analysis. She knew she was wrong, somehow. She knew that night should never come at all. She felt disturbed and ill-at-ease, guilty and stealthy. But the thought of him kept pressing forward. It rose within her and she ruthlessly ground her apprehensions away. The act was an easy one, fed with the power of her wanting. She was waiting for the night to come, keeping the day and its thoughts at arm's length.

Late that afternoon, as the coolness of the evening came stealing through the trees, pushing aside the heat of the day, she left the rock and climbed the path to the house. She had planned everything well in advance. She worked methodically, carefully, shutting out all thoughts and speculations on the night to come. She worked smoothly, coldly, accurately. She laid his dinner out exactly on time, watched him eat in that slow, deliberate way, answered his questions and shared comments. She waited until he had pushed the last of his plates away before she went about the task of cleaning up.

It was all like a puzzle, all sliding into place with amazing, skilful ease. It was amazing how perfectly her plans worked out, how they joined together in the proper places. She waited until he was ready to leave and then she accompanied him to the door. She even surprised herself with the effectiveness of her good-night. Her eyes followed him as he left. His stoop caused him to bend forward a little, creating the impression that his feet were dragging. She watched him with a detached, cool, impersonal interest.

Near the edge of the pine wall he turned once to look back to where she stood. She was there, her hand on the roof support, gazing after him. He had become quite used to this little extra she had recently contributed to their living. It gave him a solid, secure sense of right—the house, the land, and the woman waiting for his return. He made no sign. It was enough that she was there, her eyes on him as he went away. He strode off into the tunnel of the trees.

She remained motionless until she was absolutely sure he had gone from the face of the clearing. Then she turned and went back into the house, shutting the door firmly behind her. She crossed the big room and went down to the bedroom. She came around the bed and sat down before the dressing-table, gazing at her reflection in the mirror.

Her lips seemed right to-night, full, red, healthy-looking. Her eyes had a lustrous gloss to them; they caught the light and held it in myriad, little sparkling bits, like stars. Even her hair seemed to have taken on a sheen, an alive look. She sat up straight, smoothing her dress down tight and close to her body. Her breasts were held solidly in place, the full richness of her bust held secure, prisoner in the confines of the thin material. Her big waist was full and yet pliable under the probing press of her fingers. She glanced down at her big thighs swelling out from the faint dip of her skirt in her lap. She thrust her hands out before her critical gaze. They were a little red, not much, with the veins bluish across their backs. It was only in her hands that the years threatened to show. She withdrew them hastily to her lap and glanced again at her face.

Very carefully she went about her make-up. She wanted just the right dash of rouge, just a shadow of heightened color on cheeks already tinged with flush. Now a thin coating of carmine along those lips. Now press them together, even the effect, give them a smoothness; wet them for a sparkle. She parted them slowly and scrutinized the results. Just right, she thought. Not too much, but just right! She ran the silver-backed comb through her hair. It crackled, shining in the dull light. She smoothed her brows carefully, marking them a little more pronounced with the pencil. She bent forward and studied her eyes absorbedly. There were some little hair-like breaks in the whites. She sat back, closing them, putting her cool, steady fingers on the lids, waiting. After a moment she opened them and resumed her inspection. The miracle had not come about; the little fine cracks remained, red and inflamed. She shrugged her shoulders slightly. The cracks in her eyes were like the hands and the lashes that were too short. Necessary evils! She went over to the closet and took out the raincoat. She tossed it on the bed and went out into the house.

She tried the back door, making sure it was locked, secure. She retraced her steps to the front of the house. It had grown quite dark outside already. She could see no further than the edge of the porch through the double windows. She opened the door and stepped to the porch. There was a hushed stillness everywhere, broken only by the intermittent song of the crickets and the bull-frogs, joined in constant chorus. For a moment she stood listening to the night sounds. She left the door open and came back inside, switching off the light in the big room. She extinguished the overhead light in the bedroom, so that there was nothing but the glow from the little bed lamp in the corner. The room was shadowed and soft. She drew the blinds, leaving only a tiny crack along the bottoms. Ready now, she gazed round the room slowly, carefully. There must be nothing left undone. No little error in her planning rose to plague her eye. All was in order.

She slipped on her coat and went to the porch. Leaning inside she peered through the darkened house. She had left the bedroom door slightly ajar. The light from the little lamp came slanting out into the hallway, a thin, well directed shaft. The effect was exactly as she had planned. She grunted and closed the door gently, as if she were fearful of disturbing the effect she had created.

As she came near the little hut, Mamie was suddenly assailed by a multitude of misgivings. She slackened her pace a trifle. A little clutch of apprehension reached out and sought to hold her. Perhaps she ought to bolt and run back! Perhaps, it was all wrong! But her wayward feet took no heed of caution; they brooked no faltering, no suggestion of retreat. They bore her off the path and carried her lightly over the noiseless cushion of the needles. Overhead the stars were vulgar in their brilliance. As she moved into the little clump of stripling redwoods, he came towards her, emerging from the screening shadows of the little wooden shed.

His arms went round her tight; he pulled her to him harshly. His face was buried down in the sloping smoothness of her neck; she could feel the breath of him, thick and hot upon her flesh. She looked up over his shoulder for a moment, up towards the burning stars, and knew she must be right! She was smiling now, the cool smile of satisfaction.

He made no effort to speak; he held her tight against him, feeling her bigness, the searing, pulsing heat of her. The pads of his fingers went out, feeling the unrestricted velvet of her beneath the thin protection of the dress, the twin firmness of her hard against his chest.

The big, silver buckle of his belt cut against her stomach; she began to move the palms of her hands slowly across the broadness of his arched back, seeking out the contour of the muscles there. She realized with a sudden shadow of pleasure that he was trembling. She kept moving her hands slowly, as if she were bereft of sight, tracing out the familiarity of him. She held her arms akimbo and placed her hands low round his narrow waist; she could feel his body alive with her touch, shuddering with the painful thickness of his breathing. Her fingers were on the roughness of his jeans; she placed her palms flat against the firmness of his buttocks and pulled herself hard against him. There was an explosion, sharp and white and fiery, in her brain, and the lasting blindness filled her eyes. He broke away from her sharply and his fingers reached out to seize upon her wrists in a grip of steel. He moved back, into the shadows, back towards the half-opened door of the shed, almost dragging her in his wake. It was as if she were suddenly powerless, sightless with that searing flame in her eyes. She could see nothing. There was only the welcomed agony of her wrists. She could hear the raw, scraping breath of him before her. Once she thought he spoke, said something. Or was it a cry, rasping, harsh, far away?

She twisted her head slightly, glancing at him, stretched full-length at her side. His eyes were closed; there was a deep, sad look on his relaxed face. His breath rose and fell almost imperceptibly, a steady, measured beat. She looked up into the whitewashed sky through the jagged hole in the roof above them. Her body was quiet, her hunger appeased. She was completely at peace. She tried to remember how it had been before this night. But there was nothing that could be recalled; nothing remained from the past. It was as if all the past and all the future had merged together into the now, the present. They had only the present to share between them and its peace and contentment. The present could go on for ever; the future would be the present; the past was cast away, erased, forgotten.

She turned her head and looked at him. His eyes were on her. They were blue, vivid, even in the faint pale light that filtered down through the roof. There was nothing in them except a tiny trace of something sad and lonely, something that seemed to shut her away from him all of a sudden. He was just looking at her, that was all. She smiled and reached towards him, laying her arm on the hard, muscled case of his chest. After a long while he reached up and took her hand, locking his fingers in hers.

From the time she had come to him, there had been no word spoken. There had been no wild promises, no fevered expostulations of love. There had been no word, nothing but the silent unleashed backlog of their urgent desire. There had been nothing but that frantic race to tardy fulfilment. It was she who spoke when words returned.

"Why did we wait so long?"

His eyes remained on her. He made no answer. He was simply at her side, close and near, her only clue to his living in the slow breathing, the hard clasp of his fingers, the slight occasional flicker of his lids. She sent her gaze up to the accusing stars.

"All the time we been wasting with the others when it could have been like this all along!" Her words trailed off; the silence of the night dipped its folds about them. She wanted to talk; there were so many things within her that could be put into words now, at last. She felt suddenly as if he were the only person left in the world to whom she could talk, the only person who might understand the things she could say now, the things she had cupped within her for so long. But the words, the phrases refused to come. They backed timidly into the recesses of her mind and paid no heed to her beckoning. She stared into the white-fired swath of heaven and held them within her as before.

After a long while she got to her feet and looked down on him. He turned his head a little and kept watching her with steady eyes. "I gotta go," she said at last.

He rose and stood beside her. She moved away and went outside, away from the dilapidated shed over in the shadows of the trees. He followed her and reaching out pulled her to him again. She came willingly, yieldingly.

"When?"

The single word was in her ear. She pushed away from him and stared up into his hot, tortured face. With a flicker of excitement she knew the completeness of her triumph.

"Friday ... Friday night!" she whispered.

She broke away and crossed to the path. When she glanced back he was still standing in the shadows of the trees. She could see the white of his shirt, the paleness of his face and the arms. Her voice came drifting back through the woods to him, low and vibrant, full of strength.

"Friday night, Frank."

She turned and he listened to the echo of her footsteps as she went firmly down the path.

CHAPTER SIXTEEN

IN THE three weeks that skimmed by the pines put forth their flowering; over the hills there was the sweet, voluptuous smell of fertility. The earth was reborn triumphant in the new spring warmth. May had come.

It was Ruth who first noticed the marked change in him. But she said nothing. She kept her mouth shut and just watched. She watched Frank as he worked around the place. For almost a month now there had been something in him remote, listless, distant. It occurred to her that it was as if a curtain had dropped between them, shutting out the old-time intimacies. There was a smack of some intangible change, some new thing with its roots taking hold in him. She felt the creep of apprehension and dread. A tiny web of suspicion was being spun within her mind. She tried to ignore it. Only once, when curiosity slipped through the gate of her determination, had she attempted a slight foray across the newly drawn frontier of their friendship.

"Is everything all right, Frank?" she had asked casually.

"Sure. Sure, everything's all right. Why not?" he had barricaded her way.

She was a little startled, a little rebuffed. But she had persisted. "What I meant was, there's nothing gone wrong between you and Binnie, is there!"

"No; there ain't nothing gone wrong!" He had jerked the veil a little higher, screening himself from her eyes.

Defeated for the moment, she refrained from urging him. She knew that when the proper time came, if there were something really wrong, she knew he would come to her, as he had before. She held her peace and bound her fears in rigid check until that time should come.

Bill had begun to notice the change, too. He said nothing, however. Frank, while sharing his friendship, had never made a particular confidant of him. He made no effort to poach on Frank's preserve. Bill got the impression that Frank was not as intent as he had been. Bill worried about it; but he said nothing. There was one other little thing. He wondered about that. Art was not around as much as he had been. He had come to notice the absence; Art had not been around for a helluva long time! He casually mentioned this to Frank one afternoon as they worked together.

"Anything go wrong between you and Art, Frank?"

Frank had glanced at him with a shadow of surprise. "Something wrong between me and Art? Hell, no—why?"

"I just haven't seen him around for a while, that's all. I was just wondering."

Frank grinned. "He's been down in Colfax for a week or more. He's out of a job again. He's been snooping down there trying to find something!"

Bill nodded. That was logical enough. He felt vastly relieved. He glanced at Frank anxiously.

"Heard anything about that job of yours?"

"No. Nothing yet."

There was a grim silence. Then Frank laughed. "You getting tired having me around?"

Bill fended the suggestion instantly. "Lord, no! I was just wondering, that's all!"

Bill buried his confusion in his work. He had been wondering about Frank and Binnie. It was high time the kids were getting married, getting settled down once and for all, he was thinking. It was damn near six months now since they had decided. Bill had little faith in postponements. Especially where Frank was concerned, at any rate. But, again, it was none of his affair. And, like Ruth, Bill kept his mouth shut.

Things went on like this for several days. Ruth, nagged by her constant anxiety, her growing apprehension that all was not well; Bill with his sharpening doubts, his mounting curiosity. It was Sunday. Frank got himself all slicked up. Bill and Ruth stood together in the living-room and watched him go off the place in the rattling old car. Ruth came close to the edge of her concern. But she hastily skirted the speaking point. Bill felt her anxiety, saw the wonder and the concern sharp in her eyes. He left the room; he went out on the porch, down on to the path in the late afternoon sunlight and lit a cigarette. He hoped Ruth would not mention Frank. He knew she had come perilously close to it a moment ago. But there was no use; neither of them knew; neither of them could solve whatever it was. He returned to the room and sat across from her. She looked tired; there was a faint line scratched between her brows. They spent the evening in silence; each was preoccupied with the same thought.

Bill slept the sleep of the dead. Ruth lay at his side, staring up at the faint, pale outline of the ceiling. She was not thinking about anything in particular. She was blank. It was as if she were waiting for something. Sleep eluded her groping, an unwilling, reluctant shade, refusing to come to her, remaining petulantly beyond her grasp. Bill's breathing was steady and even.

After an eternity her ears picked up the sound of the model A climbing from the gate to the house. She listened to the spluttering as it pushed over the rise and the slight cough as he switched off the ignition. She slipped out from under the covers and went over to the window to peer out into the clearing. She could see the two of them, Art and Frank. She leaned forward to see a little better, a little more clearly. The two of them were going down the path towards the barn. She pulled the curtain aside to get a better look. Art was supporting Frank, half-carrying him, half-dragging him down the walk. One hand went to her breast convulsively. Frank was drunk again! For an instant she had a wild, impulsive desire to throw on her dressing-gown and go running down the pathway after them. But she knew that was foolish, impractical, unwise. She simply stood there, watching them go down the path, go away from her towards the barn. She was helpless; there was nothing she could do. Her face contorted with sympathy, darkening with the shadow of her disappointment. Bill sat up suddenly in the bed and stared at her by the window.

"What's the matter, Ruth?"

She started violently at the sound of him. She glanced over and managed to force a quick, screening smile.

"It's nothing. There's nothing the matter, honest!" she lied. "I just ... couldn't sleep, that's all!"

"Are you sick?" A frown of worry had settled over his face.

"No, silly! It's nothing. I just wasn't sleepy." The figures on the pathway were small and distant now. She saw the door to the barn open; then it swung shut and there was nothing but the unpierced blackness over the place. She took a deep, fluttering breath. She came back to the bed and stood at the side, looking down on her husband.

"Go on back to sleep, Bill," she said quietly. "It was nothing at all."

He flopped heavily on the pillow. He grinned at her. "You did give me a fair turn, standing there like that!" he chuckled. "You looked like you'd seen a ghost or something!"

She climbed into bed beside him. "I'm sorry, Bill," she said absently. She turned her face away from him and stared across the room to the opposite wall. A ghost? Perhaps it was a ghost she had seen! It was an old, familiar, well-remembered ghost from away back. Bill's breathing had already resumed its former cadence. He slept at her side.

The next morning Frank was up and around at the usual time. He came to the house and she could hear him washing up at the pump by the back-door. She went to the doorway and stood in the morning sunlight, looking down on him. He was stripped to the waist, bent over, his head under the spout, working the handle vigorously with his outstretched right arm. The water came fitfully, thinly at first, and then picked up and gushed forth in great, heavy globs. It came cascading over his head and went running down his chest and back. He darted back from the onslaught, his teeth chattering, and using the cotton shirt in place of a towel, he wiped himself down.

"Good morning!" she said brightly as he emerged from the ablution.

He glanced up at her. "God damn, that's freezing cold!" he laughed. His face, she could see, was pale and drawn, his eyes red and bloodshot. He shook out the T-shirt and flapped it a couple of times. Then he slipped the damp garment over his head and tucked the ends into his trousers.

She giggled. "Really, Frank! How in the world do you expect to keep that thing clean if you use it for everything from a shoe rag to a blanket!"

"Confidentially, between me and you, I don't!" He came up the steps and paused, one down, from her. "Ma'am, this here's my working shirt. It don't matter with working shirts. In fact, I kinda like 'em a little on the dirty side!"

She shook her head severely. "That proves you're nothing but a kid! Sometimes I just don't know! Frank, I'd sure hate to be your wife!"

He shot her a sharp, sobering glance. But he said nothing.

She had gone into the kitchen. He followed her. Bill emerged from the hallway, combing his hair. "Hi, Frank!"

"Hi."

"Sit down, the both of you. Breakfast's all ready." She started dishing up the eggs and bacon from the stove. Bill and Frank took their places at the table. Bill eyed him openly. Frank looked pretty rugged this morning, he thought, sort of pasty; those eyes of his looked like two black holes in the snow!

"Where the hell'd you go last night!"

"Oh, we hit a couple of the high spots."

"How's Binnie?" Ruth asked, her back to him, as she worked over the stove.

"All right, so far as I know."

There was something in the way he replied that snagged her attention. She paused; she half-turned and glanced at him. She covered the edging curiosity in her eyes with a rapid, meaningless smile.

"She's all right, you guess!" she laughed, giving her words the camouflage of every morning chit-chat. "Well, you saw her last night, didn't you? It was Sunday!" She had come over to the table now and stood with the plate in her hands, looking at him.

"No, I didn't see Binnie last night," he said quite clearly.

"Oh?"

"No."

Ruth shot a warning glance at Bill. She went back to the stove and the safety in keeping her back to them. She brought Bill's plate over and went back for the coffee-pot. Silently she poured each of their cups, one for Bill, one for Frank, and one for herself. She returned the pot to the stove and slid into her place across from Bill, on Frank's left.

The men ate in silence. Ruth sipped her coffee, her mind busy. Frank's hand trembled a little as he lifted the cup, she noticed. She tried to keep her eyes away from him. After all, whatever it was, it was strictly his affair. Certainly, it was none of her business. It did not matter to her what he did, with whom he went, where he went. She wondered vaguely where Art was this morning. He had come back with him last night, she knew that. But she did not ask questions. She did not want him to get the idea that she had been spying on them last night. It was Frank who mentioned Art himself.

"By the way, Art's back. I saw him last night."

Bill glanced up curiously from his plate. "Oh?"

"Yeah." Frank hesitated. "He didn't land the job in town."

"That's too bad. What's he going to do now?"

"He doesn't know yet. He says he's still looking."

Bill suddenly had an idea. "We could use him. around here for a while, Frank. That is, if you think he'd like to come." He looked straight into Frank's eyes.

Frank nodded; they both thought his face lit up with the suggestion.

"I'll sure tell him the next time I see him."

Ruth made her words deliberately casual. "When will that be?"

He glanced at her queerly. "I don't know," he said. "Anytime, I guess."

Bill got to his feet. He stretched himself slowly, yawning. She looked up at him with annoyance. "Really, Bill! I do think you might cover up that awful hole!"

He collapsed his jaws, swallowed, and grinned. "Forgive me, my love! I most humbly apologize." He came around the table, leaned down and pecked her lightly on the cheek. She smiled.

"Oh, go away!" She shoved him gently. "You're always forgiven, you ape! That's the trouble—you're spoiled!"

Frank pushed his chair back. The greyness in his face had faded a little, but he was still on the pasty side. He started to get up.

"Why don't you stay and have another cup of coffee, Frank."

"Yeah, you sure look like you could use one!" Bill observed drily.

"Well…" Frank colored. "If there's any left." He shoved his cup over to Ruth. She took it and went to the stove.

"There's always enough left, Frank."

Bill watched her pour it black, no cream, no sugar. He took a deep breath.

"I'll be out where we were working yesterday," he announced. He bent over and kissed Ruth beneath the ear. "Be good, honey chile!" He left the room.

She came back, handed the cup to Frank and sat down, her elbows propped on the table edge, watching him sip the steaming coffee. "Was it pretty bad last night?" she asked sympathetically.

"God awful!" he admitted ruefully.

"Something like that's a little hard on Binnie, isn't it, Frank?" she suggested. She held her breath lest the remark miss the target and upset the whole works.

He looked at her closely over the rim of the cup. "I wasn't with Binnie," he repeated abruptly.

"Oh yes, I forgot."

"It was just me and Art last night."

"Stag party?"

"Yeah; stag party."

She hesitated, choosing carefully, before she took her next step. "I thought you and Binnie always had Sundays together."

"We did."

It did not make sense any more, but she persisted, following her slim lead desperately.

"Was last night... something special?"

"No, nothing special." He laughed shortly. "Just a damned old-fashioned drunk, that's all!"

He set the cup down heavily in the saucer. There was a loud clink of china against china. She glanced down expecting to see the cup had cracked. But it was whole, as before. He was looking directly, thoughtfully at her. His forehead was criss-crossed with a lot of little lines she had never noticed before. Suddenly she thought, he looks old! He looks quite old! And yet he's younger than I am!

"I guess you'd better know, Ruth, before somebody else gets around to telling you," he was saying quietly.

Her stomach contracted sharply, as if a shock of electricity had gone through her. The muscles turned and griped; there was a thick, curdled taste in the back of her mouth. She wished something like an earthquake, an explosion would happen before he said what she knew he was going to say. She knew it was done, finished, ended before he had opened his mouth to speak.

"That getting married business between Binnie and me ... it's all washed up," he said flatly. He was staring at the dark blotch of coffee grounds coagulated in the bottom of his cup. "There ain't gonna be no wedding. It's all off."

Her breath snagged. His words seemed to be bouncing off the walls at her, glancing from the ceiling, ricocheting from the floor, striking her from every direction. She reached out and fastened her grip on his wrist.

"Oh ... Frank! Why?"

He looked at her. Somehow she had halfway expected to see a deep, crushed hurt, a heavy, heartbreaking misery in his eyes. What she saw were eyes gone all hard and callous, with a glimmer of something close to cruelty.

"I guess maybe it's just I ain't the marrying type," he clipped. He lifted his head a little. "What's the use of me getting married? A guy don't have to get married, not if he's smart. A guy can get what he wants any time; he don't have to get married for it!"

She recoiled from the hard dirtiness of his words. He was foreign and ugly to her for a moment. She had the disquieting feeling that this wasn't Frank, saying these things. It wasn't Frank, sitting before her; not Frank, but some stranger, some vulgar, common, unknown stranger.

"Oh no ... Frank, you're all wrong!"

"Yeah? Well, maybe. Only, I don't think so; not any more." He hesitated. "Anyway, we ain't getting married!"

He got up suddenly and left the table. She sat alone, stunned for a long time. It was so hard to put all the pieces together in the proper way. Finally she rose to her feet and went blindly through the routine of straightening up. As she worked she quickened her pace. There was something she had to do, now that she had found out! She dried her hands hastily and whipped off her apron. She ran into the bedroom and pulled her dress over her head, tossing it wildly into a corner of the room. She struggled into her plain shirt and pulled on her old jeans. She raced breathlessly through the house and burst from the back-door, half running, half walking, hurrying across the clearing towards the path that led to the river trail.

CHAPTER SEVENTEEN

RUTH had set out on her trek with high purpose. She was driven by the sudden, over-powering necessity of seeing Mamie Brandon once more. She had to see Mamie the one more time; that would be enough. She had set out on foot unconscious of the fact, conscious only that she must see, must talk with Mamie immediately. In her intense preoccupation she went stumbling, tripping along the river trail, hardly aware of the rocks or the chuckholes. Her mind lathered with her racing thoughts. All that was important was to see Mamie Brandon. As she hurried along she kept trying to think back over the things that had gone before. She tried to trace back, to see how all the odds and ends fitted together now. She raked up the days when she herself had pleaded, had begged Mamie to abandon her foolhardy plan to marry Brandon. She had asked her to take Frank then, only then she had believed it to be for his own good! She flushed with the guilt. Her silly reasoning came back and stuck in her craw. What a fool she had been—what a blind, unknowing fool! She remembered scornfully the sympathy she had felt towards Mamie in the months following her wedding. She recalled her coming along this same path last fall, how she had found her on the rock, alone, lonely, disappointed, trapped in the failure of her gamble.

As Ruth went crashing along everything in the past seemed so clear—to yesterday. Each little moment recalled went parading across the ground of her mind in review. The package of perfume that Mamie had brought her! The time in town when she had stupidly brought them together, blindly, unwittingly, unaware of the disaster brewing right before her face. Everything stood forth in bold relief. A hot, sickening flush scorched her cheeks with the very memories. Her sight, seeking, delving into the past, was out of focus to the rocks, to the holes, her body impervious to the growing heat of the embryo summer.

Mamie heard the sound of approaching footsteps. She raised herself on one elbow and peered down the trail from her lofty perch on the crest of the old rock. In a moment she saw Ruth stumbling towards her, her feet sliding, scuffling along the twisted trail. She waited until Ruth had come round the bend, had come within hailing distance. The finger of annoyance prodded her. Now she had an afternoon of senseless, idle chatter with Ruth Randall to put up with. That was something she had not anticipated.

"Hello, there!" She raised herself even higher, forcing a grin of welcome to the woman on the path ahead.

Ruth paused for a split second, glancing startled at Mamie above her. Her thinking evaporated with a puff from the floor of her boiling brain. She made no attempt to return the greeting. In a second she came forward and scaled the grade beside the rock, so that she would stand on the same level with Mamie. She made no attempt to climb the rock, to join her on its surface. She would make no move of intimacy; she had not come to share with Mamie Brandon. She stayed safe, secure, beyond the pale of personality. She took her stand and pulled herself straight and erect. She could say the things she had come to say from here. She dug her heel hard into the soft earth to ground herself; she looked down coldly into Mamie's now speculative eyes.

"I've been hoping I'd find you down here, alone like this," Ruth said in a low, vibrant voice. "I particularly wanted to see you alone to-day."

The light wavered in Mamie's eyes. Something about Ruth warned her; an alert wariness set itself in her eyes. The smile remained fixed on her face; her lips were parted, but her eyes were steady and humourless.

"Oh, so? What's up, Ruth? You look like the wrath of God!"

"There's a lot up: lots of things!" Ruth's tone was hard and a trifle nasty.

Mamie's brows arched slightly. "You got something eating you, kid?"

Ruth took her breath in sharply, as if she were storing it deep within her chest, making it ready, available for whatever demand was coming. She tilted the upper portion of her body forward a little. There was an odd little blaze flickering in the backs of her eyes.

"There's plenty eating me!" She borrowed Mamie's phrase. "I suppose you think you're sitting mighty pretty now. You're mighty proud of yourself, I suppose, now that everything's going the way you've been wanting it to go!"

Mamie got the idea right off the bat. She knew an angry woman when she saw one. Her eyes narrowed a trifle; she threw up her old defences instantly. The wariness hardened. She wondered how Ruth had found out, what she knew, how much of this jabber was pure bluff. She sent out a tiny, probing feeler.

"I'm sure I ain't got no idea what you're getting at, Ruth."

"Oh, haven't you!" Ruth swallowed the proffered bait. She seized her chance instantly. "You don't know what I'm talking about; not much you don't!" The strength behind her words threw her off balance. Ruth flung out her arms like a tightrope walker to steady herself. In a moment she plunged ahead.

"So, you have no idea what I'm getting at!" she repeated with a snort. "It's this rotten, dirty business between you and Frank I'm getting at, Mamie Brandon!"

The words shot off on a circular tour of the rocks and trees and finally came back to Mamie. So they had been found out. So that was it. She waited now, ready, holding herself neutral, solid behind the thick-plated armour of her defence.

Ruth's voice had suddenly changed. The force had rapidly dissipated and in its place there was the old note, the remembered appeal, the question.

"How could you, Mamie? What made you do it? Why couldn't you leave him alone? Why couldn't you let him have one chance when you knew all the time what it would mean to him? Why couldn't you keep your hands off him? How could you do this thing to him?"

There was the hint of rain in her voice. She's gonna start bawling like a calf, Mamie thought irritably; my God, not that! But Ruth dammed the tears and pressed forth recklessly.

"Everything was going so good for him after you were out of the way. Everything was going so right, so fine for him. All the things he wanted he was going to have. He was decent and fine and good, like I always said, once you went away and left him alone. And then you had to come back! You got your hands on him! And now..." her voice trailed off helplessly.

Mamie sat bolt upright, her legs pulled tight against her body. Anger fanned out in her cheeks. This here Ruth was getting monotonous, puling along like that! She severed the other's words bluntly.

"Wait a minute, you! Shut up! I'd take it a little easy if I was you. Maybe I got something to say along here, too. I ain't on to your beef, exactly. I ain't sure what business any of this is of yours, anyway. Okay, so you're a friend of Frank's. Well, that's damned nice of you. That's swell. Everybody ought to have a friend, I always say. Sure, it's good. Only, friends ought to mind their own goddam business and quit poking into places where they ain't got no right!"

Only the fact that her breath was spent halted her. She sucked in sharply and seized the threads once more, pacing her words a little slower.

"I don't know how much you know. I don't know what you been thinking about Frank and me, see? I don't give a damn, if you're interested. If anything's gone on between me and Frank, it's between him and me. My God, Ruth, Frank ain't no baby. He's a man, a grown-up man; he ain't no kid. You got yourself all steamed up like you was his old lady or something. Only, he ain't nothing at all to you. He ain't nothing but a hired hand on your place, that's all!"

Ruth edged a step nearer the rock as Mamie talked. She was staring at her intently, as if she were trying to read something half-concealed in the flaming eyes before her. She threw out a hand tentatively, to try to block the flow of words that kept flying up at her.

Mamie hesitated, her thinking unseated by the interrupting gesture.

"Mamie, you know it isn't right. If you'd only stop and think for a minute! You'd see it isn't, it never could be right. You've got nothing to gain like this. Oh, maybe it is a couple of minutes here, a couple of minutes there; but that's as far as it can possibly go!"

"Maybe that's as far as I want it to go!" Mamie cut in.

Ruth bit her lips. "What good is something like that? What good are a few stolen minutes when you've got days and months and years to go on after?"

Mamie turned her head away with a sudden jerk. "You're starting to sound like the Salvation Army or something!" she cried in disgust.

"I know. I know it's old-fashioned and silly to talk like that. But, no matter what they say, people like you, for all the laughing, for all the poking fun at marriage and living clean and decent, it's true, Mamie, nevertheless. You know it, too. You've been trying to kid yourself. You've just been pretending you don't believe it."

Mamie glanced at her and the corners of her mouth tightened slightly. "You know something? I got a feeling you're starting to get on my nerves!" she remarked sharply.

Ruth squatted on the side of the dirt bank. She stared across the space into Mamie's eyes. "You're doing nothing but hurting people, Mamie, going on like this. You're wrecking everything. Don't you know that? Can't you see that? If you don't care what happens to Frank, then what about yourself? What about the house up there, what about all the things you wanted so badly and got? What about Brandon and your life with him?"

"You ain't got no worries there. Nothing's gonna change! From where I'm sitting, nothing's gonna change ever. They'll be the same twenty years from now, God help me! Brandon ain't gonna change none, Ruth. You ain't got no worries on my side of it!"

Ruth kept staring at her thoughtfully. "It isn't going to be the same with Frank, Mamie, not at the rate he's travelling now. It isn't going to be the same for him. He won't be the same twenty years from now. He won't be the same a year from now; I'm afraid of a week from now."

Mamie flared slightly. "Just what in hell do you think I'm doing to him? Eating him up?"

Ruth stood up, her lips drawn against her teeth. "Yes, I do!" she cried sharply. "Since you put it that way, yes, I do! You're eating him and everything he could have been and had! Just as sure as you eat your meals! He is a meal to you, in a way. He's something you've been hungry for and now you're gobbling every morsel you can get!"

Mamie's blood began to whip. There was a froth of anger on it; it poured into the nooks and crannies of her brain. The skin was tight, painful on her temples; the rims of her eyes were bloodless. She held her tongue, letting Ruth go on, letting her get the rest of it off her chest.

Ruth's voice was sombre and serious. "You're taking all the wrong steps, Mamie Brandon. You're riding for a fall, just as sure as you're alive. God won't let you ruin everything. He won't let you keep on doing whatever you want. I don't know how; somehow you'll get paid. And when you do, you're going to be all alone, all by yourself. There won't be anyone around to help, anyone to care one way or the other. There won't be anyone who'll be able to help you, remember that!"

Mamie rasped out a sharp laugh. "Well, thanks, mother! Honest, Ruth, you got a helluva lot more talent than I ever gave you credit for. You ought to go down to 'Frisco and get on the stage or something. You're a helluva lot better than Joan Crawford, honest!"

Ruth backed away from the sting of ridicule. "Go ahead! Have a good laugh, Mamie. Go on, have your laugh now. Get all the laughs you can. One of these days you won't be laughing any more!"

Mamie's eyes narrowed on the last remark. What was Ruth getting at? Was she trying to warn her, to scare her? She stripped the remnant of the smile from her lips and her head came jutting forward, her eyes pinched into two glittering slits. "Just what're you getting at with that crack? What the hell you going to do about it?"

Ruth's laugh was shallow. "Oh, you needn't start worrying about me, Mamie. I'm not the one to give you away! What's the use? What's the use of stirring up more trouble? There's plenty around now, God knows. But you will be found out, one way or the other. You will be found out!"

"What are you fixing to do? Blab? Sure, why don't you ske-daddle up the hill and take your big news to the old man? He'd sure like to find out! He'd go for it in a big way! Sure, he might even believe you! Fact is, he might even like you after. I ain't so sure about that, but he might get to like you better'n he does now!"

Ruth shook her head slowly. "You don't see anything, do you, Mamie?" she said sadly. "You never see anything more than you want to see. You think I've just been talking. Oh, what's the use!" She lifted her eyes and stared across the gash of the creek. "It's no use. It's all been wasted."

Mamie curled her feet up close to her body. She folded her arms, resting the elbows on her knees, turning her full gaze on the woman before her.

"Thing I don't get is what's your set-up in all this? Why the big worry on your part? Why all the song and dance about me and Frank from you?"

Ruth's eyes came back to her vaguely. "I've… been your friend," she said quietly, stumbling over the half-truth.

Mamie looked at the ground by Ruth's feet and mulled that over. "Yeah, I guess maybe you have, in a way," she reasoned. "I most always figured you was." She raised her eyes and sought Ruth's face. Ruth detached her gaze and looked out beyond Mamie.

"I've always tried to be your friend… and Frank's friend, too," she said limply.

Mamie remained silent for a moment. When she spoke her voice held steady and sure. "Pretty hard job being friends two at a time, ain't it, Ruth? Especially being pals with a man and a woman at the same time. Take a hunk of free advice, Ruth. If you ever gotta make a choice, get rid of the woman. Men make better friends. That way you can keep outta things you ain't got no business in. You're a helluva lot better off that way, see?" She hesitated. "There's another choice piece I'll pass on, too. What's good for some folks ain't always so hot for others, see? Best thing you can do is live your life and let the rest of the dopes go piddling along with theirs somehow. 'Cause, you see"—she pushed her head still further forward as if to emphasize her words—"when you get all mixed up in a lot of things you ain't got no business in, sometimes you're the cookie who gets banged up worst of all, see?"

Ruth flushed. "You keep talking as if I were butting in on something, poking my nose into something where I had no right."

"Right? Right? Maybe I been thick-headed or something, only I don't figure you got no right in things where me and Frank's concerned."

"I'm his friend," Ruth repeated doggedly.

"Oh, for Christ's sake!"

Mamie sucked her underlip and regarded Ruth thoughtfully. There was a stubborn truculent silence hung between them. Suddenly a sharp flame of surprise came bursting into Mamie's eyes like the pluming exhaust of a rocket. It was a hard, triumphant look that turned her eyes into two barbed points of fire, needle-sharp in their intensity. She was leaning far forward, balancing on the ball of her hips.

"So...that's it! You're his friend." She pounced on the thought. "So you're his friend, huh? Or maybe you'd like to be, yeah?"

She let a tiny pause sneak through to underline her suggestion. Her words seemed to sail across the gap between and skid to a rest on the flat, receptive floor of Ruth's consciousness. Mamie pursued her point, sending her stream of sound rapidly, hammering the opening deep into the quicksand of Ruth's subconscious.

"Maybe it's you'd kinda like to be his friend, Ruth. I ain't never thought of that before. But maybe that's the way the land lies. Maybe I sort of ran over something, huh? Maybe you been hoping to get your friendship served up some other way. Maybe, after all's said and done, you ain't so damn different from me, after all. Maybe, in a way, you ain't even as good as me, really. Maybe you ain't as honest as I been thinking. Is that what you been carting around inside you all these months? So that's why you been watching over him like a hawk. You been wanting him right from the start, same as I been wanting him. Ain't that so? Only, the difference between me and you is, you ain't had the guts to reach out and grab what you wanted!" Her voice rang loud and strident. The words came lashing out, crashing in Ruth's shocked face, cutting at her nerves, swiping at her startled heart.

Ruth almost fell backwards. She caught herself, pulled herself straight, and stared with disbelief and horror into the two burning slits in the face before her. The back of her hand was pressed tight against her mouth. She flung her other hand out blindly, imploringly, towards the woman on the rock.

"Oh, stop, Mamie! Stop, for God's sake! Don't say that!" Her voice cracked in anguish. "Don't, don't ever say things like that!"

Mamie spat her words. She fired them across the space between like a pattern of machine gun bursts. "Why not say it? Why not come out with the truth? 'Cause you don't want to hear it, do you? 'Cause it's true, ain't it? Say it's true! Say you want me to stop because you can't stand to hear it true right out in the open? All these months, these years you been going around pretending you been 'friends' with him! Friends! Ha! Big, whole-hearted, mother-loving friend in need! You lean on your old Auntie Ruth, Frankie boy! She'll protect you! She'll save you from all the big, bad women! Sure, she'll keep you safe and sound, all wrapped up in cellophane, until the right one comes along! She'll pick out the right one for you, Frankie! It's gonna be different for you, kid! It ain't gonna be no Mamie Brandon character! No, sir! Don't you go sleeping with her, Frankie, she ain't your type! You stay away from that one! And, maybe, if you been a good boy, you can sleep with Auntie Ruthie some day! If she ever gets up enough guts to ask you. What's the matter, Ruth? Don't you like hearing the truth out in the open like this?"

Ruth's face was sheet white. Her lips were pulled back tight and dry, the color pressed from them. Her eyes were wide and staring, fixed on Mamie's face with horror and revulsion. She was rooted to the spot, unable to make her body move, unable to flee from the piercing ugliness of the words that came pounding at her.

Mamie shrilled mirthlessly. "Christ, you make me laugh! Women like you always make me laugh! Sometimes you're almost a riot! Only not quite. You got the gall to pussy-foot around, making believe you're the great big friend of man. Dames like you think they're everybody's big sister. You tell me your dream; I'll be telling you mine! Everything's gonna come out right in the end! All the time you been handing out that line of slop you been hoping someday there's gonna come a time when it's you and him cuddled up together. I'm the sucker! I'm the big sap who fell for it! There's the howl! You kinda expect a man to swallow that sort of junk, but here's the baby who's been around. I'm the character who was supposed to know all the answers. Well, you sure had me fooled, baby. All the time I been swallowing, you been hanging around for the big day when his arms grabbed you, when you'd get a free feel of his muscles! Trouble is, you ain't had the guts to reach out and grab him, Ruth! You been an awful screwball, Ruth! You shouldn't have been scared. He woulda probably jumped at the chance. He ain't nothing but a man. Men ain't so hard to get. Only, you gotta go out after them sometimes. You gotta grab what you want when it's there. I kinda feel sorry for you. You just ain't had the guts."

Ruth's eyes had gone lifeless, drained, cold. Her body was numb. She pulled her breath in slowly.

"You bitch!" she cried, severing the final thread of Mamie's words. "You honestly think just because you want him that way, that everyone wants it that way! You don't even know what it is, just to be a friend to someone! You can't understand how a man and a woman could just be friends and nothing more, can you? It's all over your head completely. That's because your head is only as high as the buckle on his belt, Mamie. You can't see any higher!" She bent forward slightly, her eyes becoming alive, singling out Mamie's face as if it were one in a crowd before her. "Do you know something, Mamie Brandon? I've just found out I hate you! I hate you more than I thought it possible I could ever hate anyone in my whole life. I hate you so much that just knowing it makes my stomach get sick. I want to throw up to try and get rid of the very thought of you. I just found out how much I hate you! I'll go on hating you, despising you for ever, hating you and your big, wicked body. I hate everything you do, everything you stand for, everything you represent. I hate you completely with every ounce of my strength!"

The veil of pretence hung in tatters on Mamie's face. Ugliness crowded in upon her features. The resentment and hurt within her came pressing into her face, shoving in from the little recesses of her jaws, setting up an autonomy over her visible surface. A little chain of dangerous, murderous fires began to smoulder in her eyes. Ruth's words held her pinned into place.

Ruth had drawn herself straight and rigid. To Mamie, sitting on the rock at her feet, it was as if she had suddenly become eight feet tall, towering above her, thrown up against the steel blue of the sky. Ruth's eyes were remote and harsh, eyes of condemnation, passing sentence.

"That's how much I hate you, Mamie Brandon. But, even hating you, despising you, there's something else I feel for you. It belongs to you, Mamie. It's the pity I feel for you. I pity you, do you hear? I pity you. Though God Himself knows why. I pity you the past. I pity you the present. And I pity you most the future you have made already. There's no difference between them for you—your past, your present, your future. They're all the same for you. For them, I pity you as much as I hate you."

She turned and ran down the sluffing dirt to the path below. Mamie scrambled to her feet, her face heavy with anger and frustration. She stood high above Ruth, staring down at her, impotent, stripped of the power to return the cut. Ruth glanced into the distorted face above her.

"I hope you pay for every last thing you have done, Mamie Brandon."

Her voice flew up and stung. Mamie took a step backwards and teetered on the rim of the rock. Ruth, her back full upon her, walked slowly, slow and sure along the path she had come.

Mamie followed her with fiery eyes, fuelled by the outraged fury within her. In a moment the figure of the other woman was blocked out by the bend in the creek. There was nothing before

Mamie's eyes but the discard pile of rocks and trees. Her fury collapsed, unsupported. Her body sagged. Suddenly she became conscious that she felt very old, very tired. She sat down heavily on the edge of the rock, letting her big legs dangle aimlessly down the side. She covered her face with her hands. Her eyes were smarting and hot; she had a tremendous, overwhelming desire to weep, to cry and scream, to fling herself wildly across the face of the boulder. She wanted to yell, to carry on, to get rid of everything that had become caught up within her. But nothing came. She pressed her finger-tips tight against her eyeballs to force the reluctant, evasive tears. But nothing came. There was nothing left in her but the weariness and confusion and a little displaced, undefined fear.

CHAPTER EIGHTEEN

RT was propped up against the frame of the door, watching him. His face was drawn and pale; his eyes were filled with the soft, moist look of sadness. He watched Frank helplessly. Art said nothing. There seemed to be so little that he could say at a time like this. And he knew with hopeless certainty that nothing he might say would change things. Frank's mind was made up, good and firm and final.

Frank was working feverishly. His fingers were all thumbs as he grabbed for the extra shirts and the other pair of jeans folded in the bottom of the drawer. He turned and tossed them with the other things to the bed. Then he straightened and glanced around. The photograph stuck in the corner of the mirror caught his eye. He reached over and pulled it free with his fingers. Him and Art and her, taken so long ago he could hardly remember when! He wiped the inside of his cottony mouth with the tip of his tongue. It was dry and there was a bad taste as well. What he needed was a drink. He laid the snapshot on the dresser and crossed the room to the pitcher beside the bed. He reached down and drew out the bottle. Uncorking it, he threw back his head and gulped heavily. He lowered the bottle with a cough. He gestured to Art, but the kid shook his head. Frank wiped his mouth with his forearm and screwed the cork back in place. He replaced the bottle.

"Bill and Ruth ain't much on drinking around the place," he commented.

Art just kept watching him. Frank wished he'd go away, get lost. It made him feel guilty, ill at ease, when he said nothing, just kept standing around looking, like that. He made an elaborate pretence of not noticing Art. He reached down and brought up the cheap suitcase and flipped it open on the bed. He ran his hand round the bottom exploringly, and then began to lay the stuff inside. Art remained there, never changing, just gaping at him without a word. Frank flushed under the close scrutiny. He glanced up at the kid sharply.

"Christ Almighty! Do you have to stand there gawking at me like that!" he barked irritably.

Frank sat down suddenly on the side of the bed, the folded pair of jeans in his hands. He gazed at Art for several moments and then wet his lips slowly.

"Look, kid! It's better this way, see? It's better for everybody if I just get the hell out. I been figuring it all out for a long time now. There ain't nothing here for me. I ain't getting nowheres, see? I got itchy feet. I don't like this place no more!"

A quick, darting flash of remorse nipped at the corner of his heart. Art's eyes were pained, bereft of understanding. Frank knew the look in them; he felt uncomfortable. He knew, too, how the kid had banked on him and Binnie for so long. It made it kinda hard, after the bust-up, the kid going right on tagging along with him like before. It would have been a helluva lot easier if he'd gotten sore and beat it himself. He took a deep breath.

"I guess I ought to try and tell you why it couldn't work with me and Binnie," he said heavily. His eyes were on the brass rivets of the jeans in his lap.

"I know," Art said flatly.

Frank raised his eyes, a little spurt of surprise in them. "Yeah?"

"Yeah, I think so."

Frank shrugged slightly and let it go at that. There was no use hashing it all over, not if the kid really knew. He probably couldn't explain it if he tried. And since the kid knew already… why explain? He looked away. Back to the curled photograph on top of the chest-of-drawers.

"Then … if you know, then there's not much point me telling you," he said simply. "You know it's better this way."

Art said nothing. Frank brought his eyes back to his face.

"It is better this way, kid," he repeated slowly, hoping for some response, some encouraging reaction. There was none. Frank got off the bed and went over to the window, bracing his legs apart, staring out into the sunlight over the clearing.

"I'm gonna get out of here, that's all. I'm gonna take me a run-out powder! I'm gonna beat it! I'm gonna go down to the valley, maybe. Maybe, somewheres even farther away than that this time. Maybe I'll head down to 'Frisco or even L. A. Maybe I'll wind up across the ocean. I'm gonna go where they don't have no pine trees and no rocks and none of the stuff you keep seeing up here." He swallowed with difficulty. His voice thinned out and was soft and distant. "I'm gonna go far away. I'm gonna go so far away nothing'll ever be able to catch up with me. I'm gonna go so far I won't even be able to remember nothing, good, bad, right or wrong. There'll be new jobs and women and lots of days and months and even years, maybe."

Art came over and stood just behind him. "Let me go with you, Frank," he pleaded. "Please! Let me go along with you."

Frank swung slowly to look at him. He was almost the same height as Frank now, the same coloring, the same blue jeans, the same shirt. There were the same muscled forearms, the same blonde hairs curling on the tanned skin. He could have been his own twin brother! Frank smiled.

"There ain't no doubt but what me and you'd hit it off swell together," he said. "Sure, we'd get along, you and me." The grateful look faded from his eyes and in its place there was an expression of intensity and seriousness. He shook his head sharply. "No, you can't come!"

"But why?"

Frank stared at him for a moment. He reached out and seized the kid by the shoulder, holding him with a firm, fast grip. "You can't come 'cause you still got a job around here to do."

"Oh hell, Frank. Puttering around here? This ain't no real job!"

"I don't mean no working job, not with your hands. I mean you got a bigger job. This here's one you gotta do with what you got here." He touched his head with his fingertips significantly. "It's Binnie, Art. That's your job. Don't you ever forget it. I'm turning my share over to you. You got to stay here and take care of her. You got to see for both of us that the right guy gets her and nobody else, see? It can't be no rummy like me, see! It's gotta be a guy who's got his two feet on the ground, who's cut out clean and good and right, like she is. That's the kind of guy she's gotta have. And you're the guy who's gonna stick around and make sure the tramps keep away." Art stared at the floor by his feet.

"It's a man-sized job, kid. It's a damn sight bigger one than anything else right now. You got a job to do just taking care of her, see? You're the guy who's gonna keep the big operators away, see?"

Art said nothing. He was still staring at the floor. Frank tightened his grip sharply. The kid winced a little and glanced at him, the trace of pain held captive in the corners of his eyes.

"You gotta promise me!" Frank demanded. "You gotta promise, Art! Promise you'll stick around until she's okay!"

He tightened his fingers and Art, the pain sharpening in his eyes, nodded slowly.

"Okay. I promise, Frank," he agreed. "I promise you I'll stick around."

Frank released him suddenly. He brushed past and grabbed at the things on the bed, cramming them hurriedly into the suitcase. Frank finally shut it, snapping the lock, pulling the straps tight and firm. He turned and glanced round the room.

"Well, I guess that's about it," he concluded. He picked up the suitcase and started for the door. He paused and looked back at the kid. There was a quick smile on his face.

"Well, come on, lead-butt! Ain't you gonna see me off?"

Art crossed over to the chest-of-drawers and picked up the abandoned snapshot of the three of them. He gazed down at his sister's smiling face, at his own lank form, at Frank—big, good-looking, swell guy, Frank. He swallowed hard. His eyes felt hot. They stung at the corners. He held the picture out with fingers that trembled.

"Here," he said almost in a whisper, "ain't you gonna take this here with you?"

Frank stared at him, seeing all the things so clearly outlined in his face. A great doorknob of a thing had wedged itself into his throat. He hesitated a second. Then he set the suitcase down and came back to the chest-of-drawers. He reached out and took the picture and looked down at it intently so that he would not have to see Art's face. After a long moment he forced himself to meet the stricken eyes.

"Sure thing!" he said lightly. "Sure, wouldn't want to leave the three musketeers behind!" He shoved the photo deep in his hip pocket and went back to the door. Art followed him silently through the barn.

The battered old model A was parked in its usual berth behind the house. Frank walked over and slung the suitcase up on to the seat. He ran the palm of his hand across his forehead and brought it away, glistening with sweat.

"Jesus, it's getting plenty hot!" he grunted.

Art unconsciously aped the gesture. It was getting hot! They stood beside the pick-up in mute, awkward silence. There seemed to be nothing to say. And yet there was so much that would never be said now. Frank stuck out his hand and managed to jack his lips up into a thin smile.

"Well ... so long, kid!"

Art seized the big, familiar hand and held it tight for a moment.

"So long, Frank … be good!"

Frank felt rooted, unable to move. Then he pulled free and climbed into the truck. He slid over under the wheel. Art had moved around the front of the truck to the side nearest Frank and stood in the sun, his legs braced apart as Frank had always stood, his hands shoved deep into his rear pockets. Frank leaned out over the side of the car and stared down into Art's face.

"There's something else," he said, capturing the kid's eyes, holding them fast and unwavering in his open gaze. "There's something else. Keep away from guys like me after this, see? Guys like me ain't no good for kids like you."

He started the engine and the sound was a roar that seemed to fill the whole mountain country. Frank backed the truck round slowly and drove out along the twin ruts that were the road leading off the Randall place.

Art stood very still. His eyes were wide, his legs braced apart, his hands deep in his hip pockets. He stared after the cloud of red dust that came rising up, obscuring the truck from sight. He stood for a long time just looking out over the clearing to the cleft in the trees where the road cut through the woods, watching until long after the dust had begun to settle again and the sounds of the engine had been swallowed up in the returning silence. Art took his hands out of his pockets and brushed vaguely at his eyelids. He sniffed once or twice. Come to think of it, he couldn't even remember when he had bawled the last time.

Ruth went out on the porch and took down the bit of iron pipe from its resting place. She walked over to the triangle and beat on it lustily several times. The clashing notes went spinning, reeling around the place, filtering off into the screening woods. She was already late getting lunch on the table because of the long hike

over to see that Mamie Brandon. She felt all disarranged, all out
of sorts, kind of mean. She did not notice them coming towards
the house. She reached out and struck the triangle viciously once
more, with savage force. The single note went zinging out into
the warm space. She stood frowning, the bit of pipe poised in her
hand, prepared.

"Hey, wait a minute, sister!"

Bill had come up behind her. Now he laughed. She wheeled
on him abruptly, startled. He backed away from her, surprised
at the unexpected sharpness in her eyes. It passed immediately.
She flung herself into his arms. He held her tight for a moment.
She pressed her face against the sweaty reassurance of his work
shirt, shutting her eyes, keeping them shut. She reached up and
touched his cheek wonderingly with the tips of her fingers as if
she wished to make sure he was solid, real flesh and blood. He
grinned, looking down at her.

"Now that's a lot better, sweetie!" he chuckled.

She shoved him away with a short laugh. "Gosh, us necking
out here in the middle of the day! The lunch won't be fit to eat!"
She scooted past him into the house. Laughing, he followed her
into the kitchen.

Art came in soberly from the back porch and took his place
at the table. Bill sat down and unfurled his napkin with a flap-
ping flourish. Ruth glanced over her shoulder from the stove at
them. The other chair was empty, the one across from Art. She
twisted her body and glanced out through the window in the
back door. She could not see him anywhere. The model A was
missing from its place, too. She turned away from the stove and
gave Art a close look. He looked funny, not like himself. He was
too quiet.

"Where's Frank?" she asked harshly, imperiously, planted by
the stove, holding the frying-pan before her as if it were a strange,
unfamiliar instrument suddenly materialized out of thin air into
her grasp.

"Oh, he's around somewhere," Bill supplied the answer a little too airily. He accompanied it with a sharp, warning glance at Art.

She looked at Bill with an edge of suspicion for a moment and then at Art. The frying-pan handle burned against the flesh of her hands and she winced. She shoved it back on the stove and with a frown reached for the plates stacked before her. That business with Mamie this morning had her nettled, unstrung! It was foolish to let it get her like this. Quickly she ladled the food out and crossed the space. She set the plates on the table. She placed her hands on her hips and as they began to eat she stared down at them both. They have the look of conspirators! she thought. Bill raised his head and glanced at her innocently.

"Not eating, honey chile?" he queried.

She felt strangely cold and dead inside. "I want to know where Frank is, Bill," she demanded icily.

He shrugged his shoulders, but he said nothing. He looks miserable, she thought with a pang. She dropped to her chair suddenly and turned her attention to Art who looked as miserable as Bill.

"Where is he, Art? Where is Frank?" she persisted.

He looked up from his plate, looked her right in the eye, and put the answer into unmistakable words. "He's gone away."

The words fell flat across the space between them. The room was heavy with stricken silence. There was no sound save the faint sizzle of the frying-pan on the stove. She caught herself and stared at the plate before Art, trying to rearrange her thoughts. She put all her force to the task, putting things into proper sequence, so that she might be able to go forward from this moment.

"Where ... where did he go?"

"Away."

"Away where? Away where? Where did he go?"

"I don't know, Ruth." Art shifted uncomfortably.

She wondered if she would ever breathe quite freely again. This was what she had feared for so long—that he might get up and leave like this one day! She had not realized before, not before this moment had she ever allowed the fear to come forth, to be acknowledged for what it was.

"When's he coming back?" she asked slowly, dreading the answer that would come, she knew.

"He isn't coming back, Ruth." It was Bill who answered this time. She shifted her gaze and found herself looking at him dazedly. For a moment she had forgotten about him, sitting across from her. All the things that Mamie had said came back sharp and pointed. A flush mounted in her cheeks. She forced the newly born memories from her.

"He's not coming back?" she echoed.

"No, I don't think so. He's gone for good this time."

She suddenly remembered the other time. A slim, desperate hope seized her. "Oh, he'll be back!" she cried confidently, sure, positive in her belief.

Bill kept shaking his head. "I don't think so, Ruth, not this time. We've seen the last of Frank Parks!"

How could that be? So flat, so final as that? How could he know for sure? "How can you be so sure?" she demanded. "Why shouldn't he come back, as he has before?"

There was a maddening patience in Bill's tone. "There's a time when a man goes and you know he'll be back. There's a time, too, when a man goes and you know it's for the last time. You just know it's the last time, that's all. A man has to have something to come back to, Ruth."

"You're just saying he won't come back!" She tried to keep the truth of reason from her. Why, she could remember him so clearly. She could see him as he was, tall and fair, strong and young, ready for whatever might come. It was not possible to imagine him gone for good. He was too vivid, too alive, too real in her mind, too much a part of her life, her everyday living, her thinking. What of all the days, the months they had shared in friendship? They counted for something, didn't they? People who were a part of your very life didn't just toss a few things into a grip and go off down the road, never to come back again. It was ridiculous, absurd! She glanced across the table, her eyes heavy with resentment, as if she held Bill Randall responsible for his going, for even daring to suggest a permanence to his leaving. "You're crazy!" she snapped.

Bill watched her closely, far more closely than she ever suspected. He knew how she had held Frank Parks up as a paragon, how she had battled and fought to keep him on the straight path of her choosing. Now he was gone, gone for good. There could be no doubt of it. No matter what Ruth felt, no matter what she wanted, she could not alter that truth. And he knew down deep that she knew that it was the truth. "Why don't you give up, Ruth?" he laid the words out to her in a single, even line.

She opened her mouth to retort. What she saw in his eyes startled her, frightened her. He knew, she suddenly realized. He must have known all along! Whatever she was going to say was unimportant now, a by-product remnant of her staggered thinking. She pulled her eyes away from Bill's and concentrated on Art as he struggled self-consciously to finish his meal. Bill went back to his food, too. The room went silent. She sat there dully, following Art's motions with sight that would not focus. Suddenly she felt the defeat, the helplessness come spiralling within her in one tremendous, all-crushing, all-enveloping wave. She felt a keen sting in her eyes; they became blurred and swimming.

She pushed herself from the chair and tried to walk normally, carefully from the room, knowing their gaze was on her. After she had left them, the sound of her weeping came drifting back from the other part of the house. It came to them, sitting alone, a lonely, vacant, abandoned sound. The two men went on with their meal, pretending they could not hear her, making believe that everything was just the same as it had been before.

CHAPTER NINETEEN

IT WAS a warm and lovely June Friday night. Mamie felt strong and alive, as she had each Tuesday and Friday in particular during these last weeks. From the moment she opened her eyes in the morning, there came that tingling, quickening excitement and anticipation throughout her whole being. She went about her work with rapid, impersonal surety, setting the house in order, getting the evening meal on the stove. Finally he came in from the outside, took his usual place at the table, and began to feed as she served him. He sat there, hunched over his plate, looking, she thought, a little older than he had the time before. He was so old, so dried-up! She saw him these days with objective eyes, comparative eyes, as if he were something quite apart from her personal life, something that belonged to the house, to the place. Since her meetings with Frank had begun, she was at her zenith, borne high on the crest, high above all this, high above the world about her. She felt good! She smiled at nothing, smiled at the broad black square of the old stove.

She smiled across the room to where he was munching away on his dinner. He became conscious of her directed gaze, became conscious of the obvious hypertension in her to-night. He glanced at her curiously.

"You look like the cat that et the canary," he commented.

"I feel good!" She shoved a lock of hair from her brow. "Yeah, I feel damn good!"

He stared at her dourly. "That's nice," he said.

He went on with his meal. She marked each forkful as he brought his head down to meet its rising. She marked the minutes' passing with the champ of his jaws, that slow, deliberate way he had of mastication, clamping his jaws together, up and down, up and down, finally swallowing the bite and starting all over on the next one. There was a sort of rhythm in the way he chewed. You could almost keep time with the steady movement of his jaws. One-two, three-four. Up and down, up and down. She waited as the pile of food on his plate slowly diminished, until it had disappeared. She snatched the plate from before him and replaced it with a thick wedge of pie. He watched her return to the stove.

After a moment she glanced back at him. He had not started to eat. She became a little impatient. Her irritation was reflected in her eyes. He kept sneaking glances at her, instead of getting to work on that hunk of pie.

"I got a surprise for you to-night," he ventured shortly.

"Oh yeah? What is it?"

"Yeah, big surprise!" He took a large bite of pie and she watched those jaws.

"What is it?" she repeated.

He cleared his mouth first. "Yeah, big surprise. I ain't going out to-night!"

Her eyes flickered for a fleeting second. She kept them rigidly from his gaze and busily started to pile the dirty dishes in the sink. Anything to give her trembling, give-away hands something to do! "Oh no? How come?" Make it light, make it casual, make it everyday plain.

"Water's gone low. Ain't no need to keep such a close watch on the line now. Once a week's enough from now on, I figure."

She frowned. Frank would be there to-night, waiting at the little shed off the path for her to show up as she always did. He'd be waiting in the shadows. Her eyes narrowed. She had to get there to-night. This old fool, he wasn't going to block her plans!

Not now, not at this stage of the game. She'd be damned if he was! It was what she wanted that counted now. She had to do something. She had to invent some excuse to get round him to-night, something he would swallow, something he would accept as gospel truth without getting all curious and, maybe, suspicious. She scraped frantically over the floor of her mind as she worked.

He was still at the table. He kept watching her with that detached, off-hand curiosity, that funny, almost uninterested way. She glanced at him from the corner of her eye. She worked rapidly, accurately, betraying nothing, guarding herself warily. He removed his gaze, and started to finish the pie, at last. She felt a little freer now. It was easier to think when he wasn't looking at her close like that. She pulled her hands from the warm water and crossed to the table, wiping them on her apron. She seated herself in a rehearsed, elaborately casual manner.

"Gees, I'm sorry. You didn't say nothing before about you were gonna be home to-night." She packed her words with regret and disappointment. She felt her way forward with extreme caution. Each word she uttered became a step tested before the full weight was applied. "You see, I kinda promised I'd drop round to the Randalls' after dinner!" She sent it winging over the space between them. That Ruth would have gotten a bang out of that one, she thought.

"Them Randalls! You sure been getting mighty damn chummy with them Randalls lately!" he observed tartly.

"No, it ain't that!" she hastened. "It's only Ruth and me, we been talking about … sewing and things like that." She had the sudden picture of Ruth and her talking about stuff like that after what happened this afternoon. "She's gonna show me how to put up some fruit this year." Score one! She knew he'd twig to that one—it was a chance to save some dough! She paused, waiting for his reaction.

Brandon shrugged with sudden lack of interest. "If you can stand that crowd, I guess it don't make much difference to me. Don't let me staying home cramp your style."

She glanced at him sharply. He had a gall, him parked on his duff handing out permission for her to do anything! She kept still. She had what she wanted—no suspicions, no arguments. God knows, she didn't go for them Randalls, either. The sudden wave was dissipated. This was no time to lose her head, to make a stink! She accepted his permission with contrived and grateful meekness. She rose and stood beside the table, the situation fast in her hand.

"I guess it's time to get ready," she said levelly. "I'd kinda like to get going before dark. That way I only got one trip to make in the dark."

He made no comment. His eyes narrowed slightly as they followed her from the kitchen. He didn't like them damn Randalls worth a hoot! She knew it, yet she kept on going back. He sure didn't go much for her traipsing around with that crowd! But, he supposed, the nights he had been gone, they must have been kinda lonely, too. And if she was gonna pick up some pointers on canning stuff, things like that ... well, he'd be a sucker to bust anything up just now. Better to wait until she got all she could, then clamp down. He sat alone, sucking the stray bits of meat from between his teeth with loud, smacking noises.

He was in the living room, engulfed in the big chair, staring into the cold fireplace when she came in. She wore her house dress, only now she had the light raincoat pulled tight around her shoulders. She caught the curious look in his eyes as he glanced up, saw them rack up a quick, thorough inventory as they travelled over her. They lingered curiously on the tan coat. She touched it gently with her finger-tips.

"It gets kinda chilly after the sun's gone down," she offered. "This coat's just about right to keep the crimp out."

She stood uncertain, not knowing quite how to get going, how to leave. The sudden hunch occurred to her that, maybe, she ought to stay home! Maybe she ought to put it off this time, just to play safe! Only Frank would be there, waiting, standing in the shadows of the shed. If she didn't show up after a while, he might even come over here, thinking maybe she was alone. God, no! Not that! It was safer in the long run, safer this way—safer for her to go ahead, to meet him just as she had planned.

"Ain't you gonna build up the fire?"

"Later on, maybe."

She shifted her weight from one foot to the other. She had put on her old shoes, caked with the dried mud of the nights before. His gaze dipped to her feet, hesitated a moment, and then he brought his eyes to her face. There was a tiny flicker of something there that made her apprehensive, just for the brief, passing moment.

"Well," he said quietly, "ain't you gonna get started?"

He had not said it as if he were trying to get rid of her. She could detect nothing, no underlying interest in his tone. He was simply opening the way for her, giving her the chance to go, to get moving if she was going to go.

She snapped out of her trance and crossed quickly to the door. She hesitated, her hand on the knob, before she pulled it open. She twisted her head and glanced at him. His eyes had gone sharp and beady, his gaze fastened to something on the floor by her feet. He was not looking at her but at some spot on the floor with fixed interest.

"Well, I'm going," she announced awkwardly.

He nodded vaguely, not taking his eyes from that spot near her feet. For some unaccountable reason she felt ill at ease, uncomfortable, as if she were standing in the chill shadow of threat. She wondered if she were right, going off like this to-night, with him home. Maybe she ought to stay this once. But the thought of Frank waiting in the shadows for her came back with force. She knew she could not stay, could not sit out the torturous evening knowing he was there all the time, waiting for her. She pulled the door wider and stepped to the porch. As she took her first steps, his head shifted with her movement. He listened to her walking across the porch. In a moment she came back and put her head in at the door. He glanced at her.

"I'm sure a dope!" She contrived a bright laugh. "Me going off, leaving doors open like that!"

She pulled it shut tight. He listened to her going across the boards once again. He got up quickly and came to the double windows behind the long table and bent forward, taking hold of the blind, pulling it to one side, peering through the window to where she stood at the head of the steps. His eyes were hard and cold and cruel, his lips thin and drawn, tight against the yellowed barrier of his teeth.

She hesitated for a second or two, wondering, fighting off that funny, constant feeling. Then she moved down the steps and started out across the clearing.

Brandon watched her until she had disappeared into the green tunnel that led to the highway. Then he moved with surprising swiftness. He hurried through the house, down the hallway through the dark kitchen. He flung open the door, rushed through the laundry room, out of the back-door, and down the steps on to the path. He crossed the space between the house and the shed near the outbuilding with quick strides, and pushed open the wooden door with a curt, blasting shove. It banged hard against the wall and hung ajar, quivering from the shock. Brandon knew exactly what he had come for. He cut across through the half-lighted gloom to the big shotgun, wrapped in its sackcloth protection, hooked against the wall. With rapid, hurried fingers he reached up and snatched it from the nails and stripped the cloth away, flinging it to the floor. He came back to the door, where the light was better, and examined the gun closely in the waning daylight. It was in excellent condition, black and shiny, with the thin coating of oil spread over it. He broke it and peered into the breech. It was empty. There were no shells.

He stepped lightly to the work-bench and, leaning forward, squinted at the shelves along the wall. The darkness was gathering fast. It was hard to see. He fished around in his pockets and located a large kitchen match. He scratched it on the seat of his trousers and held it aloft in his left hand, high over his head. There, in the flickering light, he could see them—a whole box of them, new, never opened before. He had never used any of them. He waved the match out and reaching up brought the box down to the bench. He tore off the cover, removed two of the cartridges, and shoved them firmly into the breech of the gun, hanging bent in the crook of his right arm. He reached down and snapped the barrel into place. He replaced the box in its proper place on the shelf. He could see nothing in the place now. The night had come rushing in to black-out everything. He did what he had to do by the familiar feel of things. There was a value and a reliance in system. When you had system, you knew where everything was when you wanted it.

He emerged from the shed and pulled the door shut behind him. He neglected to snap the padlock and crossed the space to the back door. He retraced his steps through the house, closing each door, turning off each light as he went. He was methodical though hurried, meticulous though pressured. Order and system prevented slip-ups, mistakes. The expression in his eyes had not changed. They were beady, penetrating, cold. Like those of a snake bursting with hatred and venom, coiled, ready to strike. The mask of murder sat his face well. He crossed the big room and stepped out on the porch, shutting the door firmly, pulling it over the warped rise. Once outside, he paused for a moment at the head of the steps, as she had done, reviewing the things prepared, finding them in order, with system. It had grown quite dark now. He could no longer make out the dark wall of trees along the edge of the place. The summer nights were hatched too quickly. Already there was the cool breath of night chill around him. He started down the steps.

It was darker by the time Mamie reached the little hut off the path. Almost dark, but not quite. She left the trail and made her way through the snagging manzanita bushes, through the close-set trunks of the adolescent redwoods to the ramshackle hut. She paused at its door and peered inside. There was no one here. She gazed around her slowly. There was no one here. Well, for once she had got here before him. She sat down on the broken doorstep and settled herself to wait. She felt agitated, a little irascible.

She found herself studying the trees that clumped around this hut of theirs. Suddenly she realized that these particular trees were quite different from the others she had come to know in the hills. These were redwoods, all of them, not pines as she had always thought they were. She had thought all the trees in this country were pines or scrub oak. But these were not like the others. These were young, stripling redwoods, huddled together in a protective group, screening the hut from uninvited eyes. Mulling it over now, she could remember Brandon mentioning them once, these trees. The only redwoods in this whole section, he had said.

She suddenly bent over and scratched her ankle. It itched like hell. Something must have bitten her. Probably a mosquito or a gnat or something. She glanced down; there was a tiny red mark on the skin, a tiny puff of swelling under the touch of her fingers. She scratched absently. Her shoes were awfully dirty, she thought, vexed, awfully dirty! The mud was caked an inch thick on them. A little sprig of green had caught between the rubber heel and the leather part. She reached down and pulled it free. It was not pine; it was a little bit of redwood. She held it in her fingers for a moment, then ran her nail down, snapping the little dried needles off the spine. She tossed the stripped remnant away and sat back waiting for him, being as patient as she could under the circumstances.

It was very dark now. The night had crept in among the trees; the blackness was a great pool about her. Once she stiffened slightly. She fancied she had heard the sound of a footstep out there on the path. She got up and stepped carefully to the trail;

she moved cautiously towards the Randall place. She might meet him coming. But there was no one. She returned to the little shed again. No one there, either. He was very late. She held herself erect, taut, listening. She thought she heard that step again. But if she had, it was going away from her, going up the path. Probably an animal of some sort, a deer, maybe. Her attention was arrested by the hut door. Hadn't it been ajar a moment ago? No matter … it was shut now. Could someone have been here and gone already? Those footsteps? It was nothing, nothing. The song of the crickets and frogs grew in throbbing, beating cadence. Aside from her own breathing, there was nothing human about her. She waited. It kept getting later and later, darker and darker. Frank was real late now! A chill of apprehension swept over her; she shivered.

Brandon walked swiftly down the road to the highway. He followed along the asphalt until he came to the mailbox with the name "Randall" daubed on its sides. The trail to the Randall place led off from here, he remembered from the old days. He flashed his light once, down to the beginnings of the path, just to make sure. Then he stepped off the highway and started up the slow incline. His expression was set, locked into a rigid form. He carried the gun easily, the muzzle pointing down to the earth before him. The woods were inky black, but he had no use for light. His feet were well-trained; they sought out their objective without aid.

Midway between the highway and the Randall place he came to a dead halt. His eyes found the little clump of redwoods. That was the place! His mind recalled the picture of the little sprig wedged in her heel, held fast between the leather and the rubber. Had she thought she could go on forever, carrying on with Parks like that? Well, she'd played him for a sucker just once too often. The jig was up; she'd made her slip. Now he would kill them both. Then they could go on from here, being together all the time for all the hell he cared. He snaked carefully through the underbrush to the ruined hut. There was nobody around! He peered through the half-opened door, flashing his light briefly. No one! He pulled the hut door and squinted around the grove. There was nobody; nothing but silence, dead, deserted silence. Frowning, he put his light to the ground. There were footprints—a man's big print... and a woman's. He had been right! He had been right! He had known it all along! The flame burst in his brain. So she was visiting the Randalls, was she. He moved quickly now, stealthily, going back to the path, turning towards the Randall place. He paused, taking a firm grip on the gun. He listened. He had thought he heard a step on the trail before him. But everything was quiet. He started to move slowly now, carefully, noiselessly, moving away from the redwood clump up towards the Randall place. The woods were humming with the sounds of insects busy with their summer living. As he approached the fence around the clearing, Brandon stepped off the path to the cushion of pine needles.

His footsteps were inaudible, padding silently. He came up to the railed barrier. He paused, shielded by the darkness, and stared round the open clearing. There was nothing, no one. He felt a keen surge of disappointment. Suddenly he stiffened. There was someone out there! Someone out there in the black had flashed a light briefly, like a signal, just once. Someone out there before him was moving slowly towards him. He was moving slowly as if he were waiting for someone, something. The blood in Brandon's body came crowding to his head. He could feel it rising, filling his throat, flooding into his temples, spilling into the caverns of his head. There was a beating, blinding, overwhelming bursting in the backs of his eyes. The savage madness of his hate for them seized him with an unrelenting, merciless grip. It swelled and boiled, bursting, erupting, drenching his system with its bitter poison. He could see the man quite clear now, even through the pitch black of night. He could see the white T-shirt, the dark blue jeans. The figure was hatless, the hair unmistakably blonde in the white, cold light of the stars. He raised the shotgun deliberately, unhurriedly, and took dead aim at the figure moving towards him. The man saw him in that instant. He stopped moving, became rooted to the spot. As Brandon pressed the trigger, he saw the man's face just once, naked in the brief, shocking instant. It stood forth, revealed in the spitting flash that burst from the barrels. He saw the man's face, saw his hand flung out, heard him as from a great distance, crying "God! No!" and then it was too late. The gun acted on its own power; it belched its charge into the darkness. One sharp, terrible, shattering blast spat forth into the face before him. The force of the explosion knocked Brandon back into the blackness of the trees.

Mamie was sitting on the broken step of the hut in the red-woods when it came. There was that horrible, splitting, stunning crash that burst from the silence around her and went spinning, rocketing through the hills. It was as if a sharp clap of thunder had been born at her very side. It was as if she herself were sitting in the epicentre of disaster.

Mamie's eyes spread in terror. An awful, rending scream of human agony and pain came slicing through the night. She was on her feet in an instant. Oh, my God! It's Frank! Something's happened to Frank! Fear threw its arms about her, smothering her within its grasp. Her breath was choked, a harsh, strangled, dry sobbing. She ran from the hut to the path and went stumbling up the blind trail towards the fence. The lights in the Randall house were bright and garish, streaming though the windows with brazen, obscene brilliance. There was somebody, two of them, running across the clearing from the house, running towards her. She stopped, her breath sharp, cutting in her chest, her hand gripping the trunk of a tree just off the path. They had got there first, those two. She could see them clearly now, Bill and Ruth, bent over something dark and twisted in the grass. She heard Ruth's stifled cry of horror. Bill was picking him up, lifting him easily, as if he were a baby. It seemed unreal, as if everything they were doing were being acted out, played out badly before her like a poor movie, performed against the lights from the house. Bill was carrying him, taking him back to the house.

She felt sick and faint. She wondered if she were going to pass out, right here, alone in the woods by herself. She couldn't let go— not like this, not before she knew! She stood stock still, clinging to the solidness of the tree for a long time. She followed them with stricken eyes as they went up the front steps, him being carried like that, his arms and legs dangling limp, like a doll's arms and legs, his head hanging, wobbling from side to side as Bill bore him away. She stayed there for a long, long time just hanging on to the trunk of the tree, fighting back the nauseous weakness in her. Finally she moved. Not back into the safe retreat of the woods, but forward, towards the house where they had taken him.

She moved close to the fence, close past Brandon, standing in the shadows. She did not see him; she did not hear him. He was standing, the gun hanging limply in his dropped arm. His eyes were blank and glazed, staring sightlessly into the darkness about him. He had not seen her, had not seen them running down from the house across the clearing, had not seen them taking the inert thing away with them. He had seen nothing in the darkness except that stranger's face, stark in the instant of the blast, then blotted out in a white sheet of fire. He had seen nothing. Nothing save that face, stamped upon his brain in the single instant of explosion. As she went past him, he turned slowly and shuffled off, moving mechanically down the path, away from that place, his feet heavy and dragging, his body stooped and broken, his face empty and slack, his eyes listless, vacant, dead.

Mamie swung over the fence. She moved with increasing rapidity now. Her eyes never wavered from the house with its beacon lights streaming out before her. Dimly she saw a man come running across the porch and jump into the truck beside the house. As she came over the rise she saw him go driving swiftly down the road that led to the highway. She tripped over something in the path, stumbling, never taking her eyes from the house. She fixed them on the open door, on the light slanting out into the night. She finally came to the steps and climbed them, slowly. Her breath was rough, the pain had come back to her side. She stepped in the open doorway and paused.

After a moment she came into the room. They had him on the chesterfield. Ruth was sitting at his side, on the floor, her arm flung across his chest. She was not doing anything, scarcely moving. She was simply sitting there, his blood on her hands, smeared across the front of her dress, her arm across him, her face slack-jawed with shock. Mamie stared down on him, her head hard-drawn back, looking down the length of her nose, her eyes filled with dread and fear.

Every little detail stood sharp and clear. His legs were half off, half on the chesterfield. His breath was very faint. There was scarcely a movement to the buckle hard upon his stomach. There was blood over the flat of his chest, blood almost black-stained on the white of his shirt. Her eyes kept rising, up, up, up. Up from the legs to the buckle, up past those splotches on his shirt, up to his neck, to his face. It was his face, his face that trapped, that froze her. That chin was not his chin—it was another man's chin, not his! She forced her eyes to go on, to see. She reached out blindly, groping for some support to catch herself. She could not pull her sight from what she saw. Waves of nausea came sweeping over her one upon the other. She swayed, her eyes bulging with the awfulness of the thing before her. There, where the nose, where the eyes had once been, there was nothing any more. There was no face, nothing save a great bloody, pulpy cavern where flesh and bone had been. The charge had torn across the face, blasting all away in a single smashing instant. Desperately she forced her eyes to move; she strained to break the grip that bound her. She knew now who it was there, the inert, bleeding mass. It was Art—his friend, that Art, her brother. She went violently sick.

Ruth had been sitting there on the floor all this time, saying nothing, doing nothing. She just sat there, staring up at Mamie almost stupidly, as if she had lost her mind. Now her eyes began to see; feeling and reason began to return slowly. The figure before her sharpened into form; she saw Mamie Brandon white and swaying in the centre of the room before her. There was cold, murderous hate in Ruth's eyes, a hatred so open, so sharp that Mamie staggered back from the intensity of it. Ruth pulled her arm from his chest. She came to her feet and stood at his side, her staring blazing eyes fixed on the woman before her.

"How dare you come in here!" She broke off each hoarse word with a brittle snap. "How dare you come in here, in this house, Mamie Brandon! Who is it you want now? Frank isn't here any more. You drove him away. He's gone. He's escaped from you! And Bill … he isn't here. He's gone for a doctor, if that'll do any good!" Her voice broke; she struggled to bring it back to control. "Is it him there? Is it Art now you're after?" She flung her hand down at the awful, bleeding hulk before them. "Is it him you're after, Mamie Brandon? Is it Art there? You'd like him. He's young, he's a man, what's left of him! Why don't you take him? He's still warm!" Her voice shattered into a wild, jumbled confusion of raucous laughter mixed with weeping. It rose higher and higher until it seemed there could be no peak. Mamie reached up frantically, clapping her hands over her ears, her eyes stark with horror. Suddenly she pulled them away and stepped forward quickly. She slapped Ruth once, as hard as she could, a stinging, shocking, lashing crack of her palm full flat across the gibbering mouth. Ruth caught her breath. The screaming had stopped as suddenly as it had begun. Her eyes were startled.

Mamie stared at her a moment and then she smiled with a hard, brittle sadness. She wheeled and went from the room. She moved across the porch and started down the steps to the path. Ruth could hear her footsteps, sharp, staccato in the stillness at first, then fainter, fading as she went away into the night. Ruth raised her hand slowly and touched her bruised mouth with the tips of her fingers. Suddenly the hate was gone. She was drained completely, her resistance broken. She slumped to the floor beside him there and she began to weep, silently, easily, for all of them.

CHAPTER TWENTY

MAMIE sat huddled in the clutch of the chair before the fireplace in the big room. There was no fire, only the blackened niche of the grate piled with dead, grey ashes of the fires from the other nights before. Those ashes were like her, she thought dully, grey, dead, and empty.

The lights burned steadily throughout the house. They glared in the kitchen; they lit the little room; they blazed in the bedroom; they were stark and obscene in the bathroom; they were shining brilliantly in the big room. The lights burned harshly, holding the shadows at bay with unyielding, uncompromising fingers. They were bright and garish, without life or warmth; they were servants, not companions.

Mamie had returned to the house automatically, somehow. She had no recollection of her return. She knew she must have come down the path as always, past the redwoods, past the little deserted hut off the trail. She must have come on blindly, past the mailbox, along the shoulder of the highway, through the old, familiar tunnel of the trees. She must have climbed the steps of this house, crossed the porch, opened the door, come inside.

Her mind was thick and muddy; she tried to think back. Things returned unwillingly, reluctantly. She could see that body with the arm thrown over it in protection. Silly, stupid Ruth Randall! Why protect the dead, Ruth? Why not shield the living?

Sitting before the empty fireplace, she shut her eyes hard until little red spirals went whirling, spinning round and round, dancing, jagging in the void. But even trying to shut it away from her like that, she saw again the sharp and terrible clarity. She saw that thing—the face, the blood, the heartwrenching, gaping smear where nose and the eyes had been. She bent over her lap sharply, striving to beat down the nausea wave, to shove away from her that sickness.

Beyond that moment she could remember little more. There was a great blank, a wide void between that moment and all that must have come since: the unimportant time; the unmarked, uncaring, uncharted time born in that dreadful instant; useless, sick, barren time. She raised her head and stared about her. She had returned here; this was home.

She had pushed open the front door slowly. She had stood still in the frame of the doorway for the moment. She had known there would be no one here in the house. He would not be here, she had known that. She had crossed the big room and switched on the light. She had gone into the bedroom and slipped off her raincoat, dropping it in a heap on the foot of the bed. She had turned on the light in there, as well, had left it burning as she went down the hallway to the kitchen. She had put the light on there too. The kitchen was deserted. It was all as she had known it would be. She had crossed the kitchen, gone out through the laundry to the back porch. Something kept pressing her forward; something kept compelling her to go from the house to the little shed by the outhouse. She had found the door unlocked; she had given it a shove, had peered through the darkness. She had taken a match from her pocket and had struck it, had held it aloft, an uncertain, flickering gleam. Her eyes widened and sought out the place on the wall where the gun had hung, wrapped in its sackcloth. She had gazed upon that wall to make sure, to confirm what she had known from the start. She had looked upon the space without anticipation, knowing full well what she would see. The space on the wall was bare. She had known all along that it would be, the nails shining, bare and untenanted. Her body had slackened, her strength abandoning her in that moment, alone in the shed. She had nothing now but reality to face. Before her lay the awful, lifeless reality of the failure of their lives together. She had turned away, sick and chilled, and had retraced her steps to the house.

The night was very dark. It seemed to grow darker, blacker than night had ever been before.

Suddenly it seemed as if she could not bear the darkness any longer. The night was like a festering wound, swollen and inflamed, rife with pain that never lessened. She hurriedly switched on the light in the little room and the one in the bathroom. Until, at length, the whole of the house was one bright, yellowish glare. The lights would stand her vigil with her. They would brace her with impersonal, harsh steadiness. She had returned to the living-room; she had taken her place before the dead fireplace; she waited for the moment that must come now. There was nothing to do but wait. She had raised her hands once, grinding the heels of her palms hard into her eyes, as if she would obliterate everything that had been kin to this night. But that had failed. What was remembered was indelible. The present had been born of the past, bound with bloody ties.

Mamie let her mind run free, untethered, to wander as it pleased. She made no effort to guide it at first, to lead it. But, guideless, it sought the ugliness of the recent hours. She tried to seize control, to press beyond the evening, to go back to other things waiting for recall. Life had been before this night. The feel of his arms about her, the closeness of him, his hard, warm body sheltering her, completing her. But the memories once brought back would not remain. They lingered as feeble shades and faded quickly, fearful of recall. A fear began to grow within her. Trying to hold the past, she failed. Frantically she forced her mind to race after them, to recapture them, these memories she must possess. But the effort was fruitless, a failure. With a sharp pang of terror she knew now the cost of this night! She struggled to recreate the image of his face before her. But all she saw was that other face that was no face at all. When she reached for the things so wanted, she returned with nothing save the memory of this single night alone.

Sitting alone in the house she had no awareness of the passage of hours. The night began to fade and daylight stole into place. But the coming of the dawn brought no release. The exchange of day for night was only a routine, meaningless. She remained as she was. The sun edged over the rim of the trees and bathed the clearing with fresh, restorative warmth. Mamie sat in her chair and waited for him. Now and then she shivered slightly, as if some chill lingered within the house. Nothing happened. No one came.

She knew vaguely he would return. Somehow, sometime he would come back. This was his place. He would return as surely as day outside had taken over from night. She found herself trying to think how it would be when he did come. The realization came to her quite suddenly that he would kill her when he came. There was no doubt.

She saw him coming up the road from the highway, emerging from the green tunnel, the gun held firm in both hands, held tight in his gnarled fingers, sloping down across his middle. She saw his face. It was dark, almost black, packed with hate and rage. His lips were thin and bloodless, a pale scar across his face. His eyes were deep in his head, two hollow caverns, two great, black holes bored into his skull, narrowed into slits, burning with the fires of murder yet undone. She stood by the double window, behind the long table, her eyes upon him as he came towards the house. His body was hunched forward, his gait slouching and shuffling. Those eyes of his were fixed on the house ahead, never wavering, never changing. In his mind was the thought held hard and positive, generating the strength for the act to come. She stood motionless, watching him approach, knowing that in a brief moment, in a few brief, final moments at best, she was to die. He came up the steps without hesitation. She could hear his footsteps already, and as he came she turned and faced the door. She heard the sound of his hand upon the knob. He stood in the squared frame of the door and she faced him, staring across the room at him, showing him she was not afraid of what he must do.

He smiled in that moment. The corners of his mouth twitched and were gathered into the slight grimace. She knew that smile, that smile that always came when he had her where he wanted her. He had her now, caught her red-handed, guilty, awaiting execution for her crime against him, against this house. No matter what happened, she would not cry out. No matter what happened, she would not beg with him, would not plead with him, would not cry out to him to spare her, would not entreat him to let her go on living. She would not scream that it had all been a terrible mistake. She would not grovel at his feet like a whipped dog, reaching out to touch his ankles, pressing her face against his legs while the tears ran streaming down her cheeks in fear and anguish and repentance. There would be nothing like that. She would stand where she was, by the table, unshakable, sure of herself. She was ready, waiting.

He saw that, saw her standing unbeaten, unafraid, ready for him. He saw her like that and the rage within him split from itself and trebled. His face grew darker, his eyes more sunken, his lips more taut and paper-thin, more bloodless than before. The throbbing in his temples increased until even from where she stood she could see its pulsing. It was as if the blood in his body charged upwards, fighting for an outlet, pushing up into his brain in one mighty surge. He raised the long barrels of the gun slowly. He pointed them at her, directly at the centre of her body, at the two full breasts that had never belonged to him. He stared at her big, rich body that he had thought was his all these months. She watched the muzzle rise until it was level with her, until her eyes were staring down into the twin caverns from which the end of her living would come spitting forth. She could see his finger tighten, squeezing the trigger slowly, firmly, finally. And then it happened—quick, loud, sharp. There was that sheet of blue-white flame, that crash, that searing, cutting, terrible pain shocking through her body. That was all. The darkness fell swiftly about her. She welcomed it, reached out and seized it to her. Blessed darkness, release, forgetfulness, draping itself about her like the dropping of great heavy curtains to shield her away for ever. He stood there, the double-barrelled gun pointing down now, towards the floor. He stared across the room at her, at her body heaped upon the boards, sprawled on the floor of his room. Perhaps there was a little trace of satisfaction in his eyes. More likely, the edge of satisfaction on his face. He stood staring at her, seeing her thick, red blood, not black like the other, but scarlet and vivid as it came gushing from the great torn, blasted hole in her breast, bright crimson flowing freely out over the rug, a thick, unerasable stain over the floor of his house.

And she knew what he would do even then—when it would no longer matter to her, one way or the other. He would go past her, bleeding there, go out through the house to the rear, to the shed by the leaning outbuilding. There he would carefully clean his gun, clean it, oil it, wrap it in sackcloth, and place it back upon the nails on the wall. You always took care of what you had, then it would last longer, do the job when you needed it, he had always said.

That is the way it would be, she knew. She sat in the big chair, waiting for it to come as she knew it must. She waited for that moment when all this would come to an end. She waited for the one slight press of his finger against the trigger, the one brief moment of agonizing pain that would be her trade piece for blessed darkness, wanted void, that moment of release and forgetfulness. She sat waiting quite calmly, quite unafraid, in the soft embrace of the chair before the fireplace in the big room and all the lights throughout the house burned bright in the midday.

CHAPTER TWENTY-ONE

THE sun sought its zenith. The heat banked itself against the resistant walls of the house. It baked the earth outside and pressed against the barrier of the building. Over towards the pines ringed around the clearing, a silver, undulating shimmer fluttered and vibrated. Within the house it was cool, almost cold. The house had become a tomb, still and quiet, hung in a pause, unmindful of time or temperature or feeling.

The sun relinquished its seat in heaven. It recalled its scorching rays and retreated behind the hills in the west. The shadows came out, edging from the trees behind the barn, cautiously at first, and then, finding no rejection, scurried forth with eagerness. They came hurrying across the clearing, their spearheads reaching for the house, seizing it with greedy tendrils, drawing it into the shade of approaching night. The lights still burned within the house as they had through the night, through the bright, hot day.

Her face had gone heavy with the strain. Deep, hard lines had come forth slowly, unhindered, on her face. Her eyes were wide and dry, dull and bloodshot. She sat almost stiffly erect, her fingers tight upon the arms of the chair. She was tense, brittle, knowing it could not be much longer now.

Night set its scenery on the stage; the dark hours took their places. There was no clock in the room; she would have paid little heed had there been one. Time was a useless thing. To use time to advantage, one must have the future against which to weigh the value of the present. It made little difference to her whether he came by day or by night. Come she knew he would. No matter when he finally came, she would be ready for him, waiting, be it by night or by day. She would show him that she could win even at this stage of the game.

She had not moved from her place. She had no hunger, no thirst, no weariness exactly. She had no particular feeling in her. Even the horror of that thing of blood and agony had receded, had become tempered and remote in her memory now. It was as if she had gone a little dead already, beyond everyday emotion.

At first she did not hear the automobiles coming up the road towards the house. Then the sounds of them touched her with cautious fingers. She lifted her head slightly, staring directly into the brick of the fireplace. What was that? It seemed as if there were a car, a number of cars approaching the house. She pulled herself together and got up stiffly. She crossed to the long table before the double-window and peered out through the screening curtain into the darkness. There were four lights coming at her, like two sets of diabolic, searching eyes. The first car came almost to the house and then swung off abruptly, past the porch steps, slanting its lights over towards the barn. The second car came up close behind the first and stopped. The engines died away and there was the distant murmur of men's voices. She saw one man get out of the first car, on the side away from the house, from the driver's seat. He moved around in front of the machine, crossing before the two beams of light, cutting them off momentarily with his body. He came across the small space to the porch steps and she heard his footsteps as he climbed up and came to the door. In a moment there was a slight, almost inaudible rapping. She made no move. The knock was repeated, this time much louder and insistent. The sharp crack jogged her into action. She started slightly, crossed to the door and jerked it open. She stood stupidly, staring up into the solemn face of a man who was a complete stranger to her.

"You Mrs. Brandon?" He made a motion as if he were going to touch the brim of his hat.

She nodded vaguely. Her voice failed to come. It seemed buried down inside her throat somewhere.

The man fidgeted a little and shifted his weight uneasily from one foot to the other. They've come to get the murderer, she thought suddenly. Well, come and get him! Find him and take him away with you! The man glanced down at his feet and then up into her face again. "I'm afraid I've got some bad news for you, ma'am," he was saying.

The other men had got out of the cars now; they were standing around in the space between the machines and the porch steps. They were all looking up at her. Their faces were nothing but a collection of expressionless, pale ovals in the darkness. Somehow she had expected to see them flushed with hate and fury. But their faces were blank, impassive poker faces. She turned her eyes to the man before her.

"Bad news?" she echoed.

He's dead, she thought instantly. That was it! A sharp, rising excited hope spun within her. Here was freedom! She felt life stir again, picking up the tangled threads within her body once more. She ran the tip of her tongue nervously along the edges of her lips.

"You say you got some bad news?" she repeated.

Say it, man! Say it! Come out with it! If he's dead, tell me! I can take it! Oh, brother, how I can take it!

"It's your husband, ma'am, it's Mr. Brandon."

The glorious feeling of freedom at last came rising swiftly. It was all so clear now—why had she not thought of this before. They had gone out after him, after the murderer! They, these fine, good men of the hills, had gone out to hunt the skulking killer down. She knew Brandon, she did. He wouldn't let himself be dragged off to any jail, to be taken off and locked up, tried, hung by the neck until he was dead. No, sir, not Brandon! He'd blow his own brains out before that. Oh, sure, you fine men, I know what you've come to tell me. It was all so simple. He had put up a fight. That was it! He had put up a fight. There had been some shooting, naturally. And now, Mrs. Brandon, you're a widow. We're sure sorry about all this, but you're a widow woman now, Mamie Brandon! She must remember to look very shocked when he told her. She wondered if maybe she could cry, just a little. There was already a hot sting in the corners of her eyes. They'd be tears of relief, of joy, of her winning; but they need never know the kind of tears they were. If she squeezed hard they could come, those tears. She turned her eyes up to the man who would give her this news and she began to play her part.

"My husband!" she cried, "what's happened to him?"

"Steady now, ma'am." He reached out and touched her arm, helpless concern in his eyes.

She closed her eyes to screen the lights she knew must be dancing there. They must look like a fireworks display, she thought.

"He's dead," she said flatly. "I know it. He's dead."

She opened her eyes. He had said nothing. She looked at the stranger who had set her free. "Tell me," she pressed, "tell me how…"

The man was staring at her with unconcealed surprise. He's the one who looks relieved, she thought sharply. He was shaking his head slowly.

"Oh no, ma'am. You got it all wrong. Brandon, he ain't dead. Leastways, not yet."

Her whole mounting exultation collapsed in one thunderous crash. The fireworks in her eyes failed abruptly. Something was wrong! What had he said? No, ma'am, he had said very plainly, Brandon, he ain't dead … She stared at him, not believing.

He was looking down at her miserably. She was sure taking it bad. He could see the pain and torture standing out sharp on her face. He put his hand more firmly, more reassuringly on her arm and his words came fast, spilling over themselves, running together in their haste.

"He's bad off, ma'am, I'll admit. He's awful bad off, I guess. There ain't no doubt of that. We just found him a little while ago. We brought him back here."

She looked dazedly past him to the men ringed round the porch steps.

"The doc'll be along in a minute or two. He can tell you better than I can."

She forced her gaze back to the man before her. The doctor would be along, he had said. She shook her head to try and clear away the confusion, the helpless feeling. They were all standing around, waiting for her to do something, to say something. She swallowed.

"Won't you… bring him in, please," she tried to keep her voice level, under control.

The man at the door turned and said something to the men below. They went to the second car and there was a struggling among them at the rear door. She glanced down over the shoulder of the man before her. She could see his legs first, his legs between them, dangling, and then the big, heavy trunk of his body as they slid him from the back seat of the car. Now they had begun to come across the space, carrying him between them like that. He looked dead to her, completely dead.

She turned and went down the hall to the bedroom. She flung her raincoat over into a corner and pulled down the bedcovers. She heard them coming, shuffling to squeeze through the front doorway with their burden, then the odd uncertainty of their footsteps in a strange house as they came to the bedroom door. She glanced up as they wedged in through the narrow opening. They laid him out on the bed. She was standing there, on the opposite side, across from them, her hands down behind her, gripping the edge of the dressing-table with her fingers, looking down on him, staring down at his body, stretched out before her.

Brandon's face was chalk-white. His eyes were closed except for a tiny slit in each eye. She could see the whites gleaming in the slots in an unnatural way that made her go slightly sick at her stomach. His hands were gnarled, lumped useless at his sides. His breath was a series of short, uneven jerks. A stubble of beard had come out on his face, a sort of dirty, greyish shadow that almost covered up the deep-cut lines around his eyes and mouth. She kept staring down at him as if she had never seen this man before, as if they had made an error and brought a stranger to her bed. He looked so useless, so clod-like, a hunk of worthless flesh to her. She felt revulsion at the sight. Her eyes were wide; her head was tilted back slightly, as if she sought to unfasten her sight from him and could not.

The man who had done all the talking at the front door looked at her. His face was kindly, his manner soft, almost apologetic. "I'm sure mighty sorry it had to happen like this, ma'am."

She raised her eyes dumbly and gazed at him. For a moment she could not make sense of what he had said. Then the meaning sank slowly through her consciousness.

"Thank you," she whispered. She felt she was required to say something more. They were all standing around the bed, gazing down at him with eyes devoid of expression.

"Where was he?" she asked, not really curious. "Where did you find him?"

The man shot her an odd, quizzical glance. He looked at the man next to him and then back at her.

"Down the road a piece," the man said slowly, his eyes fixed on her face. "He was down the highway near Colfax."

"Was he lost in the brush or something?"

"No, ma'am." There was a crippled pause. "He was flat on his face on the shoulder of the highway, ma'am. Right out there in the open. Don't know how long he must have been like that. There ain't been too much traffic to-night."

She frowned slightly, still staring down at him. "On the highway? Near Colfax? What was he doing down there?"

"I don't know, ma'am. He was there, on that same curve where she got killed—that's where we found him."

She raised her eyes slowly and turned her head to look at the man across the bed. "She … ?" she echoed.

"Yes, ma'am." He was plainly embarrassed now. He reached up and yanked off his hat and began to turn it nervously, one hand over the other along the brim. He had hands like all the rest, she noticed absently, they were gnarled, grimy hands, hands of the earth and the woods. She brought her attention back to what he was saying. "It was that there very same spot where she got killed! The very same spot!"

A flutter of sharp impatience seized her. "Who is this 'she' you keep talking about? Who is she?"

The shadow of surprise swept across his face, banishing the embarrassment. "Why … Ellen Woods, ma'am!"

Ellen! It was as if he had suddenly leaned across the space and struck her across the mouth. Why … Ellen Woods! She stared down at Brandon, lying there, dead to all appearances, but alive she knew. Suddenly she felt the impulse to laugh harshly, rudely, loudly. She had never realized he could love like that! She clamped her lower lip tight between her teeth and drew her head back abruptly. The men around the room were watching her with a kind of dull fascination, a group of impersonal, almost uninterested spectators. They heard the front door scrape over the warped place and the sound of steps coming down the hall.

He nodded and came into the room, pushing his way through them to the side of the bed. His eyes took quick stock of the figure there and came rising to rest a moment on her, standing with that stunned look in her eyes. She looked as if she were going to bust loose and get all hysterical! Dammit, he thought sourly, I'm gonna have to take care of her too!

The men moved back to one side, silent and respectful, giving the doctor space and silence. Their faces had gone serious and taut, as all faces in the presence of the authority of medicine. He felt their concern, the riveted wall of audience, the solid backdrop of awe behind him.

He pulled off his coat and hung it on the bedpost, glancing around.

"You fellows will have to clear out of here," he said brusquely. His glance shifted to her and his tone softened slightly. "If you don't mind waiting outside, too, Mrs. Brandon. I'll only be a few minutes."

The men shuffled out obediently. She came slowly round the bed and hesitated for a moment as if to take a last look at him. Then she went on out and pulled the door closed behind her.

She had a sudden desire for activity, to do something, to keep her hands busy. She mentioned something about coffee and they followed her down into the kitchen. They grouped themselves in an uneasy, silent circle behind her. She could feel them watching her with close eyes, as people always watch the bereaved or the next-of-kin at a time like this. As if they were waiting for something to happen, a little fearful that it would, yet all the while holding the vagrant, profane hope that it might. Well, if they were waiting for her to go screaming and hell-raising, they could damn well relax! she thought viciously. She'd not give them that satisfaction! She'd not give them some fresh story to tell around the hills! God knows, they had enough to talk about already in these last days! She picked up the coffee-pot. She was quite all right now, quite firm.

"If you boys'll grab yourselves a cup"—she gestured towards the cupboard to the row of cups hanging from the hooks—"I'll fill 'em up."

They went and took down the cups like a crowd of well-disciplined children. They filed past her and she poured the hot coffee. After they were all taken care of, she went and got herself a cup. She had become aware of hunger and thirst suddenly. She slid the pot back on the stove.

The man who had been doing all the talking started up again. She watched him thoughtfully as he spoke.

"It's sure funny, ain't it?" He stared down at the linoleum pattern on the floor. "Funny, how he was down there, right where that damn accident happened! I know that was the place."

She kept watching him intently. Ruth had given her a smattering of an idea how it had all happened. She hoped this stranger would go on talking about it. Suddenly she wanted to know everything; she wanted to go over to him, to grab him by the arm, to force him to begin right at the beginning and tell her everything he knew.

"When was all this?" Her voice sounded tinny in the room. The men all turned their eyes to her, all at once, all at the same time. It was so unified a gesture that it was almost as a rehearsed act. But she put her attention to the man with the information she sought. He flushed under her sudden, direct look; he had a vague feeling that he had dragged something up that was best left alone around here this night of all nights.

"Um...'bout ten years ago, ma'am, if I'm remembering correctly."

She opened her mouth to ask another question. Now go back, she was about to say, go back and tell me everything you know about everything—how it was between him and this Ellen. But the doctor was at the door, looking at her. The men all turned their eyes to him now with that curious, odd one-motion. She had to look. He ignored the others and gazed down the lane between them to where she was by the table in the breakfast nook.

"Will you come in, please, Mrs. Brandon?"

She found herself moving through them, down the silent passageway they opened for her, going to the door. He turned and led her down the length of the hallway, going on into the big room. She followed him, the empty cup cradled in her moistening palms. Her fingers were sticky against the smoothness of the warm china. The doctor had gone across the room to the dead fireplace. He stood with his back to her, hands on the mantel-edge, staring down into the black hole at the grey, lifeless embers. She moved over to the long table and set the cup down. Then she came to where he stood and took her place silently behind him.

He swung around and glanced rather sharply at her, his eyes sober. Good, he thought. She's passed that hysteria stage—it will be easier now!

Looking into his eyes she felt a revival of the old hope, taking her cue from the intent seriousness of his expression.

"He's gonna die," she said flatly.

"No, Mrs. Brandon, I'm afraid he isn't going to die." He contradicted her very quietly. "It's too bad he isn't; but he isn't going to die."

She stared up at him, not quite following his remarks. He hesitated for a second and took a deep, steadying breath.

"I'm sorry for you, Mrs. Brandon, I'm very sorry for you. You're a young woman. You've a long, hard row ahead of you. It's going to be hardest of all on you."

She thought of the row that lay behind her. She sent her gaze on past him to the little brass dog set in the centre of the mantel. None of it had been exactly what she'd call a breeze! None of it had been a soft snap! she reflected.

"What is it? What's the matter with him?"

"He's had a stroke."

A tiny terror clamped on to her heart and hung there grimly. She tried to shake it loose, but it was there, its teeth deep in her.

"Just what does that mean?" she asked dully.

He looked at her for a long moment before he answered. Had she glanced into his eyes she might have seen compassion there.

But she had turned her head and was looking away from him, looking out through the windows to the blackness thick outside.

"It means your husband is paralysed, Mrs. Brandon. A clot of blood on the brain, pressing down on a part of it, and you get total paralysis. Brandon's a bad case. Brought on, I should imagine, by what's gone on in the last couple of days." She glanced at him sharply. He nodded. "We know what happened," he said heavily. He hesitated and then went back to his thought. "Brandon's completely paralysed. He'll never walk again, I'm pretty sure. It's entirely possible he'll never speak again, ever. In many ways, your husband is dead, Mrs. Brandon, as you thought. He's dead … except for that little thread of life down there within him somewhere. Brandon will never get out of that bed again."

Her breathing was trapped in her throat. She felt a searing, sharp pain go zig-zagging through her. A core of agony formed within her, hard, insoluble, dull and gnawing. She tried to see the man's face before her, but her eyes were blind with the pain that had seized residence in her heart.

"How long?" she whispered.

He took his eyes from the face that had suddenly become old and haggard in a tiny, fluttering moment.

"No one can tell about these things. I have no idea. Years, I would say, most probably in his case. No one can tell these things off-hand. I'd say it would be a long time with him." The room was brutal with its very silence. "You see, Mrs. Brandon, he's a very strong man, physically and mentally. He won't give up easily, not without a long fight."

"How long?" she repeated as if she had not heard him.

He looked down at her and wet his lips nervously. "Mrs. Brandon, I'll be frank with you. I've known cases like this to go on for ten, for even twenty years before it ends."

She stood very still in the centre of the room. Slowly she drew herself erect and thrust back her head almost defiantly. She turned and walked away from him. She went to the opening to the hallway and hesitated for a moment.

"Doctor … " she said quietly, grasping the frame of the door, looking back at him "Doctor, there was an … accident." She pursed her lips to give them pliability, to bring back the feeling to them. "A man was shot. Tell me … is he dead, too?"

The doctor scowled. He knew now that she knew what had happened. She knew why they had been looking for him when they found him on the road like that.

"No … the boy is not dead, Mrs. Brandon," he said simply. "Death seems to have been playing hard to get up here the last couple of days." He disliked his ill-chosen jest instantly. Her eyes were no longer on him. They were on nothing, simply turned into the emptiness of the room. After a moment he went back to her question. "No, the boy is not dead. They've taken him down to Colfax to the hospital there. We'll know more later on. But, from the early reports, I'd say he'll live. Poor, damned devil. He'll be blind, of course, and hopelessly scarred. Yes, he'll live, after a fashion. It would have been a damn sight better if Brandon had killed him outright." There was a harsh, bitter note in his words. It evaporated instantly. "God knows, he'd be better off dead than to have to go on as he will, an ugly, sightless pile of a man!"

Mamie Brandon turned away from him, her face ashen, her hands making feeble motions of protest. She moved down the hallway haltingly, placing one foot before the other tentatively, as if she were making her way through a sea of glue. She moved on into the kitchen.

The men were silent, their heads turned to the door, as she entered. She did not falter. She came forward, her head held high, her eyes glazed and bright. The men parted and she passed through them, neither glancing to the right nor to the left. Only the barrier of the breakfast-nook table barred her way. She stood, her back to them, her finger-tips pressing down on the table edge, her eyes dull.

Dimly, as from a far distance, she heard them stir and shuffle as they left the room. She heard them move down the hall away from her. She heard them go out on the porch, heard the protesting rasp as someone pulled the door over the warped place, heard the click of the lock. Then the silence came cautiously back to the house. In a moment there was the sound of car engines starting and the nervous clash of gears. Then these sounds too faded and were gone.

After a long while Mamie shifted and took a deep, heavy breath. She expelled it slowly, a weary, empty sigh. She took her place at the table, her arms outstretched before her, hands palms up on the surface. She turned her head and looked woodenly through the window. The night was passing. Outside the grey light of day was rising from the earth, pressing the night back behind the screen of heaven. She let her sight wander around the confines of the place. She saw the. barn, the vegetable patch, the solid green of the tree wall beyond, the same scene, the same setting, the same as before, unaltered, unchanged. She lifted her eyes slowly from these things to the tree-tops, to the open, unfettered skies. Those skies were clouded and swollen, low and close. The bright, warm sun of yesterday was truant.

Her gaze drifted back to her hands before her, to the palms. She stared at the lines there, the deep, unbroken, immutable lines. She raised her hands before her and peered at them intently, concentrating, trying to read the message. But there was no clue, no answer. Mamie shut her eyes tight against the growing light of day. Suddenly she bent forward abruptly and covered her face, the palms flat and hard against her cheeks, her fingers harsh upon her lids. There was no sound of life in all the place.

THE END

www.ingramcontent.com/pod-product-compliance
Lightning Source LLC
Chambersburg PA
CBHW031213260626
47169CB00007B/2042